D1053111

The NERDY and the DIRTY

The NERDY and the DIRTY

b. t. gottfred

HENRY HOLT AND COMPANY
NEW YORK

Henry Holt and Company
Publishers since 1866
175 Fifth Avenue
New York, New York 10010
fiercereads.com

Library of Congress Cataloging-in-Publication Data
Names: Gottfred, B. T.
Title: The nerdy and the dirty / b.t. gottfred.
Description: First edition. | New York : Henry Holt and Company, 2016. | Summary: "A cool girl—with an X-rated internal life—and a socially inept guy prove that opposites attract in this honest look at love, sexuality, and becoming your true self"—Provided by publisher.
Identifiers: LCCN 2016001531 | ISBN 9781627798501 (hardback)
Subjects: | CYAC: Dating (Social customs)—Fiction. | Love—Fiction. | Sex—Fiction. | Self-acceptance—Fiction.
Classification: LCC PZ7.1.G68 Ne 2016 | DDC [Fic]—dc23
LC record available at https://lccn.loc.gov/2016001531

First Edition—2016

Designed by Anna Booth

Printed in the United States of America by
R. R. Donnelley & Sons Company, Harrisonburg, Virginia

1 3 5 7 9 10 8 6 4 2

(As part of the agreement with Penelope and Benedict that allowed me to publish this novel, I agreed to let them write the dedication.)

This book is for anyone who ever is, was, or will be nerdy or dirty. That should pretty much mean this book is for anyone ever born.

—P & B

"I'm invisible."

—*Penelope Lupo, 16*

"I am the center of the universe."

—BENEDICT PENDLETON, 16

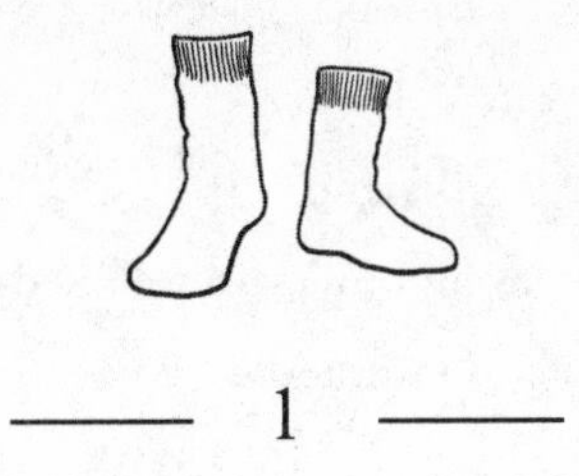

— 1 —

Benedict Maximus Pendleton

"I'M VERY HANDSOME. I DON'T REALLY THINK this is a question of opinion. I am objectively handsome," I said to Robert, who was staring at his roast-beef sandwich. He always stared at his sandwiches. This made it difficult to have conversations. I've talked to him about it. He's working on the problem.

"I agree, Benedict," Robert said to me. Toward the roast beef but to me.

"Of course you agree. You are a logical person. I am six feet one inch tall, slender but not skinny because I do fifty push-ups every morning and every night. My eyes and nose are proportional. My ears might be slightly large for my head, but my thick head of hair, which I style every day, should more than compensate. I also dress very well. Not trendy. I dress with sophistication."

"I like how you dress," Robert said.

"Thank you. I know you do. Sports jackets are woefully under-represented in the wardrobes of today's teenagers. Do you know why I am telling you this, Robert?"

"No."

"I am telling you this, Robert, because I think it is time I get a girlfriend."

"You've never had a girlfriend."

"I know! Obviously. But only because my dad told me I could not date until I was sixteen. He wanted me to concentrate on school. This was great advice."

"Your dad is very smart."

"He is. Obviously. But I turn seventeen in six days and not one girl has expressed interest in me the past year, and though some of the fault must lie in the female student population of Riverbend High School, I must also admit that, with my having been on the proverbial sidelines of the dating scene until a year ago, they might not be aware of my availability and interest."

In the several seconds it took Robert to respond, Evil Benny started talking in my head. Evil Benny is not real. I'm not crazy. It's just self-doubt. I call this voice, this self-doubt, Evil Benny because I want to make sure my better self differentiates itself from my lesser self. And Evil Benny, obviously, is my lesser self. It is easier to ignore Evil Benny if I make him a separate person. I don't actually think he's a separate person. That would make me crazy, which I have already stated I am not. I just make him separate in my head. Evil Benny says very untrue, very destructive things like "You don't have a girlfriend because you are very unlikable." So, obviously, destructive thoughts are not productive. That's why he's Evil Benny and must be ignored. I will expunge him, and self-doubt entirely, from my head someday soon. I am sure of it.

"I'd like a girlfriend," Robert said, which made me happy since it was easier to ignore Evil Benny when I could talk.

"Robert . . ." I started, but then stopped. I was about to tell him that he was not objectively handsome. Robert wouldn't have minded me telling him this. He enjoyed that I was always honest with him. But I fear my practice of being blunt with Robert since we were twelve has led me to be blunt with others, which may be a third reason for my current lack of girlfriend. Girls, see, prefer that you lie to them. So I have decided to start lying to Robert about certain things. As practice for when I have a girlfriend. Thus I said to Robert, "Yes, I agree. You and I both should get a girlfriend." Though, obviously, I would get a girlfriend first, and then my girlfriend would provide one of her less attractive friends for Robert to date.

2

pen

Let's say I was writing a book about my life.

I'm not. My real life is boring and all the crazy fantasy stuff in my brain should never, ever, ever, ever be public. So no way would I ever write a book.

But, because I read a lot and can't help thinking about this sometimes, let's say I was. And I had to figure out a way to start the book, a totally honest/unique/mind-blowing opening that would make some sixteen-year-old girl like me want to read the whole thing after they downloaded the sample on their phone. But I also had to figure out a not-too-girly beginning so boys would want to read it too, even though they're usually too lazy to read books not assigned for school. Oh, and I guess it couldn't be too honest or sexy or anything that would make parents burn my book before any kid even saw it.

So . . . never mind. I can't think of anything that could do all that. All I guess I could say was, "My name is Pen. I pretend I'm normal. The end." So, yeah, NEVER MIND. This is a stupid thing to think about.

I'm stupid.

I'm boring.

Stupid.

Boring.

Oh, and fake.

So fake. Not fake like you see on TV where the girls are all snotty yet saying nice things like "You are so pretty" even though it's clear the girls hate everyone including themselves. No, fake because I wish I could be real. I wish I could just come out tell everyone who I really am. I could just come out and say stuff like:

I masturbate a ton.

I would never, ever, ever tell anyone that. NEVER. But I wish I could. Every inch of my stupid/boring/fake body wishes I could. If I was a guy, talking about how much you masturbate would be pointless to mention. But I'm a girl in high school, so maybe it's interesting. As far as I know I'm the only girl at Riverbend who masturbates. I wish I wasn't. I wish all my friends masturbated as much as me because then I wouldn't feel like a freak.

So, yeah . . . I guess if I was going to write a book, I'd write a book about anything or anyone but me. I'd make it about someone who's actually interesting. Someone so interesting even boys would want to read my book.

So maybe it should be about a boy.

A really, *really* interesting boy.

Probably too interesting for someone boring and fake like me, but at least he'd be fun to write about. Not that I'll write anything ever. I don't even know why I'm thinking about this. Other than because math class is even more boring than thinking about how boring my life is.

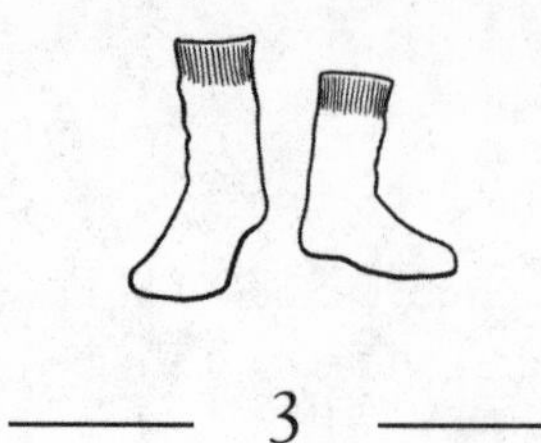

3

Benedict Maximus Pendleton

JUST AS I WAS CONVINCED ROBERT COULD BE a good ally in helping me find my first girlfriend, he said, "I want to date Pen Lupo."

"Robert, please, we have to take this seriously."

"What's wrong with Pen?" He actually put down his sandwich to say this. Having all his attention on me made me uncomfortable. For only a moment. I can handle almost any confrontation. Obviously.

I explained, "Penelope Lupo is not even in the top one hundred of class rank. In fact, she's probably in the bottom one hundred. We should set up rules for our girlfriend search. And one of the rules, obviously, is that they are smart."

"Pen is very smart."

"Robert!" I yelled. Sometimes I yelled when people were not logical.

"She is, Benedict. We used to talk all the time in seventh grade."

"Robert . . ." I calmed myself. I was good at calming myself most of the time. I had been enduring him talking about Penelope Lupo since we were in junior high and I had been, understandably, dismissive of his interest. But if I were going to get a girlfriend, I would have to learn to be patient with a girl's irrational thinking. Though Robert was usually very smart, he was not smart at all when it came to discussing Penelope Lupo, which meant he could be a good practice subject on this issue as well. Thus I stated, "I know you and Penelope—"

"No one calls her Penelope anymore."

Do not yell at him, Benedict! I didn't. It was very difficult. "Fine. Pen. I know you two were lab partners in seventh-grade science class, but you haven't spoken since we got to high school."

"She always says hi in the halls."

"But you haven't actually discussed anything at length, correct?"

Robert shook his head and picked up his roast beef again.

I continued, "That's because you have nothing in common anymore. You and I are among the top ten smartest kids at Riverbend." Technically, he was twelfth in class rank. I was third. Being third, it's my duty to be generous in praise of those lower than me. "Both of us will attend nationally ranked universities." I'll attend Northwestern. My dad went there. He's famous. I would, obviously, get into Northwestern even if my father were not a famous legacy. I would get into an Ivy League school if I wanted! But that's not important right now. What's important is, "Penelope—"

"Pen."

"Pen, sorry, is a stoner and a loser. She might not attend college at all. She will drag you down to her level. And you being my best friend, if you were dragged down to her level, you might then drag me down. We have to protect each other from making bad choices." Obviously, I just needed to protect Robert. I didn't make bad choices.

4

pen

"Penelope, why aren't you taking notes?" Mr. Bravier asked me. I didn't answer because even though I heard him, I didn't really hear him. Maybe because he was using my real name (which I hate) but more like he was a television show on in the background that I could ignore. Except he wasn't. He was my algebra teacher. He talked like an overeducated zombie. "Penelope?" he said again. Oh yeah. I heard him again. But really heard him this time. Guess I should say something.

"Yeah?" I never speak in class. Just one-word answers like that. I don't speak much in life either. I don't know how to think like normal people, so I shouldn't try to talk like them. I'm quiet. So quiet. Always. Really.

"Take notes," said Mr. Bravier.

"Yeah," I said, then put my pen to my notepad. Chances of me taking actual math notes? Zero. But Mr. Bravier didn't need to know that. It wasn't his fault somebody was stupid enough to pay him seventy g's a year to teach kids stuff they don't care about. It wasn't my fault either. I'm bored thinking about how boring algebra is—can you imagine how boring it would be if I actually paid attention?

I have a boyfriend. His name's Paul. Paul and Pen. Pen and Paul. We've been dating since eighth grade. We're juniors in high school now. So we've been dating so long we're practically married. But not really married. He's great. And hot. And nice. And he never once has mentioned my scar. Also, I should mention he's Catholic. So am I, I suppose. But he's really Catholic. We still have sex. But he hates himself after every time we do it, so we don't do it that much. Which is fine with me. I'd rather masturbate. I don't tell Paul I masturbate. He's Catholic, remember? Really Catholic. A Catholic girl who masturbates is like Satan. So I don't tell anyone I do it. Except when I have conversations with myself. Like now. I'm probably crazy. But no one knows I'm crazy because I can fake being normal so well.

So fake.

So, so, so, so fake . . .

But, you know, I'm tired of faking it. Yeah. I'm tired of it. . . .

Shit. I just had a revelation, didn't I? Or a proclamation. Or maybe I had a revelation about making a proclamation. Here it goes: "I, Pen Lupo, will no longer fake being normal. On this day, Tuesday, December 17, I will cease pretending I'm like everyone else. I'm going to be a freak. I've always been a freak. But I'm not going to hide being a freak anymore. The end."

Interesting. I guess I'm having that day old people look back on and say, "That was the day my life began," but I'll never say it like that since that's a boring, normal-person way to say it. So I'll say it this way: "That was the day I told the world to accept me for who I am or go fuck itself."

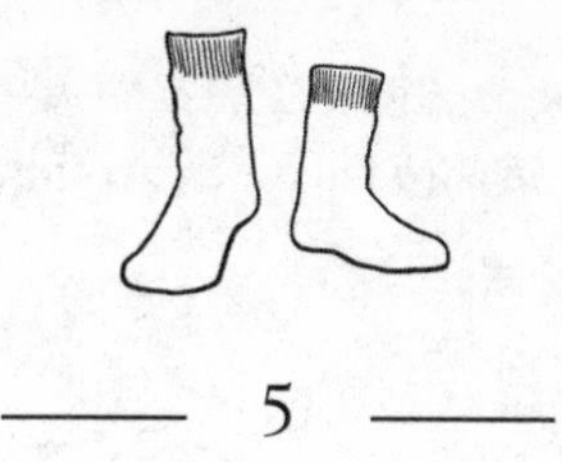

— 5 —

Benedict Maximus Pendleton

WHEN ROBERT LOOKED UP FROM HIS SANDwich, I knew he wasn't going to say anything intelligent. I know when people aren't going to say intelligent things because of how intelligent I am. His eyes were also red. My dad says no one has ever said anything smart when they're being emotional. Then Robert said, his voice cracking, "I think I love Pen, Benedict. I think about her all the time."

"ROBERT!" Darn it. I yelled again. He was being so difficult! "I now must remind you that she has a boyfriend. A BOYFRIEND, Robert. You hate when I mention Paul, so I try not to, but I'm very tired of talking about Penelope—"

"Pen."

"PEN! YES, PEN! Pen . . ." I paused. It was a good idea to pause. We were, as we were every lunch hour during the winter, in the SAC, which is short for Student Activity Center. A public place. One must always be in control when in a public place. "I'm sorry for yelling. It's just that I am very serious about getting a girlfriend. If you are going to help me, if we are going to help each other, I need you to be serious too.

And Pen is not a serious person. So please tell me you will stop talking about her."

Robert took a moment to accept I was right, nodded, then took a bite of his sandwich. Mustard fell down his chin.

"I'm glad you agree."

"But . . ." he started.

Darn it. "But what?"

"Will you at least admit that Pen is pretty? I'll never mention her again if you just admit she's really pretty."

No, Pen was not pretty. The most obvious imperfection was the scar on her left cheek. It made her look like she got in a knife fight with a homeless person. I never bring up the scar to Robert because I just don't. But that's only the first problem with her. Pen also only wore black clothes. Every day. Maybe this was in preparation for her life as a waitress at a nightclub. I don't know, but it was depressing. She also had a nose ring. A *nose* ring. That alone would disqualify anyone from being considered attractive. Pen dyed her already dark hair even blacker, which looked cheap because, as my dad has pointed out, dyed hair always looks cheap. Pen also had strange eyes. I never talked to her. She never talked to me. But when I passed her in the halls, she would look at me with these strange eyes. It wasn't the heavy mascara she wore, though that didn't help; it was her pupils. There was a light in them. A tiny sparkle. No, that makes it sound like a good thing. It wasn't. Her eyes just seemed to contain . . . madness. Yes, madness. She acted normal enough, for a stoner that is, but I promise you that behind those eyes was an insane person.

Thus, obviously, Penelope Lupo was not a pretty girl. But it was also obvious that Robert could not be convinced of this, no matter how effectively I laid out the facts. And, since I needed to practice how to lie to girls, I lied to Robert. "Yes, okay, Robert, Pen is pretty."

6

pen

I had this revelation/proclamation thing in my soul now, and as I sat in my classes the rest of the day, I was like, "Pen, this is it, this is the thing that finally makes this whole existence makes sense." Really. It felt super powerful. *I* felt super powerful.

Since I was a kid, even before I knew I was thinking it, I thought that everything was just nuts. All of it. Life. Just nuts. People say they love each other but then hurt each other; they bring babies into this world but then hate that they brought babies into the world. Just so much fake stuff. So much. And I knew it was all fake, but what the hell was I supposed to do about it? Nothing. I'm nothing. It's all nothing. But I'm especially nothing. So I just go along with it. I do the same thing as everyone else. I say stuff like "I love that dress" when I really hate it. I say, "That kid's such a dork," to my friends when I really think that kid is interesting. So I do all that.

I'm the biggest fake when it comes to all the sex stuff. Pretending to Paul that he's good, pretending to Paul that I'm this innocent girl and think just like him. After every time we have sex, really *every time*,

Paul says, "God doesn't want us to do this until after we're married. Don't you think we should wait?" And I say, "Okay," or some other thing that's super fake. And super passive. But really I'm thinking that God, if he/she/it exists, and that's a big if, doesn't give a fuck whether we have sex or not. But I can't say that. If I said that, Paul would flip out. He'd probably tell my mom since Paul and my mom tell each other everything. And then my mom, who's the craziest Catholic who ever lived, would do all her fire-and-brimstone bullshit. It wouldn't work on me, but I'd have to *pretend* it worked or else it would go on forever.

But now that was all going to end. No more fake for me. No more bullshit for me. I was going to tell everyone what I really thought all the time about everything and they were just going to have to deal. Really. Shit, it felt good. My whole body felt connected. My body is all connected, I know, but most of the time it didn't *feel* connected, but right now, as I was walking to the benches near the cafeteria where I meet Paul and the rest of them every day after last period, I felt for the first time in my whole life that my life was whole. That was poetic. Really. I've got to write that down. "For the first time in my whole life my life felt whole." It wasn't as good the second time. Still cool, I guess. But not as great as the first time I thought it.

As I'm feeling all this and thinking all this, I see Paul. My Paul. As soon as I see him, with his black leather jacket, with his dimples and his sexy stubble—no other boy gets stubble like Paul—I start to remember that I love him. It was a lot easier telling Paul about my freakiness when I forgot I cared what he thought.

Paul's family moved to Riverbend in eighth grade.

Up until the end of seventh grade, I was a dork. All my friends were dorks too. . . . Listen, I never called them dorks then and I have never called them dorks outside my own head since. I was so awkward when I was a kid I'm shocked I could walk in a straight line. See, I've had this big jagged scar down my left cheek since basically forever. It's fucking ugly. Really. I might have been beautiful if it wasn't for this goddamn scar. But whatever. I'm trying to say I don't judge dorks because I get what it means to be a dork. I just felt uncomfortable in my own skin, blah, blah, blah . . .

Forget it. The point was that I wasn't part of the popular crowd. I got good grades, cared what teachers thought, that sort of stuff. I knew it was all stupid, even then, but I didn't know what else to do with my time.

My social life, my life really, was forever changed when for Christmas in seventh grade I asked for a bunch of new clothes. I changed my whole wardrobe. I stopped wearing baggy things or dumpy blue jeans or all that bright crap from Old Navy I'd wear all the time. I wanted to wear black. Tight and black. I'd seen this singer girl from Germany with this look on YouTube and I just knew that was what I wanted to be. To look like. My mom hated buying it for me, but she still bought it for me because my mom likes to bitch about doing something and then do it for you and then tell you how great she is for doing it for you. I don't want to get into Mom's problems now. It stresses me out. Let me concentrate on explaining the Paul situation because that might be seconds away from blowing up in my face.

So in seventh grade, when I showed up to school in January dressed with my high-heeled black boots and my black jeans and my black sweater and black bra, everybody was like, "Whoa." Nobody said that, but I could tell they were thinking that. All my friends, my dork friends, thought I was playing dress-up, but I knew this was the real me. The permanent me. Because suddenly I wasn't uncomfortable in my own skin like them. And then after a few weeks, the popular kids started to talk to me. Not often, but I could tell there was a difference.

It wasn't until the summer that Iris, one of the cool girls, started texting me. Then calling me. Then shopping with me. Turns out Iris was super nice. Really. Funny how you always think people that aren't your friends are jerks but then they become your friends and then they are awesome. Iris and I became best friends that summer. She's still my best friend. Iris is blond, with long legs, and very pretty. But she totally wastes being pretty because she never once has liked a boy. She's not a snob about it. I think she may be afraid of sex. Her mom died when she was a kid and that probably screwed her up. My mom screwed me up by staying alive. Shit. No more talking about my mom. Really this time.

So Iris got me invited to Stacy Ashton's birthday party right before eighth grade started. Stacy was the queen in junior high. She got huge boobs before anyone and her parents lived in the rich Covered Bridges section of Riverbend. She was also a super-big bitch. Always knew how to insult somebody faster than anyone else. It's scary how good she is at insulting people. She's still the queen in eleventh grade, sort of, but she got fat last year and there's a big difference between a hot chick with big boobs being a bitch and a fat girl being a bitch.

So that's where I met Paul for the first time. At Stacy Ashton's birthday party right before eighth grade. As soon as I saw him, I fell in love with him. My whole body vibrated. Those dimples and flawless olive skin. Thick black hair, bright white teeth. Loud with his guy friends, but soft around the girls at the party. I never wanted something more in my life. Nothing. The weirdest thing? I got him. Like right away. That night. People made fun of us because we dressed the same. Twins almost. Except I didn't have a black leather jacket yet. But twins besides that. We started talking and he was so nice. He can yell and get bossy sometimes, but he's almost always nice to me. Like I said before, he has never once talked about my scar. Not once. Three years. Sometimes I think it's weird he hasn't talked about it, actually. But I never bring it up to him because, if somehow his brain can't see it on my face, I don't want my talking about it to change anything.

Eventually, on the night we met, we went upstairs to Mr. Ashton's home office and closed the door and he kissed me. That was my first kiss. Shit. Greatest moment of my life. So, yeah, I fell in love with Paul that night. At first sight. It happens.

So three years later, a lot of other stuff went down in school and life, but Paul and I are still together. Nobody in school can imagine us not being together. I can't imagine breathing without him. So as I see him standing there with Joey and Miller, near Iris and Stacy, I start to have a panic attack. I can't—I CAN'T!—tell him that I masturbate every day and that I think Catholicism is bullshit and all the other real stuff I think and feel. I just can't . . . because seeing him makes me feel so connected *to him*, which makes me feel less connected *to me*. And feeling less connected to me makes me feel less super powerful. Instead I feel vulnerable. Like I could break into pieces if I say even a single word. Suddenly my whole revelation starts to scramble in my head. It's not profound or life changing at all anymore. Instead it's like this disease I need to get out of my head as fast as I can before it destroys me.

So that's that. I'm not going to tell Paul what I really think. It will just hurt him or confuse him. I don't want to hurt someone I love. Above all, I don't want to lose him. But if I can't tell Paul, I can't tell anyone. And not telling anyone just makes me more fake than ever.

"Hey, babe," Paul says to me as I hug him. He kisses me on the temple. It's all the same. Nothing's changed. It feels comfortable. Okay. Cool. I guess. And I am standing there with my friends, with Paul's arm around my shoulder, and we are talking about nothing, which is what we always talk about.

And that's when I see Robert and Benedict walking down the hall. Robert and Benedict are my old dork friends from junior high. Well, Robert was. Nobody has ever been friends with Benedict except Robert. They're walking and I know Robert has this crush on me and I want to be nice, so I wave hi as Robert waves hi to me.

Except then Stacy, shooing them with her left hand, and in her bitchiest way possible, says, "Move on, Scarecrow and Tin Man, nothing to see here," and Robert is just crushed. He drops his chin to his chest, closes his eyes, and probably fights back tears as he races off down the hall. I want to tell off Stacy. I can be real with her. I can start there. Maybe I never tell Paul what I really think, but I can tell Stacy. It's not like I'd care if Stacy stops being my friend. She's told me fifty times how I should get plastic surgery to fix my face.

But before I can say anything or decide not to say anything, we all notice that even though Robert has run off, Benedict has stopped. And now he's staring down Stacy. Fucking Benedict. The kid is so weird. Calling Robert "Scarecrow" was mean and didn't make sense. But even though I never would have said it, calling Benedict "Tin Man" is not entirely inaccurate. The boy talks and acts like a robot. A super-smart and super-*super*-weird robot.

"What are you LOOKING AT?" Stacy says, saliva specks landing on Benedict's face as she steps right up into him. But he doesn't say anything or move. And she looks pretty stupid. She's short, and chubby now, breathing hard, her hands shaking at her side. All the while Benedict—despite being a robot or maybe because he's a robot—stands there, still, so still, and tall and confident. He might be delusional, but he is sure as shit confident in whatever delusions he's telling himself. Stacy yells again, "Leave, you loser!" Paul tries to reach out and pull Stacy back, but she shakes him off and waves her finger in Benedict's face. Stacy then yells, "You're such a freak!" And she laughs. Yeah. Really. Joey and Miller laugh too. Paul tries not to. I don't. Iris doesn't. But still, I feel bad for Benedict. He doesn't show any emotion because he's a robot, but somewhere inside he has to feel something, right? Worried Stacy is going to keep pummeling him into oblivion with her acid mouth, I take one step forward. Maybe to say something. I never say anything, so maybe just to stand between them. I don't know.

But then, before I can do anything, Benedict says, "Stacy, I am sorry you are now fat and will probably be fat the rest of your life, but after high school, you will have to learn to be nice because nobody will be friends with a mean fat person." Then he leaves.

Holy—

Stacy explodes into tears. No way can she breathe with how much snot is flying out of her face. She runs off to the girls' bathroom. Iris runs after her because she and Stacy have been friends since they were born. (Iris still calls Stacy her best friend, which makes me jealous if I'm being real.) Once Stacy and Benedict are both gone, Joey and Miller laugh again, though this time they are laughing *at* Stacy, not *with* her. Assholes always, I guess. Paul hits them both, not hard, but enough to stop them from laughing. I don't know what to do. Should I go to the bathroom and console Stacy? The fact is, she was a bitch and deserved, sort of, what Benedict said. Part of me wants to go make sure Robert is okay. But mostly I just want to do nothing because that's the easiest thing to do.

Then Paul, raising up his chest, says, "We have to beat the crap out of that Benedict kid now."

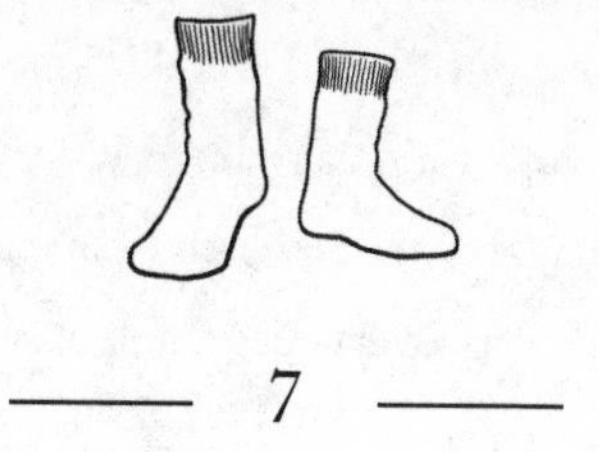

7

Benedict Maximus Pendleton

ROBERT WAS CRYING LIKE A LITTLE BOY AS I drove him home from school. Normally I would have told him to stop acting like a child, but I've been working on being more sympathetic to people who have emotions. I have emotions too. To clarify: I am working on being more sympathetic to people who can't *control* their emotions. Obviously, I can control them.

Thus I stated, "Robert, it's okay that you are sad that Stacy Ashton insulted us. But can you please not wipe your boogers on my seats?" I shouldn't have said that about the car seats. It's just that I like to keep my car clean. It's a white Lexus GS 350. It's a very nice car. It costs fifty-five thousand dollars. I didn't pay for it. Obviously. I'm only sixteen. My dad bought it. He's rich. But I'll be much richer than him someday.

Evil Benny doesn't think I will be. Evil Benny says I will never be as good as my dad at anything. He says that anything I do accomplish will only be because of my dad and everything I fail at will be my fault.

"Robert," I said because I needed to talk, "I don't care if you wipe your snot and saliva on my car." I did care, but it was good to lie now. "I only care that you know that you are better than Stacy and Pen and the rest of them." I thought this was a very nice thing to say. Being a good friend is easy.

"I don't want to be better than them," he said. Hearing him say words was better than him crying, but I wish he had agreed with me. He continued, "I want to be their friend. I want to go to parties. I want to talk to Pen."

"What happened to promising to never talk about Pen again?"

"You brought her up," Robert said.

"This is true." I had made a mistake. I hate making mistakes. I didn't know how to speak for a moment.

"Benedict, you've been my best friend since fifth grade." Robert had turned to me. I could tell he wanted me to look at him, but I had to watch the road.

"Sixth grade. We weren't best friends until sixth grade."

"Okay. Since sixth grade. But I want to have more than just one friend."

"Once we have girlfriends, we will."

"We will never have girlfriends. We are losers. We are the biggest nerds in school!"

I did NOT like hearing him talk like this. My face became really hot. It felt like it would melt off my head. I said, and said it with each word very loud and very distinct, "Maybe YOU are a loser, Robert. Maybe YOU will never have a girlfriend. But I am NOT a loser. I will have a girlfriend and you will be so jealous you will want to kill yourself."

"No, you won't. NO, YOU WON'T, BENEDICT! BECAUSE NO

ONE LIKES YOU BUT ME! NO ONE! I DON'T EVEN LIKE YOU ANYMORE! I DON'T WANT TO BE YOUR FRIEND!"

I stopped the car and screamed. I don't know how long I screamed. When I stopped, Robert was out of the car. I turned around and found him walking down the sidewalk. It was cold outside. I should drive him home. No, I shouldn't. I can't. Obviously. Robert and I are no longer friends. It's for the best. He was becoming less and less smart by the minute.

Evil Benny said I would never have a friend again. He said that no one else would ever like me. I knew this wasn't true, but Robert wasn't there to talk to, so Evil Benny had no one to interrupt him.

8

pen

"Yeah," Joey and Miller both say, nodding, agreeing with Paul.

"Huh?" I say, because my brain needs to hear him say it again.

"We got to beat him up, babe. He insulted Stacy," Paul says.

"She insulted him first." My voice is like a whisper. My whole life is like a whisper.

"She's our friend and what she said was just normal Stacy stuff. That Benedict kid said stuff you just can't say."

"You're not beating him up, Paul," I say. Shit. I never tell him what to do or not to do. You know. I always do my passive thing. He doesn't know how to react. It takes a moment, like he has to think twice to make sure he heard me right.

"Babe, you can't talk to me like that."

I, uh . . . I don't know how to get out of this. It's not like Paul is threatening me. He just isn't used to me saying anything. I had been the nicest girl he ever met. Or at least pretended to be. And now I'm telling him off. Just a little.

"Babe?"

"Benedict is . . . he's . . ." I start, and then I just have to say it. "He's not like us."

"Of course he's not, Pen!" Joey says. "He's one of the smartest kids in school!"

"I meant he's different, like, he doesn't know how to talk to people. He's school smart but he's not, like, interpersonal smart," I say. I shouldn't have used the word "interpersonal." They won't know what it means. I barely know what it means.

"Interpersonal? What the fuck does that mean?" Paul says.

"You know Steve Jobs? The guy who started Apple?" I say.

"Yeah?" they all say, with no clue where I'm going with this. I don't really have one either.

"Well, he was super smart, right?"

"Yeah," they all say again.

"Nobody talks about it, but he also didn't really know how to deal with people. If you read that book about Steve Jobs and you see what a jerk he was, you'd know he couldn't really help it because his brain was just different from the rest of ours."

"You don't read books," Paul says, so sure of himself.

"I don't read schoolbooks," I say. Shit. All three of them are looking at me like I'm a freak, which I guess I wanted. No, I didn't. I wanted to *tell them* I was a freak, but then I wanted for them to tell me their freak things and then for us all to be freaks together. But that was never going to happen. I'm the only freak. I should just be quiet like I always am.

"The book said he wasn't interpersonal smart? The guy who like created the computer and the smartphone?" Miller asks. Paul is too mad at me to speak.

"No, the book didn't say it, but I think I'm right. And maybe he created those things because he didn't know how to communicate normally like us. I don't know. Look, I just think Benedict has a hard time understanding how to talk to people. So I don't think you should beat somebody up for saying something he doesn't even know he's saying."

None of them say anything for a moment. I was this small, quiet girl who never said anything but "hi" and "cool" and "yeah" and now I had said more in the last twenty seconds than maybe ever. Not really. But it must have felt like it the way all three of them are looking at me. Especially Paul, who is breathing fast. Hyperventilating maybe. Except he's pretending he's calm, which makes his eyes bulge.

So Paul finally says, "Why are you talking like this?"

"Yeah, you are freaky," Joey says. He said freaky. It's out there now.

Paul gets very stiff except for his breathing. His neck muscles shake. He stares at me without blinking those huge eyes. He says, "Do you have secret opinions about everything, babe? Do you have secret opinions about me?" I say this one thing about Benedict and Steve Jobs and it's like I chopped his legs off. I should never say anything real ever again. And definitely not anything real to Paul or anyone I care about.

"No, baby," I say, "I just don't want you to get into trouble for beating up a kid that doesn't know better." Then I wrap my arms around him and squeeze. This soothes him, I think, because he stops looking at me like I'm this alien. Which I am, aren't I? I'm an alien because I'm not like anyone else I know. And when you're an alien, you have to pretend you're not or else all the normal people will kick you off their planet.

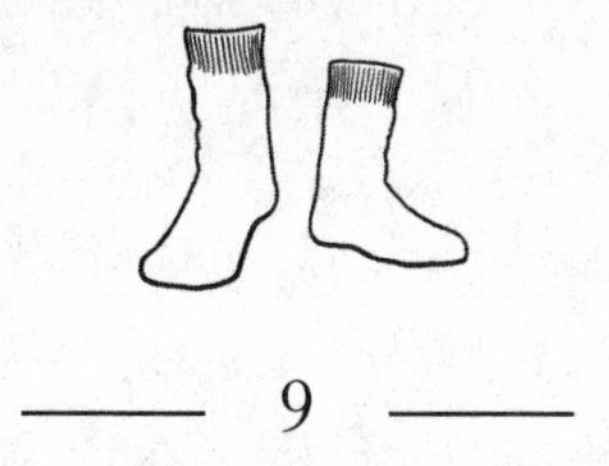

9

Benedict Maximus Pendleton

WHEN I GOT HOME, I WANTED TO TALK TO MY dad. He would have great advice. He's brilliant. I'm not saying that just because he's my dad. He's a psychiatrist and an author. He doesn't have any patients anymore unless you consider the millions of people that have read his books all his patients. That's how many people think my dad is brilliant. So it's not just me. His most famous book is called *Being a Perfect Person* and it describes in detail how one can achieve perfection through thought and action. I have read it fourteen times even though it is a book written for adults. But I'm very mature. Obviously. I'm also very smart. Obviously.

Our house is an old farmhouse in an unincorporated part of Illinois north of Riverbend. My dad made it three times bigger, though, so actually it's just a new house. It has ten acres of land, but only my mom and sister ever walk around it. My dad and I are too busy inside studying and working to walk around the yard. My dad didn't want me to go to Riverbend High School. He wanted to send me to Phillips Exeter, a private high school in New Hampshire, because he thought Riverbend wasn't good enough for me. But I wanted to go to high school with Robert. And not be far away from my dad. He yelled at me when I told him I wanted to stay. He said I was making the biggest mistake of my life. Now that Robert and I are no longer friends, it turns out my dad was right. He always is.

When I went into our house, I looked for my dad in the living room. Sometimes he would read there and eat cereal. But he wasn't there, which meant he was in his office, which was in the basement. The whole basement. I knocked on the door to the stairs. "Dad?" There was no answer. I knocked again. "Dad? Can we talk?" But there was no answer again. My dad ignored us if he was working. He was very disciplined. But I really needed to talk to him, so I knocked again. "DAD!" But there still wasn't an answer.

My mom leaned into the hall from the kitchen. "Benedict. Your dad is working." He had been working a lot recently on his new book. All day and night. He would sleep in the basement often because he was working so hard. His next book was going to change the world, he said. It has been eight years since *Being a Perfect Person* was published.

"I know but I need to talk to him."

"Why don't you talk to me?" she said.

"You're not as smart as Dad, Mom," I said, then turned and went upstairs to my room.

Evil Benny said I shouldn't have said that to my mom. Evil Benny said that a person who can't even be nice to his mom would never know how to be nice to anyone.

"But she's not as smart. She wouldn't want me to lie," I said out loud to Evil Benny, which I shouldn't have done. Evil Benny then said I was going crazy if I was talking to voices in my head.

My mother didn't have a job. She was just a mom. She was Polish but looked Asian. My dad said she probably had Mongolian in her, but my mom never talked about where she was from. She was very beautiful. This was not just my opinion. She had been a model at the auto show and other events when she met my dad.

When I was thirteen, my dad said to me, "You are developing into a good-looking boy. I was worried when you were younger that you would stay awkward. But I shouldn't have worried since I am distinguished looking and your mother is genetically very attractive. So your good looks are because I chose her as your mother. I didn't choose her for her brains. Obviously. I'm smart enough to make up for her shortcomings. But you should know that since your mother is not an intellectual you don't need to listen to her on certain topics."

Since my dad told me that, it has been hard to talk to my mom about anything. She used to be good for consoling me, but my dad's book said people should be able to console themselves. My dad's book says the most important part of becoming a perfect person is not needing other people who are, obviously, not perfect. Thus talking to my mom about Robert was not an option. She would just try to make me feel better. I didn't need to feel better. I needed advice on how to avoid this mistake in the future.

There was a knock on my bedroom door. I jumped up, very fast, and opened it. It had to be my dad. I would have been so happy if it had been my dad.

But it was not. He must still be working. It's okay. He is writing important things.

It was my sister, Elizabeth. She's in eighth grade. She's not as smart as me, but she's pretty smart for a girl. I'm not sexist. I just know girls aren't as smart. My dad said it's because they can't always think logically. Logic is the most important skill one can have to succeed in life.

"What do you want, Elizabeth?" I said. My sister walked past me and sat on my bed. She didn't say anything. Elizabeth is very tall, almost as tall as me, which is very frustrating. She also has long black hair that hangs down to the middle of her back. She is objectively pretty, which is good because pretty girls can marry more successful men than non-pretty girls. She has a boyfriend—his name is Derrick and he is black—but I wasn't allowed to tell my dad because he would yell at her. Not because Derrick is black. My dad said we should both marry people from different races because our children would benefit from genetic diversity. He would yell at Elizabeth because she wasn't supposed to date until she was sixteen. I had listened to him. But I was smarter than Elizabeth.

"What did you say to Mom?" my sister said after not saying anything for almost thirty seconds.

"Nothing."

"Then why is she so sad now? I was in the kitchen with her and then you said something and now she's sad."

"Elizabeth, I told her I needed to talk to Dad and she tried to talk to me but I told her she was not as smart as Dad because she's not."

"You're such an asshole," Elizabeth said, then left.

"I'm telling Dad you cursed," I said after her even though I wouldn't tell him. I used to tell my dad every wrong thing my mom or sister said or did, but then he told me it bored him when I told him these things, so I stopped.

I slammed my bedroom door so that my sister would feel bad about calling me an asshole, turned on my computer, and opened up my email. There was no email for me except spam. Robert usually sent me an email after I dropped him off. Usually some funny YouTube links. But I guess I won't get those links now since we're not friends anymore. It's for the best. I was getting too old to waste time on silly videos.

Usually I did all my homework as soon as I got home so that I could then play *StarCraft*, which is a strategic video game that I am very, very good at. My username is MaximumAwesome. I am ranked highly if you want to go online and see. But instead I decided I would make a list of the girls at Riverbend that I would consider to be my girlfriend. Since I didn't have Robert anymore, it was even more important that I get one.

Before I listed the names of actual students, I listed necessary qualities a girl would need to be my girlfriend:

1. TOP 25 IN GPA BUT NOT JENNY GOLDBERG. JENNY WAS RANKED NUMBER ONE IN OUR CLASS. I WAS SMARTER, BUT SHE WOULD THINK SHE WAS SMARTER.
2. SOPHOMORE OR JUNIOR. NO FRESHMEN SINCE THEY ARE IMMATURE AND NO SENIORS SINCE OLDER WOMEN WHO DATE YOUNGER MEN ARE DESPERATE.
3. A VIRGIN. I WAS A VIRGIN. IN FACT, I HAD NEVER KISSED A GIRL. IT WOULD BE BEST IF THE GIRL HADN'T KISSED ANYONE EITHER.
4. SHE KNEW HOW SMART I WAS. (*SEE JENNY GOLDBERG NOTE.)
5. SHE WAS SO ATTRACTIVE THAT OTHER BOYS WOULD BE JEALOUS.

I stopped at five because five is my favorite number. For the next two hours, I went through the yearbook from last year and considered any girl that met my five listed parameters. (Though I could not be assured of their being virgins, any girl that had a boyfriend longer than three months, like the otherwise parameters-approved sophomore Carolina Fisher, was eliminated from being a consideration.)

In the end, I was left with only two girls until allowing women in the top fifty in GPA brought my list to my preferred number of five.

I considered emailing all five in a group email but instead sent the same letter to the five different girls though Facebook. It stated that I, Benedict Maximus Pendleton, was interested in their becoming my girlfriend and I would like to go on a trial date to see if I enjoyed them in person.

I had not heard back from any of the five girls after doing my homework. Nor after dinner. Nor after my fifty push-ups. Nor after playing *StarCraft*. Nor after playing *StarCraft* an hour longer than usual.

Getting into bed, Evil Benny said I would never have a girlfriend and that I would die a virgin. He said I was a friendless loser who would be alone forever.

I tried to argue with Evil Benny, but my dad had taught me not to argue with facts.

— 10 —

pen

After we left school, Paul drove me to my dad's pizzeria. Which was normal. Neither of us said anything. Which was also normal. But the way we didn't say anything was different. Felt like there was a bomb in Paul's head. Tick, tick, tick. It was going to explode any moment and, shit, I don't know what would happen. Even if it never exploded, I could hear that tick, tick, tick in *my* head and it was driving me cray-cray-cray-zy.

After he parked in the restaurant lot, I said, "My mom wanted me to ask if you were coming to Wild Wolf again this year for Christmas break?" Wild Wolf was this lake/resort place up in Wisconsin my mom had taken me every winter since I was a kid. My dad has never come because he always works. Wild Wolf was fun when I was little, before my mom and I realized we hated each other, and then it was torture for like five years yet she still dragged me there anyway. Freshman year she told me to invite Paul, he came, and he made it bearable for both of us. Even fun again as long Mom and I weren't left alone too much.

Paul said, "You don't want me to come?"

“Of course I want you to come,” I said, quiet because I always have a quiet voice, but inside I was screaming. I cannot imagine being stuck alone with my mom in a cabin in the middle of the woods and snow. I might kill myself. I’m not kidding.

“Then I don’t know why you even asked. Of course I’m coming. We’re getting married.” Paul always talked about us getting married. And he said it most often when I knew he was mad at me. Like he was telling himself he just had to put up with me, no matter what. To be real, I think Paul feels he has to marry me because we’ve had sex. I’d be lucky if he married me. Even if it’s only because he thinks he’d go to hell if he didn’t.

Paul took my face in his hands, pulled my chin close. His eyes were so close to mine it was like our eyeballs had left our heads so they could be right next to each other.

He said, “I love you, Pen.”

“I love you too.” I always said “I love you” after he did. I said it first once and it weirded him out. So I say it second. Always.

My dad’s restaurant is called Penelope’s Pizzeria. It’s named after me. Which sucks because I feel like I’ll have to work there until I’m dead.

Besides the terrible name, the pizza is great. Really great. My dad is the chef and, really, it’s the best in all of Chicago. Yeah, I’m his daughter and biased but only a little. The pizza really is so good and it’s normal pizza, thin crust, not the thick stuff that the rest of Chicago likes. He grew up in Brooklyn and only moved here, to Riverbend, because my mom made him. It’s a long story and really boring. The short version is that my dad hates it here and my mom hates that he hates it here. They have fought about it every week or more since I can remember. All parents fight, I’m sure, but it still su-u-ucks.

I work the cash register at the restaurant four or five nights every week. It's cool. My mom complains that I work too much, but I'd rather work than do homework. My mom says that's why my grades suck. She doesn't use the word "suck." She says "my grades suffer." She says no college will want me. My dad tells her that he didn't go to college and he's very successful, and my mom then explains that owning one pizzeria does not make him "very successful" and then he tells her she should get a job if she thinks she could do better and then she says she stopped working to raise me and then they fight about all that. It's boring when they fight and even more boring thinking about them fighting.

"You're late," my dad said as I walked into the kitchen. He said it loud, over the sound of Frankie doing the dishes and Juan folding boxes. They worked almost as much as my dad, which was every day. Every day except Thanksgiving, Christmas, and the Fourth of July. My dad's a large guy. Yeah, maybe fat. Like his second chin is bigger than his neck. But anyone who worked in a pizzeria all day and made pizza as good as my dad's would be fat. I try to tell him he's got to lose weight and he always says, "I know, I know," but he doesn't really listen.

And I wasn't really late. I was never late. I have this strange thing with being on time, actually. But my dad liked to say I was late because he just likes to say things. Especially in front of his other employees, always proving I don't get special treatment because I'm his daughter.

"I'm on time, Dad." I kissed his cheek and messed up his hair. He likes when I do that. He's really just a big kid. Which is great, right?

"If you're not early, you're late," he said, and then he turned his back to me and sank his hands into mozzarella under the hot water. Most people who put hands in water that hot would go to the hospital. Not my dad.

After we closed at ten, I swept the dining room and then sat at a table and almost started reading a book that I was supposed to read for English class but instead I texted with Iris about how Stacy was doing and how Paul and the boys wanted to beat up Benedict but we had to stop them. Iris agreed with me, but she'd probably agree with Stacy if Stacy tells the boys to really beat up Benedict.

Since my dad's gotten into two accidents in the past ten months from falling asleep at the wheel, I always drive home. I actually have a car—a silver Beetle—but my mom drives me to school and Paul drives me to work so I can drive my dad home. It's not my dad's fault he crashed. He works too much. He's the hardest-working person I know. The hardest-working person anyone knows.

Our house is part of an old development by the grade school. It was the nice part of Riverbend before they built Covered Bridges. My mom bitches about the snobs in Covered Bridges, about the trees they cut down to build it. But my mom just wishes we could afford to live over there.

After I parked the car in the driveway, my dad made himself a plate of cheese, went to the living room, and got into his La-Z-Boy in front of the news. He loves watching CNN. He has CNN on all day at the restaurant and all night in the living room. If the news isn't on, he'll talk about it as if you didn't watch the same segment he just did. I love my dad, so it's almost cute. He'll fall asleep in the La-Z-Boy as soon as he's done eating the cheese. He only goes up to bed after the sunlight wakes him in the morning.

After I kissed my dad good night, I went up the stairs to the bathroom. My mom was watching TV in her bedroom with the door closed. She actually likes all the good shows, the same shows I watch, but we never watched them together or talked about it. I tried to be quiet walking past her door, but she heard me and yelled, "Don't forget to wipe the sink, Penelope! I saw toothpaste in there this morning!"

I ignore her when she calls me Penelope. I fucking hate my name. She loves it. That about sums up my mom and me. Not really.

After peeing, I brushed my teeth, left the toothpaste there for a second in the sink, but then cleaned it. Better to just do what my mom says sometimes or else I'd go crazy. I already am crazy. But I'd go the kind of crazy I couldn't control.

Then I went to my bedroom, locked the door, and turned on Pandora. I don't like music with words. I like some of it, I guess, just most of the time I like to listen to really experimental, trippy stuff by artists no one else has heard of. It just lets my mind leave my body and then my soul leave my mind. That sounds cheesy, but I'm being real.

After I texted Paul good night, I got under my covers, took off my underwear, and then put a pillow between my legs. I can orgasm about fifty different ways—with my fingers or the faucet in the tub or even just rubbing my legs together if I concentrate—but using a pillow is my favorite.

I don't like looking at porn. Not real porn anyway. Sometimes I'll look at magazines like *Vogue* or the Victoria's Secret catalog. I'm not a lesbian. Lesbians are cool. I'm just not one. See, I don't imagine doing anything to another girl. I imagine *I am* that girl, that beautiful model, and how sexy everyone thinks I am. Imagining everyone finds me sexy turns me on more than anything.

Once in a while, I'll think about a boy when I masturbate. Never Paul. I made myself do it once, but I couldn't orgasm. This makes me feel like a terrible girlfriend, but how can I tell my body to get turned on by something if it doesn't?

I can't even tell my own head some of the boys I've imagined. Like I know I'm a freak, but I should be put in jail for having some of these thoughts in my head. Teachers and Iris's dad. Shit. I can't believe I admitted that. Like, if they tried to kiss me in life, I would cry and report them to the cops. But sometimes when I'm masturbating, faces just come into my head and my body just shakes and I don't stop it. After I orgasm, even I want to go confess I'm a sinner. Then I realize I could never tell anyone any of this.

I'm.

Such.

A.

Freak!

Really. Shit. It's okay. It's not okay. But I can't be different, I've tried, so even though I'm not going to tell anyone—not ANYONE—about what goes on in my head, I'm not going to hate myself anymore. Well, at least not hate myself as much as I usually do.

(Okay, I know I said I didn't but as long as I'm admitting everything, there have been a few times I've thought about being with a girl. Usually that androgynous girl Zee in my class. It's hard to explain. All of this is hard to explain.)

As I was lying there on my bed, thinking all this, the music playing, pillow between my legs, I started to imagine Benedict. Fuck. See? I just can't stop crazy things from happening in my brain. Why would I think of him? He's such a dork and so awkward. But not awkward like Robert or like I was. Or am again. But Benedict, he's awkward like he doesn't belong here. You know, among normal people. But he doesn't seem to care he doesn't belong. Everyone else, me, Paul, Stacy, Robert, and everyone, we all care about belonging. I care so much I'm willing to spend my life pretending to be someone else.

But Benedict doesn't give a crap, does he? He doesn't. And even though he's this robot, he was this sexy robot today. Because he's a *real* robot and not a *fake* person like me. And being real is really sexy. Really. Yes.

My body shook, twice, and I fell asleep two seconds later.

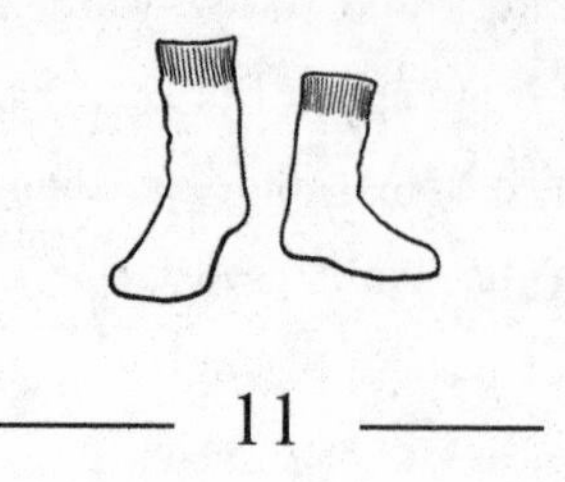

— 11 —

Benedict Maximus Pendlet . . .

WHEN I WOKE UP THE NEXT MORNING, I CHECKED Facebook on my iPhone before I got out of bed. An email! Success! One of the five girls had written me back. Sophie Gutierrez. She was in my top two, so at the first sight of her name, I felt satisfaction. But then I read what she wrote: *Don't be weird, Benedict*. That was all. I almost asked if this meant she would go on a date, but then decided this did not mean she would go on a date.

I was not sad. Sadness is not productive. But my head felt as if there were a large object on top of it, crushing my skull. There was nothing literally on my head. My head was safe. Obviously.

After showering and dressing, I found my mother in the kitchen. She had made me egg whites and English muffins. This was my favorite breakfast. I should have apologized for saying she wasn't as smart as Dad yesterday. Instead, I said nothing, not even good morning, and started eating. When Elizabeth entered, she said, "Good morning, Mom," and then, "Thanks for breakfast."

I should say thank you too, but now I felt bad for not saying it before my sister. So instead I remained silent and looked at my phone. There was nothing on my phone I wanted to look at, but your phone is a good place to look if you want to avoid eye contact.

When we were finished eating, my mother said, "We aren't going to Hawaii this year for break."

"Why not?" my sister asked.

"Because your dad wants to go to Wisconsin."

"Wisconsin's not warm!" Elizabeth whined. "I need to get a tan! I'm so pale!" My sister was always nice until she didn't get her way. Then she was a baby.

"Why Wisconsin, Mom?" I asked, very calm. I enjoyed Hawaii, mostly because I could order as many virgin piña coladas as I wished. But if Dad wanted to go to Wisconsin, I was sure this was the right thing to do.

"There's a lake he went to as a kid. He wants to show both of you where he spent his winters."

"No, he doesn't," Elizabeth said. "He hates nature. He just wants me to be pale."

"Why would Dad care if you were pale?" I asked.

"Shut up, Benedict."

"Don't say 'shut up,' Elizabeth," my mom said.

"What is the name of the lake?" I asked.

"Wild Wolf." Since I already had my phone out, I looked it up. It was a resort, sort of. Not fancy like we were used to. There were pictures of cabins with large fish hanging on the walls. "It doesn't look very nice," I said. Elizabeth yanked the phone out of my hands. I yanked it back.

"I'm not going," Elizabeth said.

"Yes, you are. But you can bring a friend if you wish," my mom said. "And Benedict, you can bring Robert."

Elizabeth whined louder than usual, "It's like three days away! And anyway, no friend of mine is going to want to go up to freezing-cold Wisconsin with my weirdo brother and weirdo Robert!"

"Elizabeth!" my mom yelled.

"Robert won't be coming. We aren't friends anymore," I said. Both my mom and sister snapped their heads toward me as if I had turned into a gorilla. I hadn't turned into a gorilla. Obviously.

"Benedict, but . . ." my mom started, but she did not know what to say. My sister looked down at her plate. She felt sorry for me. Having your younger sister feel sorry for you did not feel good. I was not doing a satisfactory job of controlling my emotions this morning. I must work on that.

I said, very confident, "I am very okay. I am better than ever. Robert was no longer adding to my life in a way that benefited me."

"Benedict . . ." my mom started again.

"I am fine. Tell Dad I am excited about going to Wisconsin." I then stood from the island counter, scooped up my backpack, and drove to school. I would be very early because I didn't need to pick up Robert, so I drove through his neighborhood just in case he called. He didn't.

I went to my locker even though I bring all my books home every night and carry them around all day. But sometimes you need somewhere to go so you don't look lost. After opening my locker and rearranging some folders so that I appeared busy, I closed it and turned to walk toward first-period AP English.

The rest of the students in the hall had all moved toward the lockers. No one was walking in the center except me. This was very strange. Obviously. Then three boys moved to the center and started walking toward me. It was Paul Barbo, Joey Plint, and Conrad Miller.

Everyone called him Miller because he didn't like the name Conrad. They were all friends with Stacy Ashton, whom I had insulted yesterday. Thus, logically, this meant they were here to hurt me as revenge for what I had said. The three boys spread out as they walked toward me, far enough apart that I couldn't walk around them but close enough together that I couldn't walk between them. The smart choice would be to turn and walk the other way. Or to stop and press myself into the lockers like the other kids. But then everyone would think I was a wimp. I wasn't a wimp. But I didn't want to get beaten up either.

The first time I got beaten up was in sixth grade. His name was Kyle. He punched me in the face in the bathroom because he said he didn't like how I answered questions in class. My nose bled all over the floor and mixed with my tears. I told the teachers what he did and then Kyle got in big trouble. When he came back to school after being suspended, he had a bruise on his face. He told everyone that he had fallen skateboarding. But Kyle's dad had coached us in soccer, so I knew he was very mean and had probably hit Kyle. In sixth grade, I was happy his dad hit him. But now that I'm older, I realize I'd rather be a kid who gets punched by another kid than a kid who gets punched by his dad. Obviously the best kid to be is the kid that doesn't get punched at all.

After Kyle, I got beaten up four times in junior high. I didn't tattle on them like I did Kyle, just in case. No one had tried to hit me since high school started. This is probably because I'm taller and I do push-ups. But I didn't know how to fight, so even if I was taller than Paul, Joey, and Miller—I'm going to call him Conrad, okay?—they probably *did* know how to fight. Joey was on the wrestling team. So he really knew how to fight. I kept walking toward them, but I walked slower because my imagination could feel their fists hitting my face and that made it hard to walk normal speed.

With Robert no longer my friend and none of the girls I had emailed wanting to go on a date with me, I decided that I should just run the other way and not care that everyone thinks I'm a wimp. No one likes me anyway, so I might as well be someone no one likes who doesn't get punched. But then, just as I was logically explaining to my body how we should turn around and flee to safety, my mouth yelled, "AAAAAAH!" and my legs ran toward the boys, and my arms twisted my backpack off and swung it into Joey's head. He wasn't expecting that. I laughed. I don't even know why. I must be crazy. But maybe I was happy because the other kids in the hall all clapped. But then Paul tackled me. He was on the football team. He did not play much, "rode the bench" I believe is the vernacular, but my body said he was still good at tackling because I was thrown hard into the floor. Paul straddled my chest and pinned my arms down with his hands. I tried really hard to move, but I couldn't. Then Conrad kicked me in the thigh.

That hurt

so so so so so

much.

Then Joey, who was mad that I'd whacked him in the head with my backpack, kicked me in the side. As much as getting kicked in the thigh hurt, getting kicked in the side hurt five trillion times more.

I couldn't breathe.

I still couldn't breathe.

And I still couldn't breathe.

If you can't breathe, you die. So I guessed I was going to die. I should have run. I should have run and then when I was rich and famous when we are all grown up, I'd exact my revenge by hiring assassins to blow up their cars. But now I was going to die.

While I was dying, Paul said, "Never talk to any of us again, retard," and then he pulled back his fist to hit me. Gosh, it's mean to hit someone while they are dying. But then I heard:

"Paul! Don't!" He turned and I, sort of, turned too. It was hard for my eyes to focus. You get blurry vision when you are dying, I guess. I did manage to see that it was Penelope. Paul's girlfriend. Robert's dream girl. She was running toward us. Before Paul could hit me, Penelope pushed him off me. Now all the kids watching laughed. Paul didn't like getting laughed at.

"WHAT'S YOUR PROBLEM, PEN?!" Paul yelled at her, and then he lunged toward her but Joey pulled him away and pointed down the hall. I think teachers were coming because everyone was trying to pretend nothing happened.

Penelope got on her knees and leaned over me. "Are you okay, Benedict?" she asked. I couldn't talk because I was dying. But I did notice that she smelled. Well, first thing I noticed was her scar. It looked different up close. But then I noticed she smelled. I don't mean she smelled bad. But she had a scent. It was very distinct. I had not been close to Penelope since junior high, and I don't remember her smelling like this. I don't remember any girls smelling like this. It was a nice smell. It was like flowers and fresh laundry and something I couldn't determine. I've always liked the smell of fresh laundry. I guess I also liked flowers. And this currently undefinable third component too. She asked again, "Are you okay?"

Even though I was surprised I was still alive, I somehow managed to speak and I said, "I'm dying." But it came out very wheezy and high-pitched.

Penelope smiled, which I thought was not very nice at first but then realized it calmed me down. She said, "You just got the wind knocked out of you." Then Penelope rubbed my chest for only a second. It felt almost as good as getting kicked felt bad. I think it also helped me breathe again. At least the two seemed to happen at the same time.

A teacher then leaned over and yanked Penelope off me and to her feet. A second teacher, whom I didn't know but I think taught woodshop, leaned over me and asked if I was okay and that's when I started to cry. Darn it, Benedict, you turn seventeen in five days. Seventeen-year-old boys should never cry even when dying. But I think my breath coming back made me realize I *wasn't* going to die and knowing you are not going to die when you thought you were might be even scarier than actually dying. That doesn't make sense, but my brain isn't working optimally at this moment.

Both Penelope and I were taken to the dean's office. I had never been there. Only people who get in trouble go there. And I never, ever got into trouble. Obviously. Penelope and I were seated next to each other and told to wait here until Dean Jacoby arrived.

The office was small and dark since the blinds to the courtyard were closed. There was a big computer that looked so old my iPhone probably was ten times faster.

"It smells like cigarettes," I said, which I didn't mean to say out loud. I didn't want to speak to Penelope. For at least five reasons and probably more.

"Totally," Penelope said. Saying "totally" made her sound not very smart. Which I already knew. Then she said, "I'm sorry Paul and those guys jumped you like that."

The mature thing to say would be "I'm sorry I told Stacy she was fat," but my brain and mouth didn't want to work together this morning. Perhaps they never worked well together. Thus I said, "I'm sorry you have a boyfriend like Paul."

I didn't look at Penelope, but I could tell she was sad by the way her body slumped in the corner of my vision. Then she said, "Yeah," and then we were quiet until Dean Jacoby arrived twelve minutes later. During those twelve minutes, I didn't look at Penelope even though I wanted to say something nice because I could tell I had made her sad. My dad's book talks about how it is not our job to make other people happy, that we must fight compromising ourselves for the sake of others' feelings. But I felt sad that Penelope was sad. This was very confusing to be sad because someone else was sad. I really needed to talk to my dad about controlling these feelings.

There was another thing about those twelve minutes we waited in silence in the dean's office. Even though we didn't speak, and we didn't look at each other, I could still smell her. Those flowers and fresh laundry and that mystery smell almost made the cigarette stench go away. It almost made the pain in my side and leg go away too. But it didn't make my sadness go away. Her smell might have even made the sadness worse. This didn't make any sense.

12

pen

Shit. Pushing Paul off Benedict made Paul super pissed at me. I had never seen him look at me like that. He hated me. I mean, *hated* me. And now, once Benedict told Dean Jacoby that Paul, Joey, and Miller had beaten him up, Paul would totally blame me for getting caught. Then he'd dump me. My whole life would be over. Except for like the tiniest one second, I thought, I'd be free, right? I'd be free. . . . Then I hated that feeling. I don't want to be free. That's stupid to think. Everyone wants to be free. But not if free meant my whole life would change. Because, man, I like my life. I mean, yeah, it's not perfect—my parents fight, my boyfriend doesn't know the real me, I'm getting C's in all my classes—but, like, I'm cool and my boyfriend's cool and my friends are cool.

I mean, what the hell were you thinking, Pen? You should have just let Paul and them beat up Benedict and stayed out of it. So stupid. I mean, shit. Now I'm sitting next to the robot in the dean's office and I can't even look at him because he's so weird and I, of course, can't stop thinking how I got off thinking about him last night. And I know how stupid and weird I am for having thought about Benedict like that. I mean, sitting next to him I can't even imagine saying two more words to him! But of course sitting next to him and thinking about the dirty thoughts I had last night starts turning me on because I can't control anything about myself and then I feel like such a freak I want to kill myself.

Dean Jacoby strutted in after making us wait forever. He had the smug, creepy grin he always has. Like he's got naked pictures of you in his house or something. After sitting on the edge of his desk like he's so goddamn important, he said, "Hello, Ms. Lupo. I thought you promised you wouldn't be making any visits to my office until next year?"

I was about to say "I'm sorry" or something except Benedict spoke first. "She helped me. She should be given praise by you, not judgment." Shit. Benedict the Robot just told off Dean Jacoby. No one ever tells off Dean Jacoby.

"I don't know you and I don't like your language," the dean said.

"I am Benedict Maximus Pendleton. I'm ranked third in the junior class. I do not ever curse, so I am not sure why you would not like my language."

"Christ," the dean said. Benedict was getting to him. I tried not to smile. But, man, it was sweet to see Jacoby sweat. "Just tell me why you're here. Penelope, you go first."

But Benedict spoke before I could think of how I could lie without getting in trouble. He said, "Another student and I ran into each other, accidentally, in the hallway. Penelope helped me up." The robot was lying for me. He was protecting me. And protecting Paul. And me and Paul. Shit. Not expected. My brain didn't know how to rearrange my assumptions in my head. I mean . . .

"Benedict, I asked Penelope to speak first. Do you have a problem with authority?"

"Not if it is competent," Benedict said.

Dean Jacoby's face was turning that purple color that means he's about to yell. Like really yell. But he held it in, and even though he wasn't breathing normally, he said, "Penelope, I was told there was a fight. What happened?"

Benedict said, faster than me like always, "I just told you what occurred."

"DO YOU WANT A DETENTION?!" Jacoby couldn't hold that yell in for long, I guess. Benedict looked like he just got slapped. Then the dean said the most asshole-ish thing I had ever heard him say. "I can see your face is red from crying, kid. You think lying to protect Penelope and her loser friends is going to make you popular? It's not. And if you think they can make you cry, wait till you see what I can do."

I so wanted to tell off Dean Jacoby, for a hundred things he had done and said to me since I got to The Bend, but mostly for making fun of Benedict, who wasn't used to getting bullied by a jerk-off adult like Jacoby.

Except Benedict, fucking crazy Benedict, said, "I will make YOU cry when I report you for smoking on school property."

Jacoby was about to explode. Literally. You could see his ears shaking super fast. He stepped toward Benedict, but said to me, "Lupo, get out of here. I see you again, I'm kicking you out of school."

I'm free to go . . . I should go. I should. But now I didn't want to leave Benedict, like I was afraid Jacoby might hurt him, like really hurt him, so I said, "Dean . . ."

"GET OUT OF HERE!" he yelled at me. Shit. How do angry nutballs like this get put in charge of kids? But now I knew I definitely couldn't leave Benedict. He was shaking too. Just fricking terrified.

Jacoby shaking out of rage, Benedict shaking out of fear. No way could I leave them alone. No way. I knew what Jacoby was capable of.

"He's got social problems," I said. It sucks Benedict heard me say this, but I figured it was better than leaving Jacoby alone with him.

"Lupo, you are out of here in three, two, one." The dean grabbed my arm, with those pudgy dirty fingers of his, pinched me hard, then ripped me off the chair and toward the door.

"No, I don't," Benedict said, loudly, then he said it quietly under his breath. Then he said it a third time and that third time made the dean let me go. Jacoby looked at both at us. He hated his job so much right that second.

The dean said, "Both of you get out of here. I don't want to hear anything from either of you about anything, you got it? I don't care what the hell is wrong with you." He shoved a pointed finger in Benedict's face, then said one more time because he was the meanest dickhead on the planet, "Not a word."

I grabbed Benedict, who was either too afraid or too unaware to move himself, and pulled him out of the office with me. Once we were in the hall, it felt like we had just escaped an underground jail cell. The light and air were so plentiful they made me dizzy. Like gonna-puke dizzy.

Then Benedict stopped me. Looked like he might cry again. Shit, I didn't want him to cry. His gaze got even more intense. Not like he was about to cry, but like . . . shit. He's going to kiss me. For real. Like people get that look in their eyes where they just have to kiss you. Paul never has it. But you know, like I've seen in movies. That crazy lust in their eyes and then they just lunge at each other. I mean, I wasn't feeling that. I mean, not really. But I can't say I didn't like seeing Benedict look at me like that. Like really liked it. God, I'm so screwed up. The kid was . . . never mind.

He didn't kiss me. As soon as he started talking, I realized how stupid I was for thinking he wanted to kiss me. Maybe I'm the one who is bad at interpersonal stuff. I gotta stop using that word. He said, like he knew what I was thinking, "I don't have problems. I'm very smart." Then he let me go and walked away. Yeah.

Paul was super mad at me for pushing him off Benedict. Even after I explained how Benedict and I lied to the dean and never mentioned his name, Paul was still super angry. Paul grunted at me, like he couldn't bother wasting words on me, and went out with the boys at lunch, leaving me with Stacy and Iris.

Once we were in Iris's car, Stacy said, "You're such a bitch," and ignored me the entire ride through the Taco Bell drive-through and back. Iris still talked to me, but not like usual. You could tell she was more worried about not pissing off Stacy. So I just sat in back and wished I was a different person. This all sucked. So much.

After school, Paul grabbed me under the arm and dragged me out to his car. He kept twisting the skin of my arm. It felt like flesh would tear off, and I never told him to stop. Just take the pain, Pen. It's okay. Paul would never really hurt me. Right? Once we were inside his car, he put the volume all the way up on an Eminem song and then he yelled at me. "If we hadn't had sex, I would totally break up with you, Pen! But I love you and we're going to get married. But we're going to hate each other like your parents hate each other unless you stop acting like such a cunt."

My boyfriend had just called me a cunt. Paul had never called me a bitch or even a jerk before. Ever. And now he had called me the c-word. Jesus. He also said my parents hated each other, and even though it's true, it sucks to know your boyfriend knows. I wanted to yell back at him. I felt so small and pathetic and I just needed to yell to make sure I still existed. I would tell him how he never listens to me or asks me what I think. Tell him that he's brainwashed by his parents and religion. Tell him I've never heard one original thought come out of his brain in three years. But I didn't say any of this. I just nodded. I didn't cry. Shit, I never cry. I mean, I did all the time as a kid when my parents would scream at each other. The only thing that made them stop was my crying. So I never wasted it on anything less. So no, I didn't cry. I just nodded. Just agreed with everything he said.

"How you going to make it up to me?" he said as he put his car in drive and exited the school parking lot. I knew what he meant. Every time he got mad at me he would get turned on. He's a freak too, I guess. We all are maybe.

So I put my hand on his crotch and started rubbing. Then he turned down a side street, found our usual dead end next to the golf course. We had come here at lunch a few times before. He undid his jeans and pulled them down to his knees. Before I even undid my seat belt, he put his hand behind my head and started guiding me down toward his crotch. It's not like he shoved me down there. But, I don't know, I guess I made it up to him.

Which is such bullshit. I mean, I like giving Paul blow jobs sometimes. But I hated doing it now. I hated me. I hated him. I could totally hurt him—

"Watch the teeth, baby," he said.

Yeah, I can't hurt him like that. So I hurt him by thinking of someone else while I did it. He would never know. But I would know.

I wish I could control who I thought of but I just couldn't. The only face that would enter my head was Benedict's. Still better than Paul. But this Benedict fantasy thing felt too wild, too weird, even for me, and I just had to stop it before . . .

Before what? It's not like anything could actually happen. Ever. It's just my imagination. My freaked-up imagination, but still, it's not real.

Nothing about me is real.

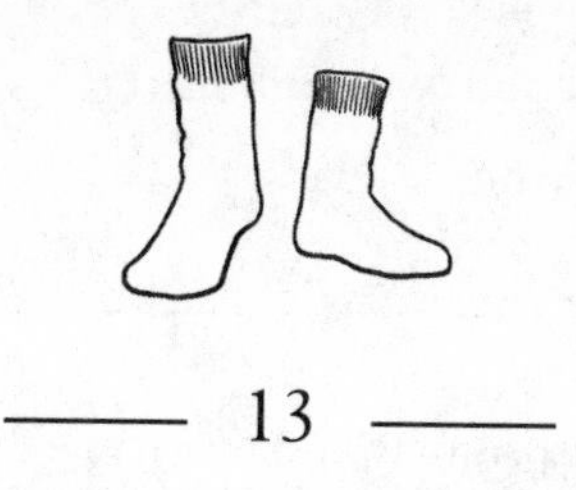

— 13 —

Benedict Maximus Pend . . .

OTHER STUDENTS LOOKED AND POINTED AT ME the rest of the school day. I did not enjoy this. I considered screaming at every guilty person but then determined this would only make my situation worse. It was especially difficult at lunch since I could not sit with Robert in the SAC. The Student Activity Center is technically meant to be for the use of all students, but the only people who actually use it are members of student government. Robert had run, unsuccessfully, for junior class president. I'm rather positive the only votes Robert received were his and mine. But Kristen Redding, who had won, appointed him as a special representative, which gave him and me, by my association with him, the unofficial permission to eat in the SAC. Which he would do without me now. He would make new friends quickly because Robert is a very good person. Except when he dumped me as his friend yesterday. Besides that, he was the best friend I can ever imagine having.

Thus I took the lunch my mom put in my backpack and ate on the bench outside the library. I was alone. I will get used to this, I am confident. But it was not pleasant today. Not at all. People were looking, pointing, whispering to each other about me. My body still felt the pain of getting kicked, and without Robert to speak to, Evil Benny just said the worst possible things.

His main topic, not surprisingly, was telling me that Penelope was right, that I had social problems. And, Evil Benny said, "social problems" really just meant I was a loser. A dork. The biggest dork in the school. Just like Robert had said.

I had heard this before. I knew I was different. My dad told me that "all great people are different," so most days I didn't mind being different. I often took pride in being different. But it was very hard to take pride in being thought of as having problems by someone like Penelope. Because Penelope was not smart. That's not nice for me to say. I always think not-nice thoughts about people who make me think not-nice thoughts about myself.

I very much didn't want to be different today. I was very tired. My brain could not focus. I almost left school after lunch but decided this would not be smart. Instead, I waited until after last period and then ran to my car. I must have looked strange running to my car, but I just needed to leave school as fast as possible.

I drove home, going over the speed limit the entire distance. I needed my mom. Yes, it was okay that I needed my mom. It had been an especially bad day, so needing your mom on an especially bad day was acceptable. Except her car wasn't in the garage. I had forgotten she took Elizabeth to her club volleyball on Wednesday.

My dad wasn't in the living room. I couldn't decide if talking to him now, in my current state, would be beneficial. My father is brilliant, but he has little patience for weakness. And I was feeling very, very weak. But I just couldn't go up to my room and be by myself. I was so alone up there. So alone at school. So alone everywhere.

I knocked on my father's basement door. "Dad?" I asked. There was no answer. "DAD?" I yelled.

I shouldn't have . . . but I tried the door. It wasn't locked. It was usually locked. Maybe he hadn't locked it because he wanted to talk to me.

I opened the door and descended the stairs. I grew nervous. It was confusing to be nervous. But I hadn't been in his basement since I was ten. Perhaps longer than even that. Yet I still stepped downward. Anything was better than being alone for even a moment longer.

Once at the bottom of the stairs, I realized the entire office basement was dark. I said, "Dad?" There was no answer. I worried he was hurt. I turned on the light.

My dad has given speeches all over the world. My dad has received thousands of letters from people who thank him for changing their lives. He's really important. He's the opposite of me. Well, that's what Evil Benny says. But it was true I was just a high school student with no friends and no girlfriend and my dad was a famous, rich author. Maybe Evil Benny was correct in this case.

The basement looked different from when I was ten. Smaller. Which I suppose would make sense since I am bigger. There used to be pictures of us on the walls. A painting of a bird my mom had done. But now those pictures and the painting were gone. Now the walls just had typed manuscript pages in rows, fastened by blue painter's tape. The black leather couch I remembered was still there, but now it had a pillow and blanket folded on it. A large metal desk faced the light well on the far wall, across from the stairs. It was as big as a Ping-Pong table. There were books stacked in organized piles as high as my waist against the walls. My dad sat in his chair, which has such a high back I couldn't see his head. But I could see his left elbow on the arm of the chair. So I knew he was there.

"Dad?" I said, but my voice sounded very whiny. Like when I was ten. Maybe I was ten again. That's stupid to think.

"Benedict," he said, but didn't swivel the chair toward me. He didn't sound whiny at all. He sounded very adult. Very important. Like he was a king. When he didn't say anything else, I almost went back upstairs. He didn't want me here, I could tell, but I needed him. I did. I hate admitting that.

Because I didn't want to say something pathetic, I said, "Why were you working in the dark?"

That caused my dad to swivel in his chair toward me. This made me excited at first, but then I saw his face, saw how his forehead was scrunched up and his eyes were dark, and his nose had flared open like it did when he was mad but trying not to show he was mad. "This is my office, Benedict. This is where I work, Benedict," he said. He also said my name a lot when he was mad but trying not to show it.

"I know," I said. I should leave. I should. But maybe he'll stop being mad and then talk to me.

Instead he said, "If you were my employee, Benedict, and not my son, I would fire you."

I nodded. He was right. I almost cried again. But I didn't. My dad would think even less of me. So I nodded again and went back up the stairs.

Exiting onto the main floor of our house, I found my mom and sister waiting there. My mom still had her oversized sunglasses on and her gigantic purse over her shoulder. These made her look like a movie star. But she was just my mom.

"You were down in Dad's office?" asked Elizabeth, wearing her volleyball practice clothes.

My mom said, while looking at me, "Elizabeth, go get showered. I'll take us out for an early dinner."

"But I want to go into the basement if Benedict gets to go! I want to see Dad too!"

"Elizabeth, go shower. Now." My mom could speak very effectively sometimes. Once Elizabeth had walked upstairs, my mom stepped past me and closed the door to my dad's office. She then took my head into her two hands and looked at me. Her eyes watered. She tried to smile. But she was not very successful. She asked, "Why'd you go down there?"

"I . . . wanted to talk to him."

"That's where he works. You know you can't disturb him," she said. These were not consoling words. My mom used to be good at saying consoling things, but maybe she was out of practice. But then she pulled me in and hugged me. "I'm so sorry, Benny." She called me Benny when I was a child. My dad told her to stop, so she did.

"I screwed up. I'm a bad son."

"No, no you're not. Not even a little bit. And . . . you should be able to go say hello to your dad. Every son should be able to say hello to his father whenever he wants. But do you understand that your dad is different?"

"He's important," I said.

"He's different," my mom said, but she had said it in a way that made it sound like "different" and "important" weren't the same thing.

The three of us went to dinner at the Cheesecake Factory. My sister wanted to go get pizza at Penelope's Pizzeria, but I said no way. I didn't tell her why.

During dinner, after we had eaten the brown bread but before our entrées came, I asked my mom, "Do I have social problems?"

Elizabeth laughed before my mom could speak. My mom said, "Elizabeth, don't you dare." Then my sister stopped snickering.

"I'm smarter than you," I said to my sister because I wanted her to feel bad like I felt bad.

"Smart is as smart does," she said.

"It's stupid is as stupid does, stupid," I said.

"I changed it. Artistic license."

"Elizabeth," my mom said. She could always make my sister shut up just by saying her name. Then my mom turned to me, reaching across the table and taking my hand. "Benedict, you don't have problems, you're just different."

"I don't want to be different anymore."

"What happened?" she asked. Part of me wanted to tell her about how I had no friends now, and no girlfriend ever, and how I got beaten up. But I didn't want to talk about being so pathetic anymore.

"Nothing."

"Benedict," my sister started, "you wear sports jackets and nice pants like you're going to church."

"We've never gone to church," I said.

"Ugh, I mean, like as if you were someone who went to church. And not just that, but it's like styles from 1985. You just look like someone who doesn't know what planet he's on."

"I know what planet I am on!" I don't even know why I yelled this.

"STOP TAKING EVERYTHING SO LITERALLY! GOSH!" my sister yelled much better than me. The tables around us got quiet for a moment. But then went back to normal. Nobody wanted trouble at a Cheesecake Factory.

"Both of you cannot yell like that," my mom said in a hush.

"I'm sorry," Elizabeth said.

"I'm . . . sorry . . . too."

Evil Benny said I was a hopeless loser who took everything literally and was so stupid I couldn't even see how stupid I was.

"Elizabeth," I said, because it was better to talk than listen to Evil Benny.

"Yes?" She didn't want to speak to me, like everyone else, but she was my sister, so she had to, I suppose.

"I . . ." Part of my brain wanted to say something. But another part of my brain, or another part of me, wouldn't let me. It was like my whole existence was malfunctioning.

"What, Benedict?"

"I . . ." My neck felt warm. Like a rash was growing and going to spread out over my body and then eat every inch of my flesh. Just like that.

"Are you all right?" my mom asked, squeezing the hand she had never let go.

"I . . . want . . ." Each word felt very big and impossible, unable to fit outside my mouth.

"Can you just speak already?"

"I want . . . your . . . help."

Both my sister and mom were silent. Evil Benny laughed at me. He thought it was so funny that I asked my younger sister for help. I wish I could take it back. I wish I could go back in time and be a different person.

"Of course she'll help you," my mom said.

"Yeah, totally. You mean like . . . I don't know, what kind of help?"

"Dressing like I'm not going to church. And talking to girls."

"And helping you know what planet you're on?" Elizabeth was being clever. My dad said clever people are masking their lack of intelligence. But maybe intelligent people are masking their lack of cleverness.

So I said, with as big a smile as I could manage, "Yes, helping me know what planet I am on."

14

pen

Sex.

Xes.

Exs.

Sxe.

Xse.

Esx.

S.E.X.

I think about it. Yeah. A lot. I know this. I know I'm a freak because of it. *I KNOW OKAY.* But when I think about thinking about it, I'm actually shocked everybody doesn't think about it as much as I do.

I mean, our bodies are programmed to want to do it. By God or nature or the universe or some other power that made all of us. It's how humankind keeps from going extinct! That basically makes it the most important thing in the world, doesn't it?

Yeah, it does.

But ALSO, we all feel ashamed about thinking about it and doing it and talking about it. So this thing "sex" that makes it possible for humans to actually be alive is something we are taught *not* to feel good about. How screwed up is that? (Well, not everyone has been brainwashed into feeling like crap about sex. There are people on HBO and stuff that seem perfectly comfortable talking about it on camera. But most everyone else is. Like my family and my friends and teachers and politicians and priests and TV newspeople and anyone else kids might look to for advice.)

And then maybe because our bodies want to do it because of nature and our minds don't want to do it because of religion or morals or whatever, sex becomes confusing, which can make it more exciting, and that excitement makes it even more confusing and back and forth until no one really wants to talk about it in a real way and so everyone just guesses or judges or represses.

Knowing all that, how can I not find it fascinating? This act that requires odd-looking body parts to get weird and wet and combine together and makes everyone feel uncomfortable at least a little is the one thing that keeps our species on planet earth.

I mean, HOW DOES EVERYONE NOT FIND IT AS FASCINATING AS ME?!

Oh, Pen. Because other people have better things to think about, I guess. Or maybe because if they thought about it as much as I think about it, they'd get horny as much as I get horny and then everyone would masturbate as much as me and no one would do anything else and all of society would stop functioning.

Like now. No way could I do homework now. No, no, no, no, no way. My head's got all these thoughts and images and my body is throbbing and fu-u-u-u-u-u-u-u-ck, I'm going to look at his pictures on

Facebook, aren't I? Yes, I totally am. I fall back on my bed, tap on my phone, open the app, search my friends, type his name:

Benedict Pendleton.

We're still friends from the time we first signed up in junior high, and even though I barely post on it anymore because my mom's on it, I bet Benedict uses it still. Of course he does.

Of course.

Oh-my-god, he's such a dork. He's got pictures of himself in a suit standing in front of his fancy car. Oh-my-god, he's got pictures of his computer game scores. With him in black sunglasses pointing at the screen like he's the coolest person in the world for being good at a silly game when it actually makes him the least cool person in the world. How can someone be so oblivious to how the rest of us at school behave and dress?

And,

AND,

AND OH-MY-GOD,

HOW CAN THAT SOMEONE TURN ME ON SO MUCH?!

I keep swiping through his pictures while my free hand—not even knowing what it is doing—digs under the top of my jeans, doesn't even unbutton them, maybe if I had unbuttoned them I could have stopped or closed the door or gotten under my bedcover or SOMETHING but instead I just keep swiping through the pictures and touching myself. My underwear is drenched and it is so gross, sex is so gross, my body is gross, but it's so sexy when I feel gross, like the more animal and disgusting I am the more my body gushes. *FREAK.*

Of course I keep touching and swiping pictures and touching and then I stop on this one close-up of just Benedict's eyes and the top of his nose and I feel like he is in the room with me and it is eerie and

I hate it and I keep looking at it. I mean, those eyes are not the eyes of a human! They are empty! They go on forever! It's a Tin Man stare! Like he's got no soul! Or he doesn't think you have one or he's going to steal yours or I don't know it's so creepy I can't breathe right!

I'm moaning, I don't even know I'm moaning, IF I KNEW I WAS MOANING, I WOULD HAVE STOPPED.

But I don't know, and my body is lifting off the bed, not really, but sort of, and this orgasm is going to be the best orgasm of my life and am I crying? I don't even know, but my body is humming, yes, humming, crying, moaning, humming, and body shaking and MOANING and . . .

A shadow at the door.

Then a voice.

A screaming voice.

My mother's screaming voice.

"AAAAAH! AAAAAH! AAAAAAH!" These screams of hers are sirens, sirens that knock over buildings, sirens that kill dogs, sirens that mark the end of the world.

My body finishes, my moans stop, all joy stops, and as soon I can dig my voice out of its deep-freeze mortification, I yell, not even half as loud as her, but as loud as I can, "I WAS SINGING, MOM! I WAS SINGING TO A SONG ON MY PHONE!" This is insane. But what else could I have said? My mother is the biggest Catholic ever to be a Catholic who thinks all people that aren't Catholic are demons going to hell. She doesn't want the truth, that she just caught her sixteen-year-old daughter masturbating to pictures on her phone; she wants any lie she can grasp on to to delude her into believing I'm not a dirty-slut-heathen-Antichrist.

But her screams don't stop. Words start forming. "PENELOPE! PENELOPE! HOW COULD YOU! HOW COULD YOU!" Then back to guttural wails. As if her organs are being yanked out through her nose. She is pacing in the hallway. She can't look at me. Can't even look in my room. I get to my feet and wipe my fingers on my jeans and move toward the door.

I'll hug her, I'll calm her down. Yeah, that'll work. Do that, Pen.

My mother gets like this—I mean, never *this* bad, but gets hysterical once a month or so. Usually over my dad yelling at her or me ignoring her, and if I just grab her and wrap my arms around her, she usually starts settling down.

But just before I step into the hallway, I stop. I look. My mother in her pink muumuu nightgown that hasn't been taken off in three days, her neck craned toward the ceiling, eyes clenched closed, arms shaking toward God, surely asking him what she did to deserve such a horrible daughter.

If she had walked into my bedroom and found me dead instead of masturbating, my mother would have had a nice, contained, respectful cry. She would have called Father Jeremy and he would have come over and they would have held hands and prayed to Jesus at the side of my bed. Then she would have worked tirelessly to throw a very elaborate funeral where she would have repeated, "She's with Jesus now, she's in Jesus's arms now," and she would have loved how everyone felt sorry for her, how they all thought she was handling her daughter's death with "God's grace."

And that vision, that vision of my stoic mother at my funeral contrasting with this madwoman throwing a temper tantrum because I had my hand down my jeans . . . I don't know. I cracked. Something in me cracked. I always tried to appease my mom's craziness.

But—

"FUCK YOU, MOM! FUCK YOU FUCK YOU FUCK YOU FUCK YOU FUCK YOU!" I spent most of my life wanting to tell my mom to fuck off. This was the first time I actually did it.

She stopped her yells, turned toward me. No more hysteria. Just pure rage. "AAAAAAAAH!" And she charged at me like a rabid elephant and I slammed the door in her face and locked it. She hit the frame and yelled and pounded and demanded I let her in.

My dad, who probably wouldn't have woken up from his La-Z-Boy downstairs if you stabbed him in the leg with a steak knife, started yelling at her, "WHAT'S ALL THIS YELLING?! WHY ARE YOU SO CRAZY?!"

And she yelled back and he yelled louder. And my mother told him he was the worst husband and I was the worst daughter and then he said no, she was the craziest bitch alive. It got more vile from there.

It had been a while, but I knew their yelling match was going to end with someone getting hit, so I put my earphones on and turned the music so loud that I couldn't hear my own thoughts.

When I was about five, my mom got pregnant. You can't imagine how happy I was. Even when I was that young, I knew my parents were nuts, but to have a baby brother or sister that I could talk to and hold at night when they fought? This was all I asked or prayed or thought about. I wanted this baby so much I'd cry at night wishing for it.

But then my mom got sick and went to the hospital, and I stayed with my aunt for a week. When I finally was allowed back home, all I wanted to know was if the baby was okay.

And my mom said, "God made me give the baby back to him." She didn't say it with sadness, or even like she was trying to make me feel better. She said it like she was warning me. Like maybe God could make her give me back too. She never mentioned the baby again. My dad never mentioned it at all. I never asked.

But for years, I'd have dreams of my mom coming into my room while I was sleeping, holding this dead fetus, asking me if I wanted to hold my baby brother. (Always a boy in the dream, I don't know why.) And I'd say yes because—even though I was terrified—I had to protect the baby like I promised, right? But when I'd reach out, the baby would turn into a pillow and my mom would put it over my face . . . and I'd wake up.

That night, even though my door was locked, I couldn't sleep, couldn't even stop staring at the doorknob. I kept waiting for my mom to break in and give her horrible, masturbating daughter back to God.

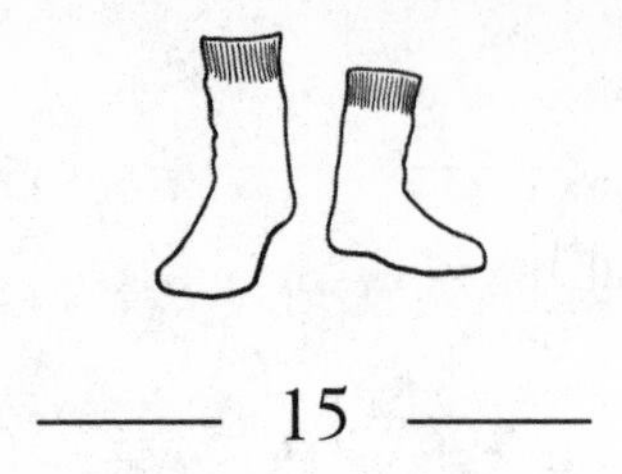

— 15 —

Benedict Maximus Pe . . .

AFTER I GOT BEATEN UP ON WEDNESDAY, Thursday and Friday at school were not very positive experiences. I still was sure people were laughing at me, even if they were only doing it inside their minds. Robert still hated me and I hated him for hating me. That's not precisely true. I hated myself for having a best friend who hated me. Evil Benny has more to say about this, but I'm trying to ignore Evil Benny.

Penelope Lupo was not in school either day. There was a rumor she tried to kill herself and was in an insane asylum. I would have believed this on Tuesday, but after what happened in the dean's office, I don't. But I'm not very smart right now, so I don't think I should believe what I don't believe. That makes no sense. I apologize for not being intelligent anymore.

Usually I did not notice, or care, whether someone like Penelope was in school or even alive. But I kept thinking about her smell and even though I should be able to stop myself from thinking about something so unimportant as a girl's smell, my "powers of self-empowerment" (from chapter four in my dad's book) were not very powerful at all right now.

I did have a secret in my head that I would repeat over and over if my mind became too dark with destructive thoughts: Christmas vacation started Saturday, and when I returned to school in January, I would be a new person. My sister and mom, after I asked for help, spent the rest of our dinner at the Cheesecake Factory planning how they were going to give me the "biggest makeover in history" during the break. My mom reminded me that I was great just the way I was but that sometimes you have to change some things so other people can see it as well.

That's what good moms are supposed to say. But the truth was, at this current time, I was a worthless, friendless loser. But maybe if I changed so that other people stopped thinking I was a worthless, friendless loser, then maybe I'd stop thinking I was one too.

At lunch Friday, I ate in the library bathroom because no one ever uses it because no one even knows the library has a bathroom. Except me. And Robert. And, I learned halfway through my peanut butter, banana, and honey sandwich, the weirdest kid in the junior class: Gator Green.

"Oh," he said as he swung open the bathroom door and saw me. "What are you doing here?"

"Eating lunch," I said, which was true even though it sounded ridiculous.

"Oh." Gator used to be a popular athlete in junior high, but then his dad died and he got strange. For instance, right now he looked like he was having a conversation with an imaginary friend. I should say that I'd probably get strange if my dad died too. (Evil Benny says it would be difficult for me to get much stranger than I already am.)

"Do you come here often?" I asked. This made me sound like we were on a bad television show about people who don't know how to talk to girls. Which, obviously, we don't know how to because if we did we both wouldn't hide out in a bathroom no one else knows exists.

"Yes, I come hang here when I need to be alone."

"Me too," I said, even though this was the first time I had come here without Robert. Then we were both quiet. I kept taking small bites of my sandwich and looking mostly down at the floor. Gator, whose real name is George but for some reason prefers to be compared to a giant reptile, didn't do anything but stand there, staring at me. He was thinking, I'm sure. But mostly it felt like he was trying to teleport me out of his special bathroom with his eyes. This was just another sign that I don't fit in anywhere anymore, even with a kid who doesn't fit in anywhere either.

"I'm going to go," he said. "Do you think you'll come back here often or do you think this will be your only time eating lunch alone in the library bathroom?" He didn't say it like that to be mean. But I wanted to cry anyway. When you lose intelligence, like I have, you gain emotions. This is a terrible trade and I don't recommend it to anyone.

"I . . . don't know."

"Oh. Okay. Well, if you decide you'd like to come back, maybe we will work out a schedule so we don't come back at the same time."

"That's fair," I said even though, again, my eyes began to well with tears.

"See ya, Benny," Gator said, then turned and left. Him calling me Benny reminded me we were friends, sort of, back in third grade. Except then girls started liking him in fourth grade, and if girls like you, then you can't really be friends with someone like me who girls don't like. Someone who, as was recently proven, girls will never like. But now girls don't like Gator anymore, so maybe we can become friends again. I was very desperate. Very, very desperate. But Gator doesn't seem desperate like me. Or, like my sister says, like he doesn't know what planet he's on. He just seems like he doesn't belong on this planet at all.

During seventh-period AP U.S. History, the teacher Mr. Rice started class by saying there would be a new student joining us in January and she was here today to introduce herself.

Because I was walking everywhere with my head down (so I wouldn't see if anyone was mocking me) I hadn't noticed the new girl standing by Mr. Rice when I walked into class. Because if I had been looking up, I would have noticed that the girl of my dreams would soon be attending Riverbend High School.

"Hi," the girl said as she stepped forward to address us. She had blond hair. Golden hair. Her hair was not made of literal gold, obviously, but it's a metaphor for how valuable her hair was to my senses. I enjoyed staring at it so much I think I was getting dizzy from its sheen. She wore a teal dress with small straps and high white heels, which made her look like she was going to a wedding in June and not to school in December. She had rosy cheeks, bright white teeth, and blue eyes that said to me, "Hi, Benedict, I am the manifestation of your romantic ideal and now you will spend the rest of your life obsessing over me." And I said, "Okay," but not out loud.

Her actual words, to the class, were "My name is Allison Wray. I'm from South Carolina and my mom got transferred to Chicago for work and everyone said Riverbend High School is the best school and so I'm really excited to be here and meet you all." Then she giggled, which was nice because girls who giggle are probably nice to socially awkward boys like me. I couldn't know, of course, how smart she was without seeing her class rank from her previous school, but considering that she was transferring into our Advanced Placement history class allowed me to give her a high probability for intelligence. The old Benedict from two days ago would have felt very confident that the arrival of my perfect female specimen was a sign that my life itself was going according to my perfect plan. But seeing her now only felt like a reminder that no girl like her would ever consider me and I am probably a delusional lunatic for thinking for even one second that she would.

After she introduced herself, she sat next to me in the front row. Let me repeat this so I can grasp it more completely: She sat *next to me.* Since I had been staring at her, without blinking, from the time Mr. Rice introduced her, I must assume she thought I'd be a friendly new face to connect with. She couldn't have known, obviously, that I was the last person in Riverbend High School she should befriend if she wished to be anything other than an outcast.

"I was so nervous. Hope I did okay," she whispered to me. Even her whisper had a small Southern accent that made me think of pretty wives in lawyer movies.

If only my sister had already started her lessons on how to be normal, I might have said something normal back to Allison Wray. Instead I said, "Because you are attractive and well spoken, I'm sure you will have a very fulfilling time here at Riverbend and you will go on to a very successful life."

Then Allison Wray, the new girl and my dream girl, tried to hide her confused and maybe even frightened face as she turned ahead toward the teacher. She never looked my way again for the rest of class.

(Nor will she for eternity! Evil Benny said with a cackle. He had never cackled before. Maybe as I become less smart, he's becoming more evil.)

When the final bell rang, every student at Riverbend High School raced and yelled with one another to celebrate our school-free next two weeks.

Except for me. Obviously.

I went back to the library to take out books my dad wouldn't yell at me for reading. (He doesn't allow any fiction written in the past ten years because he said most of it will be irrelevant within eighteen months. He's probably right. Of course he's right.) I also looked in the bathroom for Gator even though I knew he wouldn't be there. Mostly, I was just wasting time out of view from everyone else. So I couldn't see how happy they all were and they couldn't see how sad I was.

Even though my dad's book talks about how you should never care about what other people think about you because other people only stand in the way between you and greatness, I decided that only works if you are a genius like him. I'm not a genius. A genius would never have lost his best friend, would never have gotten beaten up, would never have asked out five different girls and gotten rejected by all of them. A genius would have been able to say something funny to Gator Green to make him my friend and something charming to Allison Wray to make her my girl.

A genius would never be anything like me.

(Evil Benny didn't say anything. Not right away. Then he said he might take a vacation because I was doing his job for him.)

16

pen

After the big fight with my mom and trying to ignore her fight with my dad, I fell asleep even though I thought I wouldn't. Your body does all sorts of things you can't control, I guess.

Usually when I woke up on a school morning, I'd hear my mom in the kitchen, maybe on the phone, maybe making me eggs if she was in a motherly mood. But the house was quiet. A quiet that made me squirm in my skin. When I was a kid and I'd wake up to the house this silent after my parents fought the night before, I'd always picture walking downstairs and finding their bloody, lifeless bodies.

On Thursday morning, this mad sense of relief sunk into my chest when I thought of my parents' deaths. This makes me the devil, right? Maybe my mom's right. I'm going to hell for sure.

But when I went downstairs after my shower, I didn't find my parents dead. Didn't find them alive either. Waiting for me, sitting on my mother's ugly-as-bird-poop floral couch with his hands on his knees and staring ahead with his usual empty gaze, was Jeremy the Priest.

(That's what my dad always calls him. Or else "Jeremy your mom's boyfriend." She did spend a lot of time with him, but my dad didn't really think they were having an affair. Jeremy's at least seventy, probably liked guys a million years ago before he gave up all that for the church. And my mom is the least sexual person ever born. Last night was proof of that.)

"Good morning, Penelope," Jeremy the Priest said. He always wore these tiny black glasses that were probably fifty years old yet I always thought were kinda stylish.

"Where are my parents?"

"I think your father spent the night in a hotel," he said. The only person who knew even half as much of my parents' shit as me was Jeremy. You'd think this would make me trust him more. Nope. The opposite. He said, "Your mom called me late last night and told me what happened."

Kill me, kill me, kill me. The priest knows I masturbate. *Kill me!* First, I'm going to throw up. My knees dropped, hit the carpet. Jeremy rushed over.

"Are you okay?"

Nothing came up. "I just want to go to school." I was hyperventilating. I'm a mess.

"Your mom asked me to take you to the church's recovery center in Gladys Park."

I CAN'T BREATHE. "I'm going to school."

"Penelope, I know your mother is not very understanding." Jeremy the Priest spoke with this wheezy lisp. It made me think he was always a breath from keeling over. Like me right now. "But you can talk about whatever you want with the counselors. About what happened last night . . ."

Pain. Pain. Pain. I'm not going to talk to anyone about how my crazy Catholic mother caught me masturbating! I don't even want to talk about it with the voices in my head. I yelled, even though I never yelled at Father Jeremy, "I'M GOING TO SCHOOL." I yanked away from him, stood, and went to grab my keys from the bowl by the front door. They weren't there. "Where are my keys?" That's when I looked out through the front bay window and saw my mother standing on the street, waving my keys with this possessed pride. Standing next to her, out of his patrol car, was Officer Roberts. My mother's other friend bought with praise and free pizza. "She told the cops?!"

Jeremy the Priest stepped behind me, whispering, "No, no, no, no. She told Officer Roberts that you had experimented with teenage drinking and were resisting help."

"Isn't that worse?!"

"Officer Roberts is only here to ensure you come with me, Penelope," Jeremy said.

My life sucks. Sucks. Sucks. Suck-suck-suck-sucks. My two choices: Try to escape this forced trip to some religious nuthouse and maybe get arrested? Or go with the priest and maybe end up in a straitjacket?

Father Jeremy said, "I know this isn't easy, but it's probably for the best. I think you and your mother need a short break from each other."

Only intelligible thing he had said so far. My lungs almost started working normally again. So I said, "I'll go."

After I packed a small bag of clothes, I got into Jeremy the Priest's old black Cadillac that smelled like cigarettes from 1974. As we backed out of our driveway, I refused to look at my mother. She'd either be proud of herself or ashamed of me and I didn't want to see either.

On the drive, Father Jeremy didn't ask any weird questions or attempt any lame lecture. I said thank you in my head. I texted Paul, told him that my mom was sick and that I wouldn't be in school today or tomorrow so I could help take care of her. (This wasn't true. But it wasn't not true either.)

He asked if we were still going to Wild Wolf Resort on Saturday. I said yes even though I had no idea. My mother might not be able to stomach a week in a cabin with her slut-whore-deviant daughter. I sure as hell didn't want to spend a week with my crazy-zealot-bitch mother, but I was a kid and I didn't get a whole lot of choice in anything.

The "recovery" center was a big old brick office building across the street from one of Gladys Park's fifty churches. Jeremy the Priest got out with me and led me to the front gates. The white plastic sign over the entrance read RECOVER IN CHRIST'S LOVE.

Walking in, I made a decision: Screw it, I'm tired of fighting a fight I can't win. I give up on ever being real. On ever being me. You want me to pretend to believe in you, God? You got it. You want me to think you know everything, Jesus? Fine. Done. I'm yours. I'll never masturbate again. I'll never think about sex again until it's time to make a baby so that baby can join your legion like me. Fine. I surrender.

So, yeah, I spent two and half days amazing the balls off the counselors. Told them what they wanted to hear. Didn't talk about masturbating. Talked about "focusing on what's important." Didn't talk about my mom being nuts, talked about my "not being mature enough to see her wisdom."

I was brilliant. Either that or everyone there was an idiot. Who cares?

They took away my phone when I checked in. Since I was "surrendering," I didn't stress it too much until I woke up Saturday morning. Then, yeah, suddenly it felt like a year had passed. My friends could have moved, the school might be sucked into a black hole, cars might be flying. But seriously, I felt out of joint with my existence. Like, who was I now? Then I had this thought that didn't feel crazy:

Paul was going to dump me.

Oh. My. God. He was. I don't know why I thought this, I mean he said we were going to get married! I'm sure everything's fine. I'm sure. THEN WHY AM I SO SURE HE'S GOING TO BREAK UP WITH ME?

I need my phone. I need my phone now. I went to the front desk, but they said I couldn't get my phone back until my mom checked me out three hours from then. The one boy that ever liked me and would ever like me was going to dump me and I couldn't stop it because I didn't have my phone.

It's okay, Pen.

No, it's not.

It's not okay at all.

NOT! AT! ALL!

Paul was the only thing in my life that made me feel like I should be alive. I can't remember one bad thing about him right now. Not one thing because he's my reason to live! Yes! He is! If he wasn't my boyfriend, why would I need to be alive? I wouldn't! I don't care if this doesn't make sense to you, it makes sense to *me*.

Oh. My. God. I need my phone.

I need my phone.

I need my phone.

I need my phone.

AND I REPEATED THIS IN MY HEAD FOR THREE

HOURS. I'm not kidding. I wish I was kidding. I wish I was normal. But I'm fucking insane.

When my mom did finally arrive just after ten a.m., I was delirious. I kept up my "I love Jesus and he loves me" act, but my brain was eating itself with visions of Paul going out with other girls, like Iris or that sophomore Peggy with the big tits. And me being alone, and then shriveling up into a tiny old woman in like one day. I had to stand still and smile while the counselors told my mom how I had a major breakthrough and they were excited to see me fulfill my potential now that I was back on God's path.

Only after she heard all this, not before, did my mom wrap me in this big, showy hug. She sniffled, choked up, repeated how she was glad she had her "beautiful daughter back." Yeah, yeah.

"I love you so much, Penelope."

"I love you too, Mom." Yeah, yeah, give me my fucking phone.

My mom talked as we drove away, like talked and talked and talked, and I think it was about how my dad had agreed to go into marriage counseling and our family might be saved by my descent into darkness. Great. I wasn't listening. First couple texts from Paul were all nice, then about him being horny, then him getting worried, and—I SHOULD HAVE NEVER AGREED TO GO TO THAT QUACKHOUSE—there it was:

PAUL

So I just left your house. Your mom told me everything . . .

"YOU TOLD PAUL EVERYTHING?"

"WHY ARE YOU YELLING?" my mom yelled back. I ignored her. Read more:

PAUL

. . . that you had a crisis of faith and needed to spend a few days concentrating on your relationship with God.

Yeah, okay, whatever, I did that, okay, maybe he's not breaking up with me . . .

PAUL

. . . which is why I'm not coming to Wild Wolf with you and your mom this year . . .

"PAUL'S NOT GOING WITH US?!" It was going to be just me and my mother for a week! We'd kill each other. This wasn't even a joke.

"PENELOPE, STOP YELLING AT ME!" But I just ignored her again.

PAUL

. . . and considering how you were acting on Wednesday, talking weird and acting weirder, I think we should take this next week while you're away as a break . . .

"PAUL BROKE UP WITH ME, MOM! HE BROKE UP WITH ME!"

"I'm not going to even talk to you, Penelope, until you stop acting crazy."

PAUL

. . . but if the center and god
and jesus really make you
back into the old Pen, then
I'm sure our love will return
too

Breathe. Breathe. Breathe. OH-MY-GOD I CAN'T BREATHE.

"Why are you breathing like that?" my mom asked. But it was getting worse. She yelled because that's so helpful: "WHY ARE YOU BREATHING LIKE THAT?!"

I couldn't stop—or I don't know, but I think I said I needed to go to the hospital. And my mother screamed in horror like she was the one about to suffocate from a broken heart.

So, yeah, it was a panic attack. I'm crazier than my mother. Whatever. Blah, blah, blah, I can't even remember what the doctor said, but when we got back in the car, I realized we weren't even going home. We were just driving straight up 294 to Wisconsin and on to Wild Wolf Resort.

I was too mortified to even ask if she'd packed clothes for me. After she was sure I wasn't going to have another psychotic break, my mom explained that she didn't tell Paul about my "activities," just that I needed some spiritual guidance. She said, "He's a good Catholic, and

I'm sure when he realizes you're a good Catholic again, you two will be back together."

That's right. I'm a good Catholic now. Or at least I was pretending to be one. But, really, was there much of a difference? Was I pretending any less than my mom? Or Paul? They didn't know if any of that crap was true any more than I did. Maybe every religious person in the world is faking it. No one has any real proof! Just a bunch of books thousands of years old, so old no one can make the people who wrote them admit they made all that shit up. Doesn't that mean everyone's pretending? Yeah. Probably. They might not admit it like me, or even be aware of it, but, yeah, we're all faking it just the same.

So all I had to do was keep up the act and I'd get Paul back. Right? Yeah. At least the next week at Wild Wolf Resort should be easy. There wasn't even internet in the cabins. Six days of snow, books, and sleep. I could almost envision my deviant soul starving to death from the lack of temptation.

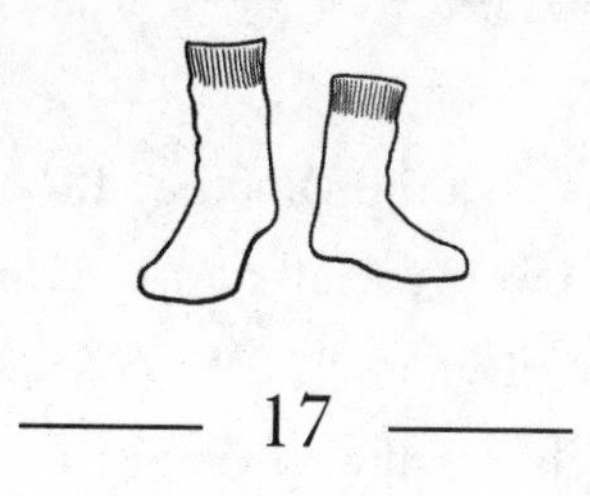

— 17 —

Benedict Maxim . . .

AFTER SPENDING AN HOUR IN THE LIBRARY after school let out Friday, I walked out to the parking lot. It was empty, which made me imagine everyone had died in an alien attack and only I was left. This was more fun to think about than reality.

But then someone said, “Benedict,” as I opened the door to my car. I said “someone” because I wanted to pretend I didn’t know who it was. But it was Robert. He was the only best friend I’ve ever had, so obviously I’ll recognize his voice until I die.

“Hello, Robert,” I said, like I was annoyed at him, because I want Robert to think I don’t need him even though I want Robert’s friendship back more than anything else in the history of my life.

“I’m not here because I want to be friends again,” he said. I think if Robert had thought for a thousand years how to say the meanest thing possible, he wouldn’t have been able to come up with something so mean. Only by not thinking about if something is mean can you say something that mean.

“Me either,” I said, even though, obviously, that was a lie.

"I'm here because I know you were in the dean's office on Wednesday with Pen and I wanted to know if you know what happened to her."

"No, I don't," I said, but then I noticed Robert begin to step away from me so I said, "but we're friends now, so I can find out."

"You're friends with Pen now?"

"Yes," I said, which was also, obviously, a lie. When I was smart and confident, I never lied. Now that I'm dumb and pathetic, I lie all the time.

"I bet you're going to fall in love with Pen now that you get to know her."

"Penelope's not my type at all." This was true. I did not mention Penelope's smell, which I'm not sure was something I liked anyway. In fact, all my problems started after I ran into her and her friends on Tuesday, so maybe Penelope's smell is my kryptonite. (Kryptonite is Superman's one weakness. My dad says people who use cultural references to make their point are lazy and incompetent. He's probably right. Of course he is.) In order to stop thinking about Penelope's smell or my incompetence, I said, "In fact, I met my dream girl today."

"Allison Wray, the new girl?"

"You met her too?" I asked.

"Yes, she was in my statistics class. When I saw her, I thought you'd like her. She looks like the blond cheerleader from *Secret Service High*. Even her boobs are just as big." We both held back a snicker because, obviously, Robert and I are embarrassed to think about boobs. *Secret Service High* was a show on Netflix about a high school that trains kids to be spies. The biggest girl character is a Florida cheerleader named Kelly. I told Robert last year I was going to marry her after I made my first million dollars. At the time, I thought of this as inevitable. Now I realize I'm probably a chemically unbalanced person who should be on medication. Except Kelly-the-blond-cheerleader's real-life twin was now going to school with us and I'm not sure if that proves I can predict the future or that I'm insane or both.

Because I didn't want to think about my mental stability anymore, I said to Robert, "I was too nervous to talk to her," even though I had never, ever admitted to being anything less than the most perfect person in the universe to Robert.

"Really?" Robert said. He had a small grin on his lips that showed me he liked me admitting my flaws.

"I'm not perfect anymore, Robert," I said.

"You never were perfect, Benedict."

My face got hot and red because I hated that he said this even if it was probably true.

Robert then said, "But I think us admitting we are dorks might help us become less dorky."

I couldn't say anything because all facts pointed to the conclusion that Robert was more perceptive of the truth than I was all along, which made my brain not know how to use my mouth.

So Robert spoke again. "Allison's very nice. I'm Facebook friends with her now."

"Really?"

"Yes. I bet she'd like you if she got to know you."

"I know Pen would like you if she got to know you." I had no idea if this was true, of course, but I don't think Robert knew if Allison would like me either. We were just telling each other nice things to make ourselves feel better about being dorks.

Robert said, "What if, Benedict, you can help me become friends with Pen and I can help you become friends with Allison?"

"I think that's a great idea."

"I think so too."

I wanted to invite Robert over to play Xbox like we usually did on Fridays, but I was too scared he would say no. I'll wait until after I get Penelope to be his friend; then he'll say yes for sure. And then we'll be best friends again, and then maybe Penelope and Allison will come over too, and it will be a double date and everyone at school will know how impressive I am for having a beautiful girlfriend and I'll say to myself, "Benedict, remember those few days before Christmas break when you thought you were stupid and pathetic?" And I'll say back to myself, "No, I don't remember that at all."

After Robert and I said good-bye in a way that I think we were both thinking we'd be best friends again soon, I drove home humming to songs on the radio. I didn't know any of the words because I like to listen to NPR usually, but I think humming to popular music is a sign that I might be close to being happy again.

But when I walked into the front door of our house, my dad was sitting in the living room eating cereal. I say "but" because it's hard for me to be happy around my dad even though he's my hero. I had not seen him since Wednesday, when he told me I was fired for going into his basement office without permission. (Not precisely true but my emotions, which remained in charge of me, said it felt true.)

"Hello, Benedict," he said without looking up from the book opened on the table. "Will you sit down with me?" I nodded and did as he asked. He continued: "Your mother and sister are shopping for some items for our trip to Wild Wolf tomorrow, so I thought this would be a good time for us to talk."

I nodded again. Maybe if I didn't say anything, my dad wouldn't be able to tell I wasn't as smart as I used to be.

He kept talking. "Your mother sent me a long email yesterday regarding how I spoke to you when you came into my office, and while I contend I have the right to my private work space, I do acknowledge that it is understandable for a son—you—to yearn to speak to his father—me—during moments of distress."

I waited a moment to see if he had more to say. He didn't. So I nodded again. He then reached down to his side and placed three books on the table between us.

He said, "My publisher continues to send me their contemporary fiction despite my well-stated position that they have no value. But I understand that some of the books are very popular with teens these days, and perhaps if I allowed you to read them, you would have a better grasp of your peers' limited thinking."

My father was still disparaging the books and teenagers as a whole, but I considered this a major breakthrough in my relationship with my dad. He was giving me permission to try and be normal! Maybe it was because he realized I was not a genius like him, but at this moment, not even that bothered me. "Thanks, Dad."

He nodded, stood, and disappeared back into his basement office. I took his cereal bowl to the sink and then took the books he gave me to my room. I began reading at once, choosing author Forest Jackson's *If Only Girls Weren't Everything I Wanted I'd Have Nothing to Do with Them*. I liked the long title and I knew it was being made into a movie. Reading a book before the film is released might prove to have social currency. Yet only fifty pages in, I knew reading this book would be more than just a talking point. The main character's name was Theodore. He was very intelligent and verbally eloquent and very appealing! His only flaw was that he didn't know how to talk to girls! This book was about me! I wasn't a misfit-outcast with no redeeming qualities. I was just like the lead character in a book that had sold millions of copies and would be made into a major motion picture!

I only stopped reading, briefly, when my computer beeped with an email. It was from Robert. He had sent me some funny YouTube clips. They weren't that funny, but that's not what was important. It was a signal the life I liked so much only a few days ago was back even though I'd been sure it was gone forever.

Then he sent me another email, telling me he had sent a suggestion on Facebook that Allison Wray and I become friends. My powers of self-empowerment had returned and were coursing through my body! Maybe my life would be even better than it had ever been before.

(Evil Benny opened his mouth, but I said, "Not listening to you!" And he went away.)

Now that Robert had connected Allison and me, it was my turn to help him become friends with Penelope. After we got back from the family trip to Wisconsin, I'd probably have to call her and ask to meet. Secretly, obviously, so Paul didn't find out (and beat me up) and also so Robert didn't find out (and discover she wasn't really my friend). And then I'd have to plead with Penelope to at least pretend to be interested in Robert so that he could, again, be my best friend and so that Allison Wray, my dream girl, could be my real girl.

I was sure by then, I'd be back to being my disciplined and evolved self and not be distracted from my extraordinary destiny by something so small as what Penelope Lupo smelled like.

18

pen

On the drive up to Wild Wolf lake, I texted Paul fifteen thousand times. I'm not exaggerating. He finally just said, *I love you but we need this time apart.* It made me wish I was dead, but what could I do but survive this week in the woods with my mother and then go back and promise to be an amazing (and mute) good Catholic girlfriend who still gave him blow jobs in his car? Nothing. Nothing. Nothing. Nothing. Nothing. NOTHING.

Anyway, the lake is a five-and-a-half-hour drive into middle-of-nowhere Wisconsin. Outside the resort, there's only white people, trees, snow, fishing shops, and more white people. And me. Me with my black hair, my black clothes, and my skin so dark olive most people think I should be deported. When we stop for gas on these trips, the men think I'm going to steal something and the women think I'm going to steal their men.

But the resort itself isn't bad. Twenty-seven cabins on the edge of the lake with a lodge in the middle. Nature so pure it almost gets me high. Cross-country trails for miles (that I never use, but still). Deep, epically soft couches in front of huge fires. And endless comfort food during mealtimes at the lodge. (I indulge in the homemade soups and freshly baked breads; my mom devours the multitude of breaded and fried meats.)

We always stay in cabin 13 because it's closest to the dining room entrance, which is fine with me because the far cabins are a little too close to the endless forest, which I remain convinced contains animals that could eat me and ghosts that could do worse.

My mom *had* brought a bag for me. She didn't do a terrible job. Packed my skirts even though she thinks I'm an idiot for dressing up to go to dinner at a place that has dead fish stuffed on the walls.

Mom also made a trip to Barnes & Noble and bought the next ten books on my Amazon wish list. (It's this secret peace offering we have. First: She acts nuts. Then: Without admitting she acted nuts, she goes and buys me stuff. Last: I forget she acted nuts.)

After we had unpacked, my mom took a nap in her bedroom. I started a fire and grabbed one of the new books, only then I decided I'd rather reread the last Millie Dragon novel on my phone. Zelda Zowie, the author, is my favorite writer—probably my favorite anything—in the universe.

Millie Dragon is a high school chick in Los Angeles who can see another dimension where all her classmates are haunted by demons. What makes it different than all the other YA supernatural crap out there is that Millie isn't trying to be a monster-fighting hero nor is she waiting to have her existence validated with the love of some brooding yet sensitive dude. She basically decided the only way to help her friends is to tell them there are these demons they can't see that follow them around trying to control their lives. She tells them that the demons can't be killed but that the demons can be made less dangerous if you learn to talk to them. Her friends think she's crazy, but Millie cares more about telling the truth than what other people think of her. (Basically the opposite of me, I guess.) Yeah, when I explain the books it makes it sound like a simple metaphor, but that's why Zelda Zowie is a brilliant novelist and I can't even get a C-plus in English class.

Whatever. The books are great. I don't care if you believe me. The sixth book comes out on Christmas, and that means, for that day at least, I'll be able to forget about getting dumped and having a shitty life.

When I was showering before dinner, I thought about masturbating because I have this weird enjoyment of getting off under hot water when it's super cold outside. But then I remembered I was trying to become a different person now and so instead I just killed time layering my mascara until I was full-throttle emo-goth. My mom, now awake and whining that it was taking me forever to get dressed, took one look at me and said, "I'm too hungry to care if you look like you're about to kill yourself."

"Thanks, Mom."

The Wild Wolf lodge is more than just the dining room. In the very front, when you first enter, is an office and small shop with stuff like shampoo and stupid souvenirs. Then off to the right is a big room with Ping-Pong and pool tables, out-of-date video games like *Donkey Kong*, and a giant mounted seven-foot bear on its hind legs. Not just the head, the whole body. (Like even the penis. Yeah. Really.) Why a family resort thinks a stuffed dead animal is an okay thing to have in a game room, I don't know. Oh, they call this room the Bear Room. Very creative of them. There are also some stairs to a loft that has a cableless television. It has a DVD player now, which is futuristic compared with the VHS player they had up through eighth grade. During the summer, when more families with younger kids visit, I think the Bear Room must get a lot of use. But it's always empty when my mom and I come during winter break. At least empty enough that last year Paul and I got half naked in the TV loft.

The dining room, to the left of the office, has just as much 1960s wood paneling as everything else except the panoramic windows overlooking the lake make you feel like you are floating above the ground. Like you're on a spaceship hovering above an alien ice planet. I'm not going to lie: It's awesome, and even during the worst weeks stuck up here with my mom, that view almost always makes me feel like the trip was worth it. Yeah.

So all this was routine, right? Driving up to bumblefuck Wisconsin, unpacking, reading while my mom slept, walking over to the lodge for our first dinner of the vacation. No Paul this year, which sucked for a bunch of different reasons, but I had come up here without Paul my whole life before two years ago, so it wasn't *that* different. It was almost cool that I kept growing older yet this trippy Wild Wolf Resort was like a time machine back to when I was a kid.

Yeah, right, so routine. The same. Year after year after year. Comfortable sort of. Predictable of course. Yeah, all that.

And . . .

Yeah . . .

Right . . .

I CAN'T FUCKING BELIEVE THIS!

I follow my mom into the dining room, toward our two-person table against the window, and I'm not even thinking about looking anywhere but outside that awesome window—honestly, it's better than any drug I've ever done—but then I get this knot in my gut, like I should look across the dining room. That there's someone here other than just middle-aged couples from suburban Milwaukee.

So I look. And I'm like, for that first second, "Oh, hey, there's two kids here this year." Unusual, but not impossible. There was a boy named Kip that came during my fourth- and fifth-grade years and it was sorta fun. (He was cute but I was ten and when you're ten you don't think about doing anything other than playing Ping-Pong but he moved to New Jersey or somewhere and I never saw him again.)

SO YEAH, UNUSUAL BUT NOT IMPOSSIBLE.

You want to know what IS fucking impossible? That *he* would be here. No, no, more than that. Any other student from Riverbend? That would and should have been impossible.

But Benedict FUCKING Pendleton?

That *he* would be here was like frogs falling from the sky or dead people rising from their graves or . . . no, no, again, still doesn't work, because all that crap people have imagined before so even those things can't even compare to the incomprehensible presence of this social-misfit kid here at Wild Wolf Resort. Because this kid was, sort of, directly responsible for me spending two days locked up in religious jail, responsible for me getting dumped by my one and only boyfriend ever, and responsible for ruining my life. Right?

Because this kid, this Benedict, was BY FAR my most bizarre sexual fantasy obsession and I've had a lot of bizarre sexual fantasy obsessions. A LOT.

And now he was here at a resort where there is nothing for me to do . . . except obsess about him more.

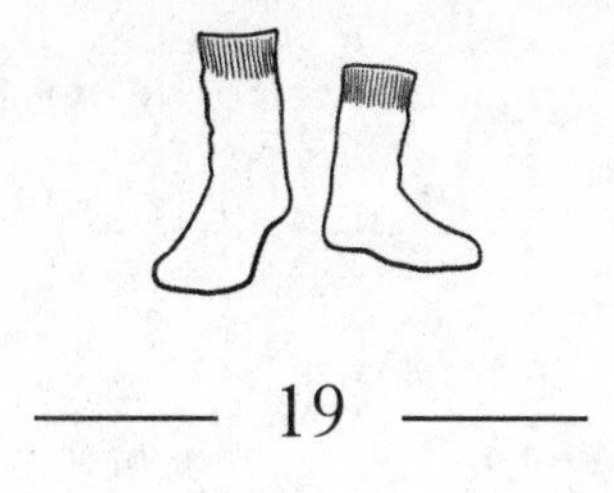

— 19 —

BENEDICT

MY SISTER COMPLAINED THE ENTIRE DRIVE UP to Wild Wolf Resort. "I want to be on a beach," Elizabeth would say. "I want to be somewhere warm," she'd say. "This is going to be the worst vacation ever." My mom (who drove because my dad is a very unskilled driver) tried to say things like "Keep an open mind" and "This is very important to your dad."

My father, who has the superpower to not get sick while reading books in the car, ignored both of them for the first three hours and twenty minutes. His ability to ignore distractions might be another superpower of his. (I use superpower not literally. Obviously.) But then, after another extended rant by Elizabeth that "life isn't fair," my dad closed his book, turned to the backseat, and said to my sister, "At this exact moment, a young child somewhere on our planet is being beaten to death by a metal rod. The last unconscious thoughts of this child, before it stops breathing, will be, 'Why did my mother bring me into this world if she hates me so much?' This child, if it weren't dead, would agree with you, Elizabeth, that life is not fair."

This shut my sister up for the rest of the ride.

In my sister's defense, the resort itself *was* rather archaic. No one with my father's bank account and without his nostalgia would come here. I feared the cabins and lodge might collapse after the next heavy snowfall. No one even bothered to plow the roads down to the pavement and my mother slid the Mercedes SUV into a snowbank as we parked at cabin 1. Our housing was on the edge of the forest, and the trees and growth surrounding it appeared primed to swallow it whole once spring arrived. All this being stated, I must say that once we stepped outside, the fresh, cold air delivered an intense rush of adrenaline into my lungs that I've never experienced before. It made me wish I could yell like a face-painted warrior in a movie where the men wear kilts and carry swords bigger than their legs. My father would never approve of such a thing, but even the urge to do it was exhilarating.

By the time the four of us had unpacked, it was time to go to dinner. My sister got back in the car, thinking we would drive the quarter mile down to the lodge. But my father instead started walking along the lake without a word. I held open the car door until Elizabeth reluctantly followed him. The wind coming off the frozen lake did put an unpleasant chill into my bones and my feet were rather wet from the snow by the time we arrived at the lodge. I would never complain, obviously, but I was starting to long for the Four Seasons on Maui, where the only season was warm.

The lodge, though just as dated inside as out, did provide much-appreciated relief from the cold. The dining room provided an inviting view of the lake that was so calming they should sell videos of it to people who want to stare at serene nature scenes.

After we ordered, my mom read through the brochure the front desk had provided. The list of activities were: fish in the snow, walk in the snow, ski in the snow, and snowmobile in the snow. Elizabeth could not contain a whine, and though usually I would have enjoyed witnessing my father's disapproval of my usually perfect sister, someone was entering the dining hall that, at first sight, looked remarkably like Penelope Lupo.

Only when this person looked back at me with the same sort of astonished recognition did I realize that, however improbably, this was not a girl who looked like her, *it was* Penelope Lupo herself.

"She's pretty," my mom said.

"She's actually not," I whispered even though I could not stop staring at her.

"She looks more out of place than I do," Elizabeth said.

"Her name's Penelope. She's in my class at Riverbend."

"I don't know how you can say she's not pretty, Benedict. I think she's very pretty," my mom said.

"She's also way too cool for you," my sister said.

"Elizabeth. Remember, you're supposed to be helping your brother."

I said, "She has a big scar on her cheek, a nose ring, and poor taste in clothing. Her eyes are too close together. She dyes her hair. She's too skinny. Also, she's not very smart."

"Benedict, don't say things like that."

"But, Mom, you were the one who was insisting she was pretty. I was explaining why she isn't."

My dad, who had been looking at the menu during the entire

Penelope discussion, turned and said, loudly enough that I'm sure Penelope could hear him, "Benedict's right. She's not attractive." I hated that my dad said this even though he was agreeing with me. Then he said, "What's the name of the girl you showed me on your phone?"

"Allison Wray."

My father added, "Allison is much better suited for you. This girl here is obviously from a broken home and will have certain developmental issues because of it."

"Samuel," my mom said, with a look toward my father. She didn't like when he said things like that out loud, even if he was right. I think Penelope could tell we were talking about her because she changed seats with her mom so that she faced away from us.

Despite this, and despite my not finding her attractive and despite my father surely being correct about her, I could not help myself from looking toward Penelope for the entire meal.

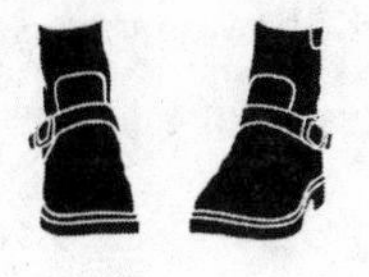

20

Pen

"Penelope, that handsome boy keeps looking at you," my mom said.

"He's not handsome." My crazy mom finding Benedict attractive only made me feel more freaky about my freaky fantasies.

She said, "How do you know? You're not looking at him."

"We go to high school together."

"He must be very popular with the girls."

"He's a fucking dork, Mom."

"Penelope! Watch your language."

"He's a dork. Okay? Like the biggest dork in school."

"Oh, I just don't understand how that's possible. He looks like a young Warren Beatty."

"Who?"

"Never mind. But I think he likes you."

"He doesn't. Trust me."

She said, "No boy looks toward a girl the way that boy is looking toward you unless he likes you."

And, shit, I had to turn. I don't, I just don't—WHY DO I HAVE TO LOOK?—but I did and my mom was right, he was blasting those gray eyeballs of his at me like he was some starving animal. That would make me his prey. Which is so dumb to think but it also turns me on because I am losing my mind.

Benedict didn't even look away when I looked at him. What kind of person doesn't look away when someone looks at them? I couldn't take it anymore. I turned away from him again. You know what else my mom was right about? And I would NEVER admit this to her or ANYONE, but, crap, the kid really was handsome. Like, let's say I walked into the Wild Wolf dining room but I wasn't from Riverbend, Illinois. Instead I was from Madison or somewhere. Doesn't matter. What matters is that I had no idea what Benedict was like. Didn't know he was such a social nightmare. A robot. The Tin Man. Like this was the first time I had ever seen the kid in my life. You know what I would think? *He's hot.* That wavy hair. Those wide shoulders. Those stupid metal-gray eyes that don't blink. Hot. Like objectively hot. Not like Paul is hot. No, Paul is hot because he knows how to dress, and he can get stubble, and he's so, I don't know, cool. But Benedict would be hot like . . . because he just looks like a guy who doesn't know he's hot, who doesn't give a crap about dressing cool or being cool, or about anything other than just existing. Now, I know Benedict's not that. I know he's not. I know he probably should be on meds he's so awkward. But if I didn't know that, my mom would have been right. That he's handsome and every girl at The Bend should be in love with him.

"Is he Catholic?" my mom asked, breaking me out of my little obsession trance. Of course she would ask that.

"I seriously doubt it."

"Well, that's why you and Paul are perfect together. A common faith is the greatest bond."

"Yeah."

"It is what makes my marriage to your father so strong."

Yeah.

After dinner, I walked the fifty yards back to the cabin with my mom, but then said I wanted to watch a movie back at the lodge. "Fine, leave me here alone," she said, doing her abandoned-puppy thing, but I ignored it and left.

So, yeah, I went back, into the Bear Room—which was empty, of course—and I turned on the TV in the loft only to finally admit to myself that I had no desire at all to watch a movie. I went down and sat on one of the couches near the Ping-Pong table because from here anyone who peeked into the Bear Room would be able to see I was here.

Not that I wanted anyone to see me. I didn't.

I'm totally lying to myself.

I have to.

If I didn't, I'd hate myself for being so lame.

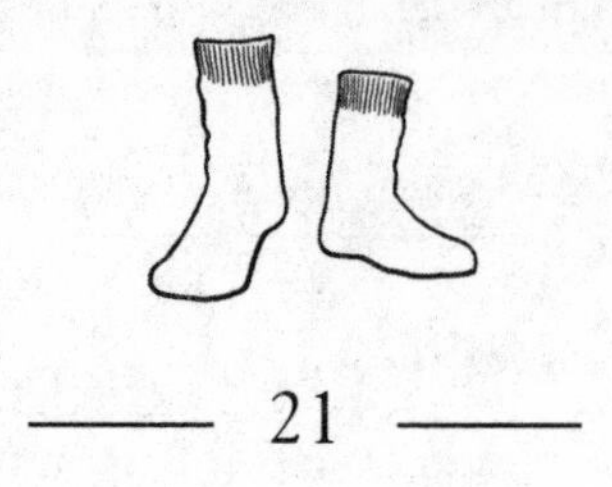

— 21 —

BENEDI . . .

"SHE'S LEAVING," MY MOM WHISPERED AS Penelope stood with her mother and exited the dining room.

"I don't care." This felt untrue. Odd.

"You're done eating. Why don't you go see if she wants to watch TV?"

"Mom!" my sister whined. "Only I'm allowed to give him advice on how to talk to girls."

"Then give him advice!" my mom said.

"Why would Benedict need advice?" my father asked. I much preferred the idea of my "makeover" when my father was unaware of it.

"Benedict asked for my help on how to not be such a dork."

"Elizabeth."

"Benedict is not a dork," my father said. "Are you a dork, Benedict?" The manner in which he asked made me feel that if I said yes, my dad would immediately disown me. I know this is not rational.

Before I could answer, my mother said, "No, he's not. He's just . . . shy."

"I'm not shy."

"He should be *more* shy," Elizabeth said.

"Genetically," my father began, "you are superior to every other student at Riverbend High School. You should not be shy. You should be confident and popular."

"Samuel . . ." my mother said

"It doesn't work like that, Dad," my sister said.

"I no longer wish to talk about this," I said.

"Then we won't," Mom said.

But my dad was now focused on the topic. Once focused, my dad could not let go until everyone agreed with him. He said, "I was criticized for not being involved three days ago. Now I am involved and being told not to? Benedict, my father was an alcoholic who abandoned us before I was ten years old. My mother, who never even graduated from high school, was a receptionist at an appliance store. Despite this, I was president of my senior class and captain of the gymnastics team. You are the son of a brilliant, bestselling author and a former model. There is no justifiable excuse for you not to be well liked by your peers. In fact, you should be the envy of them."

Both my mother and sister tried to defend me, or at least find a "justifiable excuse," but I knew that my dad was right and that the only way to end this incredibly painful conversation was to say, "You are right, Dad. I will work harder to be more popular at school."

"Benedict," my mom said, and tried to reach out.

"No, Mother." I stood, recoiling from her hand as if it would poison me. "I will see you back at the cabin. I'm going for a walk."

"It's too cold . . ." my mom started, but I ignored her, exited the dining room, and walked out through the front door of the lodge.

Before I had made it ten steps, I heard, "Benedict," and turned to find my sister shuffling her feet to catch up to me. She did not slow and soon was wrapping her arms around me in a hug. Our last hug was . . . I don't remember. Possibly never. That's improbable yet felt true.

I said, "You are feeling that much pity for me that you are hugging me?"

"I feel sorry for us both. Dad can be an idiot."

"He's brilliant."

"Sort of, but he's also an idiot." She pulled back. "Remember when I was six and I told him I wanted to be president and he said that girls can only be married to presidents? And then I cried for like an hour until you told me you'd vote for me?"

"No, I don't remember that."

"Well, you did. So come back inside and play Ping-Pong with me."

"I don't see how these two things are related."

"It's cold, Benedict! Don't argue with me!"

"Okay."

I followed my sister back into the lodge but stopped as I stepped through the doorway into the recreation room. There was only one other person there and that one person was sitting on the couch looking at her phone and that one person sitting on the couch looking at her phone was Penelope Lupo.

"Elizabeth . . ." I started, wanting to state how I knew she had tricked me into playing Ping-Pong with her so she could subtly encourage me to interact with my classmate. But before I could say anything more, Elizabeth yelled, "Benedict! Ping-Pong!" She grabbed the paddles from their mount on the wall, which also happened to be next to

Penelope. My sister said, "Hey, I'm Benedict's sister, Elizabeth. He said you guys go to The Bend together?"

"Yeah," Penelope said, only half looking up from her phone. It was very dismissive, I thought, and it made me feel that even if Penelope and I were the only teenagers in the world she would probably still be too cool for me.

But my sister would not be deterred as easily, asking, "What's your name?"

"Pen."

"Pen. Awesome name." My sister started hitting the Ping-Pong ball back and forth with me, which was nice because then I didn't have to think too much about how incompetent I am at talking to girls, even a girl I am not at all attracted to.

"My full name is Penelope."

"That's awesome too."

"I fucking hate it." She laughed.

Elizabeth laughed with her, which is a smart thing to do if you want people to like you. "The best pizza in Riverbend is Penelope's Pizzeria—do they like give you free slices if you show them your driver's license?"

"It's my dad's place. So yeah."

"That's super awesome!"

"Yeah, maybe." A now-smiling Penelope put her phone down. Which was astounding. My thirteen-year-old sister had befriended a popular girl from my class in three minutes.

I should say something to Penelope. A normal person would say something by this juncture. My baby sister had done all the difficult work in establishing a rapport. It should be easy for me to say anything—even something meaningless would be acceptable. So I should. Yes, you should, Benedict. Yes, I know. . . .

Even though convincing Penelope to become Robert's friend was the first step in regaining his friendship, which would lead to Allison Wray becoming my girlfriend, which would lead to becoming popular, which would lead to my father's respect, which would lead to an exceptional life, the pressure to communicate like a normal person with a girl was constricting my chest muscles to such a degree that I assumed I was about to have a heart attack and die. Being popular is not very useful if you are dead.

"Do you play?" Elizabeth asked Penelope, because I had failed to say anything.

"Not really."

"I'm sure you're better than me." My sister then flopped herself down onto the couch, pressing the Ping-Pong paddle into Penelope's hands. For a moment, I assumed Penelope would find a reason not to play with me. In fact, she would probably say she needed to go back to her cabin. I should state a reason I needed to leave first. This would give me the upper hand in our battle for whatever it is it feels like we are battling for. But my inability to speak remained a problem.

Except Penelope didn't say she needed to leave.

Nor did she offer an excuse not to play with me.

Instead, she stood, paddle in hand, and then positioned herself on the other side of the table from me. For the first time, she looked at me. I looked at her. She smiled at me. I smiled at her.

I'm not attracted to Penelope at all. I'm sorry for repeating this so often but . . . strange. I'm not sure *why* I'm repeating this so often. Perhaps I've watched too many romantic movies. My dad tells me they exist only to make the masses forget their lives are meaningless. He is probably right. Of course he is. But right now, all those romantic movies have me thinking that *if* I were attracted to Penelope, and if she were attracted to me, this would be a very promising beginning to a romantic relationship. But Penelope has a boyfriend, a boyfriend who beat me up. And I am attracted to Allison Wray. *And* Robert is attracted to Penelope. I have told Robert repeatedly, for years, how unattractive Penelope is and perhaps that is why I am repeatedly telling myself this now.

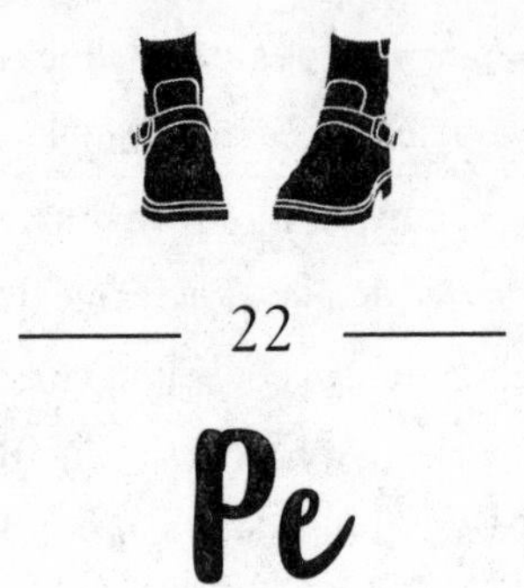

22

Pe

"Right about now is when you hit the ball to her, Benedict," his sister said after we had stood there for the most awkward ten seconds of my life. Elizabeth and I laughed a small laugh. Benedict didn't laugh. Just stood there, stiff. I've never seen Benedict laugh at anything. He'll probably grow up to be a serial killer. Anyway, yeah, so he did snap out of his daze and hit the ball toward me.

I mean, what the hell. I've gone to college parties, to huge concerts, to festivals in cornfields where everyone is high and half naked. And now, on a Saturday night, I'm playing *fucking Ping-Pong* with the biggest dork in high school, with his junior high sister watching, and you know what? You know what? I'm giggling. Not like loud or even on the outside at all. But I have this little giggle inside me. Like there's a little girl, an innocent girl, maybe only ten or eleven years old and she's not thinking about appearing perfect or about her parents fighting or her boyfriend calling her crappy things, all she's thinking is, *It's fun to play Ping-Pong with a cute boy.*

EXCEPT BENEDICT ISN'T CUTE.

He's not.

He's odd, clueless, and I don't know—a hundred other things that make me want to strangle that giggling little girl inside me.

I don't say anything while we play. Neither does Benedict. Of course he doesn't. And even Elizabeth can't bullshit a bridge between us anymore. Silence starts creeping under my skin like a disease, into the whole room, and everyone can feel it, and someone needs to say something soon or else the windows might shatter from the quiet.

Wait. Oh-my-god. Benedict's going to speak . . . I can see it forming in his head, in his eyes, here it comes, he's opening his mouth, and . . .

He says, "How'd you get that scar?"

I don't cry. Remember, I don't cry anymore. But you know who went from being a giggly love-crushing dork to a heaving, teary mess? That little Penelope inside me. Fucking loser.

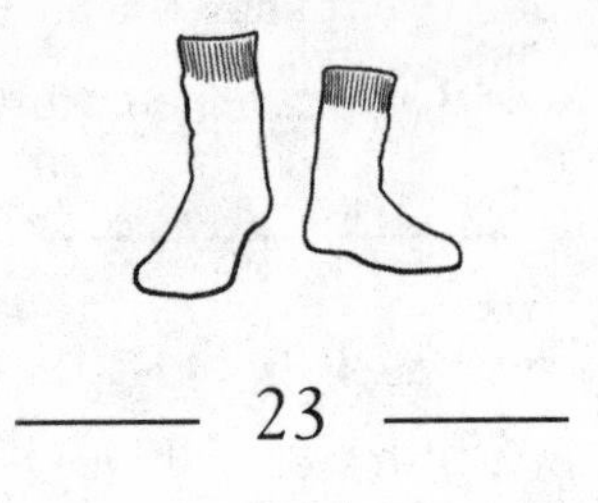

23

BENE . . .

EVEN BEFORE MY SISTER SAID, "BENEDICT, YOU don't ask that!" I knew I shouldn't have asked about her scar.

(Evil Benny, who had been dormant for some time, screamed with glee, "You're such an idiot!")

The old me and the new me had been debating very intensely on what to say. Both old and new knew that I had to say *something*, but while the new me insisted I ask something meaningless such as "Is this your first time at Wild Wolf Resort?" the old me insisted that asking meaningless questions doesn't benefit anyone. It would be disingenuous to ask a question I did not care about the answer to even if the asking of the question made that person more comfortable in my presence. The new me said that's exactly what I needed to do. But the old me had been curious for years as to the origin of that very distinctive scar. And I think I had been concentrating so intently on why I needed to continue to believe Penelope wasn't attractive that the scar had become the focal point to concentrate on my lack of attraction. . . .

24

P

I keep hitting that Ping-Pong ball, but really I'm just waiting for my body to crumble into five thousand pieces. I mean, look at my life:

One, I've just gotten dumped by my awesome, popular boyfriend.

Two, I've been sexually fantasizing about the biggest dork in high school.

Three, this young, innocent Penelope inside me is acting like she's full-throttle in puppy love with this dork while we are playing Ping-Pong.

Four, this dork—WHO IS RETARDED AND I HATE THAT I EVEN THINK THAT WORD BUT I HAVE TO BECAUSE HE IS—doesn't say anything, not one word, until the first and only thing he says is, "Hey, let's talk about that grotesque disfiguration on your face that is the only thing I can think about because it is so hideous."

Five, I'm so numb to anything real, so dead inside, that I just keep hitting the ball back and forth and back and forth and screw this—SCREW THIS, I'm getting my mom's keys and I'm driving myself straight back to Riverbend and I don't care where Paul is or who he's with, I'll throw myself at him, I'll get him so turned on that he'll beg for me back, beg for my body, beg to marry me and save me from my mom and Benedict and myself. . . .

"Pen, Benedict, he's, uh . . ." Elizabeth says, picking up the ball from behind me. I look up, realizing that I actually did stop playing. I'm just standing there like an even bigger idiot than I was when I kept playing. His sister can't find the words to explain her brother. No one can. Look at him look at me. He's not human! He doesn't even know what he said! No clue! Why am I here? Go home. Go home.

"Penelope . . ." Benedict starts. Fuck, he's even calling me by the name I fucking hate. GO HOME NOW, PEN. He starts again, "I mean, Pen . . ."

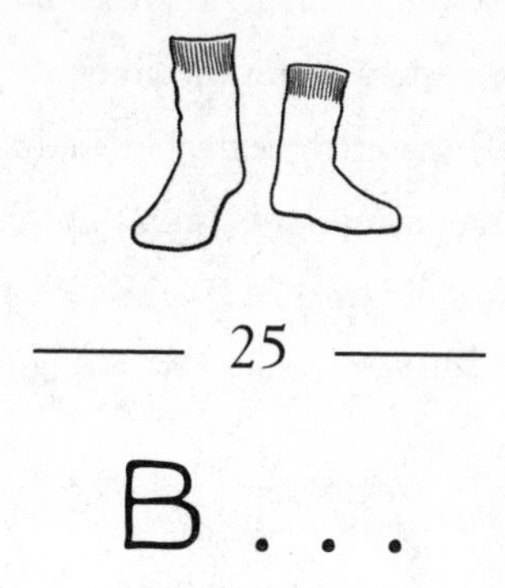

25

B . . .

THE NEW ME WAS TELLING ME TO APOLOGIZE; the old me was telling me I should remain steadfast. Elizabeth was begging me with her eyes to say anything. My mom's voice was telling me I'm not a horrible person even though I know I am. Robert's voice was telling me we will be dorks forever if I don't repair things with Penelope. And my father's voice was telling me that Penelope is not worth my time, but also if I don't become popular, then my entire life is a failure.

But growing louder than all these voices was Evil Benny. Just cackling and cackling. He didn't even need to speak words. Just laugh and laugh at how I was on the brink of literal insanity.

I came to the conclusion that this is not exaggeration. To clarify: I'm not saying I'm losing my mind because it's a metaphor for my feeling overwhelmed or confused. I'm say I'm losing my mind because I can actually sense the detachment between it and my own consciousness. I did not know how to stop all these screaming voices in my head. I could not function normally, not even in my not-entirely-normal normal way. I did not know how to do anything besides stand at the

Ping-Pong table, watch Penelope Lupo try desperately not to cry, and wait for a permanent psychotic break to take hold.

Understanding that these were my final moments of sanity, the fear of embarrassment that had rendered me unable to talk to a girl disappeared. I did not want my final words to be false, not falsely apologetic nor falsely boastful. They should be true. True in a truly new way.

So I said, "What you said in the dean's office . . . you were correct. I have social problems."

After she took several seconds to register that I actually said what I said, Penelope's internal pain seemed to ease. As did my sister's external stress. Saying these words out loud, and seeing the effect on others, also seemed to pause my descent into madness.

So I continued, "I should have asked you a meaningless question such as 'Have you been to Wild Wolf before?' But my body feels very uncomfortable when I ask meaningless questions even though it would have achieved my desired effect of forming a bond with you. Instead I asked about your scar . . ."

Both Penelope and Elizabeth flinched. But I had to stay the course of truth.

". . . which I was genuinely curious about because it is so unique. If I didn't have social problems, I would have known better than to ask this. I have asked my sister to help me, but I think you can see her lessons haven't started yet."

— 26 —

Pen

What the hell, right?

I mean, crazy-crazy-crazy Benedict. He basically says the most asshole-ish thing ever because he's too oblivious not to say it, and as I'm standing there ready to evaporate from pathetic-ness, he goes and says the most real thing I think I've heard anyone say ever.

And suddenly it makes sense.

Why I fixated on him so much. Because it's so hard for me to be honest with myself, with my friends, with Paul, and yet I could see this purity inside him. This ability to say things I could never say. He even explained it. Said his body is uncomfortable asking bullshit questions. My body gets uncomfortable with being real; *his body gets uncomfortable being false.*

I forgot about his scar question. It didn't even bother me anymore. In fact, it was worth it because it led to him saying what he said. Which led to me finally understanding my obsession with him.

"It's cool, Benedict," I said, which was lame because of how generic it was after how unique what he said was. But I'm not him. I'll never be him. I can only be my quiet, invisible, fake self.

Elizabeth said, "I promise to speed up my lessons." Which was funny, or at least a relief, and she and I laughed. And, damn, so did Benedict. I've never seen the kid laugh ever.

"I'm laughing at myself," he said. Of course he would point this out. "I think this is the first time I have ever done so." Which made Elizabeth and me laugh more, which made him laugh more, like this over-the-top robot laugh. And he was on a roll so he said, "My laugh is very awkward, isn't it?"

And that sent us all into a breathless fit of laughter, which, I don't know, I hadn't experienced since maybe the first time I smoked pot freshman year. Tonight I guess I was high on Benedict's craziness. Or realness. Or whatever combination of the two he was.

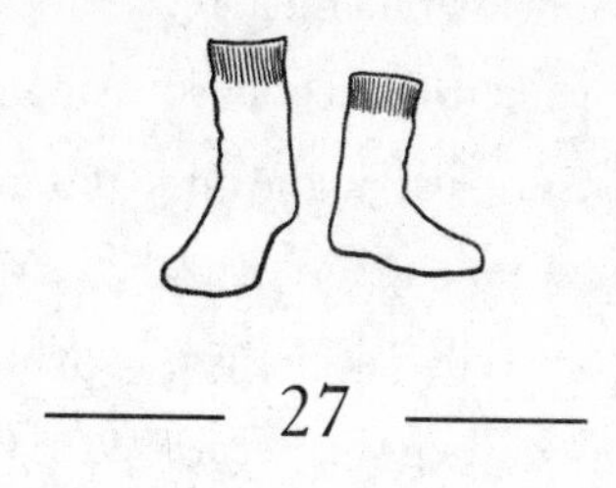

27

BENEDICT

PENELOPE, MY SISTER, AND I STAYED IN THE lodge for another hour playing Ping-Pong, talking about the resort and even a little about school. I tried to make the occasional self-deprecating reference to my social problems, which always resulted in their laughter, which I enjoyed.

After Elizabeth said she was tired, I said I'd walk her home, and then Penelope said she should go too. Penelope's cabin was next to the lodge, so after we said good-bye, my sister and I had a long walk back together.

"Benedict!" she said, loud but whispering, once we were a few cabins away from Penelope's. "Not what I would have advised, but I think you did an amazing job tonight. After saying the worst thing ever with that scar question, you were brilliant. I mean, Benedict, I was so proud of you." She shoved me into the snow because that's how siblings often display their affection.

Getting up, pushing her back but not too hard because big brothers can't do that, I said, "I came to the conclusion that the confession of my imperfections was the only way to repair the situation." I did not elaborate about being on the brink of a mental breakdown.

"Well, admitting your imperfections was perfect. If you ever get into trouble like that again, just do the same thing."

I said, "I appreciate your support, Elizabeth. You have the opposite of social problems. You were a social genius when you established a connection with Penelope when we first arrived in the recreation room."

"Benedict, are you saying that I'm just as smart as you?"

"I was *not* saying that, but now that you have said it . . . ummm . . . I . . . yes. You are smart in a different way than I am, which I now value much more highly after the past week."

"That's the nicest thing you've ever said, brother."

"I will work harder to say nicer things to you more often."

"Also work on saying nicer things to Pen. Because she totally likes you."

"No, she doesn't. She has a boyfriend."

"I don't care if she has a boyfriend; she likes you."

"She has a boyfriend. Also, Robert likes her. I need to establish a friendship with Penelope so that I can then make her friends with Robert and then Robert and I can become best friends again."

Elizabeth stopped walking, turned, and faced me. She grabbed me by my shoulders. She was very serious. "Benedict, I know I said she's too cool for you. And I know you did a great job of talking about your social problems. But you and Pen, you two have this thing. I don't even know what it is. But it's a thing."

"No, we don't. She's not attractive at all."

"She's like the sexiest girl maybe ever!"

"She has a boyfriend. And Robert is my best friend."

"Oh, jeesh, are you being blockheadish again? You were being so honest back at the lodge. Can you really not see it?"

"Elizabeth, just because I am trying to improve my communication skills with my peers doesn't mean I will abandon logic."

"Oh, god, forget it, fine. Let's just get back to the cabin. It's freezing." She spun back and started to jog. I let her go on ahead. I was enjoying the winter air. For some reason, it didn't feel as cold walking back as it did walking to the lodge. Which is odd because it was later at night, and logically, it should be colder.

28

Pen

My mom was asleep by the time I got back inside the cabin. It felt later than it was. It always did up here at the lake. But it wasn't even ten. It was a Saturday night. Back home, my friends and I would just be getting our festivities going. But here there was nothing to do.

Screw it, I'll just get in bed and masturbate a million times.

But once I had changed and gotten under the covers, I didn't really feel like it. Not that I wasn't turned on. I was. I always am because I'm a freak. But I didn't feel like masturbating. So weird. So I tried to read more Millie Dragon on my phone. I couldn't really do that either.

Oh-my-god. I'm just going to think about Benedict, aren't I? Yeah. I am. Not even in a sexual way! But thinking about hanging out, playing Ping-Pong, watching a movie together, talking about whatever. This is so weird! Having bizarre sexual fantasies was normal for me! But this, *this*, I couldn't even understand.

But . . . yeah . . . okay . . . I don't know. Screw it. I can't stop. I'm just gonna think about telling him things, telling him about how my parents are nuts, tell him how religion is bullshit, about how I want to be real like him but I can't. Tell him about my sexual fantasies, about how I fantasize about him . . .

As I'm thinking this, thinking about being real, and honest, and totally connected to someone, to Benedict, I'm just aching, just throbbing, but I don't know, I don't want to let it go, I just want to feel it. I want to keep thinking about talking to him, keep feeling my body enjoying that thought. . . .

And then I faded away and slept. I never fall asleep that early, but I did, and I slept deep. No dreams. Nothing. Just sleep. Just rest. Just calm.

In the morning, I woke up in time for breakfast. When Paul was here, we'd stay up late in the living room (my mom wouldn't let him stay in my room because she thinks I'll be a virgin until I'm probably dead), and my mom wouldn't even bother to ask us to breakfast because we'd be passed out until close to lunch. But I heard her moving around the cabin, so I called out, "I'll go to breakfast with you."

When I came out of my room, she said, "It's very strange to see my daughter up with us nonvampires."

"I went to bed early."

"You didn't watch a movie?"

"I ended up hanging with that Benedict kid and his sister."

"Oh, reeeeaaaaaally?" my mom said. I decided I'm never telling her anything ever again. "What did you doooooo?"

"We played Ping-Pong, Mom. Don't be weird."

"It's not weird to want to know what your daughter did!"

"Okay, fine, let's just go to breakfast."

Wild Wolf has the best oatmeal maybe in the world, and as soon as I'm eating it, I'm regretting not waking up for it the past two years.

Sitting there with my mom, relaxed, well rested, enjoying breakfast, even enjoying us talking about silly stuff like TV shows, my head flashes back to a couple nights ago when she caught me masturbating and she flipped the hell out and I told her to fuck off and then some ugly shit must have gone on between her and my dad and I wished they were all dead. I mean, when I see shit like that happen in movies or books, the characters all change and the whole plot changes. It's like: "This fight will make everything different for our hero!" But not with me. Not with my family. We're yelling and fighting like lunatics one night and eating oatmeal together the next morning. Not literally the next morning, but close enough.

Anyway, after we're done eating, my mom and I drink coffee and look at our phones since the dining room is the only place you can get Wi-Fi or any service at all. There are no texts from Paul, which doesn't even make me feel anything. I mean, I don't feel good about it, but I don't feel any worse about it either.

Iris did text me a few times, telling me she missed me. That was nice. But then Iris asked if I wanted to hear what Paul was doing, which made me think Paul was going out with other girls, which made me want to kill every girl I've ever seen him looking at. I guess this makes me a homicidal maniac. Love's great. I'm kidding. It sucks.

"Should we go shopping this morning since you're up?" my mom asks, in the middle of my mind's murdering rampage.

"Sure," I say. At least half our vacations up here were spent driving to small towns in the area like Minocqua and Boulder Junction and buying local crap like handmade sweaters and homemade soap. I enjoyed it more than I would ever admit to my mom, but, I don't know, if I left with her, then Benedict . . .

Never mind. *Never mind.*

Like, as I'm having this thought, he walks in with his family. It feels so awkward, like last night didn't happen at all or the opposite extreme, like we had sex and can't even look at each other, only then I see him stop and, I don't know, talk to himself maybe. Then he marches right over to our table. Oh-my-god, I'm going to pass out from all the embarrassment rushing to my face.

"Hi, Mrs. Lupo, my name is Benedict Pendleton. I go to school with your daughter. I'm introducing myself because I'm working on not being socially awkward."

I laugh because I'm going to laugh every time he says that no matter how many times he does.

"Penelope, don't laugh!" my mom screeches.

"No, it's okay, Mrs. Lupo. I like when Penelope laughs. Hope you had a lovely breakfast and I look forward to talking again soon." Then the kid leaves.

My mom, who tries to be nice unless she's condemning people to hell for being sinners, can't even help but say, "Okay, you're right. He's a little dorky."

"A little?"

"Yes, okay, Penelope, maybe more than a little. But he's also adorable."

"He is adorable," I say softly, but not in my head like I thought I was going to say it. I don't think I've said that word ever. "Adorable." Gross. What a stupid, geeky word. But I said it, I guess. And my mom gives me that look. Like she knows I'm going to get myself in trouble. She's right. She's so right.

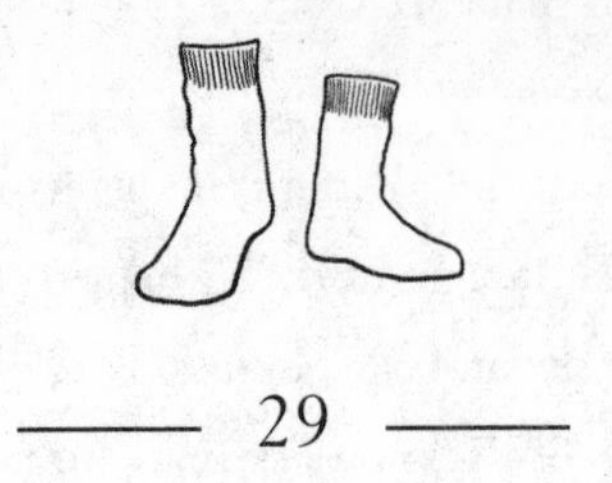

29

Benedict

MY DAD NEEDED TO WORK ON HIS BOOK, SO after breakfast my mom, Elizabeth, and I went for a hike along the service road that circled the lake. All three of us wore three layers each so we wouldn't die of frostbite, except the sun was out, the hike was strenuous, and we all ended up sweating so much we were carrying our jackets by the time we arrived back at our cabin. We were repeatedly passed by cross-country skiers, which looked like more fun and less work, so I told my sister we were going skiing after lunch.

"No, I'm not."

"Go with him," my mom said.

"You go with him."

"I'm old. I need to rest."

"Fine," Elizabeth said, "I'll go if you ask Pen to join us."

"Fine," I said, before I could think of a logical reason that I shouldn't ask her.

"Oh, my," my mom started, "should I be aware of something?"

"No, Mother," I said, "Elizabeth is only helping me practice being normal." But my sister and mom exchanged a look that suggested they didn't believe me.

At lunch, after I turned off my ability to hear Evil Benny or any other voices besides the ones saying, "Do it, Benedict! You'll be great!" I approached Penelope and her mother at their table.

"Good afternoon, Mrs. Lupo and Penelope." They both smiled. They found me humorous because I am awkward.

("This should make you feel like a moron!" Evil Benny said because he has access to my mind even when I think he doesn't. But I decided not to let it make me feel like a moron. Evil Benny didn't know how to respond to that.)

"Good afternoon, Benedict," Mrs. Lupo said.

"Hey," Penelope said.

"My daughter only speaks in single words."

"I know, but those single words often contain a great deal of meaning." I knew this was a nice thing to say even before Penelope's mouth formed this miniature smile. Maybe after I say one hundred more nice things like this it will make up for my question about her scar. I went on, "Penelope, my sister and I are going cross-country skiing this afternoon and would like to know if you would join us."

"I, uh, don't . . ." she began.

"She would love that," her mom said.

"Yeah, okay," Penelope said.

"Yes, great. They rent skis down at the boathouse. Should we meet there at two p.m.?"

"Okay," Penelope said.

"Great. See you then." And then I walked away. Though Penelope was just a friend, and probably just a friend because we were the only high school students at Wild Wolf Resort, it did feel, on some level, that I had just successfully asked a girl out on a date for the first time.

I tried not to let this triumph go to my head, but as I ate lunch, I began to think I, once again, was the greatest person in the world. When contrasting this thought with my near collapse as a functioning human being last night, I could not help but laugh at myself. I've found I feel better after laughing at myself and am going to try doing it more often.

After lunch, in our cabin, I tried to think of topics of conversation to begin with Penelope while we cross-country skied. Elizabeth was very good at this, so I would only need a few, but I didn't want to be unprepared. Then I worried I was going to be late for my date with Penelope even though I know it's not an actual date. I like to be early because I don't like to waste brain cells being worried about being late, so I told Elizabeth it was time to go but she refused to get up from the couch.

"It's not even one thirty, Benedict! It's going to take us three minutes to walk down there!"

"It takes at least eight minutes, Elizabeth. We've done the walk five times now and it has always taken at least eight minutes."

"Fine, eight minutes. I'll leave at one fifty-two, then."

"No, we must leave now."

"No, we *must* leave at one fifty-two."

"I'm going now. I'll check out the skis and make sure everything's in order. You promise you'll be there by two p.m.?"

Elizabeth formed this little grin on the right side of her mouth. Then she said, "I promise I won't let you down." I didn't like how she said that at all, but now it was almost one forty and I was far too concerned about being late to worry about anything else.

— 30 —

Pen

If I had Benedict's number, I would have texted him I couldn't go skiing with him. I mean, fuck me. Really. There was like fifteen minutes where I was kinda into it. Like, "it's cool to do something different." But then I remembered I HATE doing anything athletic and I HATE being cold and this was both those things AT THE SAME TIME. Right? Right! Like I said, fuck me.

But I couldn't text him. And I couldn't show up and tell him, "Hey, can't go because I'm sick or whatever," because he'd be able to tell I was lying, and even though I know I'm a liar, I don't want him to know. I just don't.

Oh, and also, yeah, ALSO, I had no snow pants, so I had to borrow my mom's white puffy overalls, which were five hundred times too big for me, and my black jacket barely fit over them and it all made me look like a huge marshmallow that was charred on the top half. Seriously. I had to walk bowlegged and they made a swishy noise, and if there ever was an outfit that would make a boy not want to have sex with you *ever*, I'm sure this was it. Not that I wanted Benedict to want to have sex with me. I didn't. I mean, maybe I did. But not for real. I loved Paul. I needed to get Paul back. Paul, Paul, Paul, Paul . . . he's my everything, yeah, everything, and I kept thinking about this, I made myself even. . . .

But I walked, or swished, my way out of the cabin anyway. The boathouse was down on the water on the opposite side of the lodge from us, so it was a lot of swishing. Like, I'm sure everyone at the resort could hear me. If someone was making a video of me doing this and posted it online, my life would be over. No one would ever want to be seen with me again in public. That's how ridiculous I looked! Why did I say yes?! What-the-hell-am-I-doing? Why does Benedict make me do and think the dumbest things ever?!?!

"Hi, Penelope, Pen," he said when he saw me. He ran to the top of the boathouse stairs to help me walk down them because it was that obvious I couldn't move like a normal person. He, however, looked *so* normal in his snow pants and jacket. He even looked like a jock. It's like I've entered an alternate universe where Benedict is popular and normal and I'm the one with social problems who can't even walk down stairs by herself. He said something about his sister being late, but I was just trying not to slip and break my butt in half.

Inside the boathouse, there was some old guy with a red beard and something red on his hands—oh, wait, that's fish guts, awesome—and he was getting out ski shoes and putting them on the floor for me to try on. Of course the fish guts got inside the shoe and I'd throw up if I thought it would make all this stop. Benedict was very helpful, I think, saying nice things, I think, but I was sweating now just from trying on shoes and so mortified by everything that was happening that I couldn't even really pay attention to anything.

Eventually, with the ugliest shoes in the history of shoes on my feet,

I walked back outside and had to do the stairs without Benedict's help since he was carrying all our skis and poles.

At the top, Benedict laid out the skis near the beginning of what I think was a path into the woods. I'm pretty sure the boathouse fish-guts guy said how to put the skis on, but I couldn't remember a thing. Like, not even how to talk. Benedict could tell because he handed me the poles, told me to use them for balance, and then got on his knees in the snow and lifted up my feet and snapped the shoes into the skis.

You know, as I was watching him do this, I just had this weird thought. What if, back in eighth grade when I decided to start wearing sexy clothes and makeup and make myself popular and all that . . . what if, instead, I just stayed a geek. A dork. Yeah. And studied, got good grades, and never had any friends, not really, but then now, right now, since I got to Wild Wolf, everything happened sort of the way it happened. I'm sure it would be different, but sort of the same. And this moment, right now, with Benedict, who my dork self doesn't think is dorky but actually thinks is awesome and super smart. Yeah . . . and that dork self, who I kinda am right now in this marshmallow outfit, would be looking at this handsome, smart boy down on his hands and knees in the snow just to help me, as if he was some kind of knight-in-shining-armor crap. Dork self wouldn't think "crap" because she probably likes stupid fairy-tale shit. Like that dork self would be so in love with how handsome and helpful and kind and confident this boy was being. . . .

"How do you feel?" he asked.

"Huh?" I said because my brain was off in fairy-dork-land.

"How do the skis feel? How's your balance?"

I looked down. I wiggled around. I didn't feel like I was going to fall, but I hadn't tried moving yet. "Okay, I think," I said.

"Good. I've never done this either, so we can learn together."

"Is your sister coming?"

"About that. I've come to the conclusion that she's not going to show up. She tricked me, I believe. Will it not be fun without her? We don't have to go if you don't want to."

My out!

But not really. And screw it, I don't want an out anyway. But I've hesitated and Benedict can tell I've hesitated. . . .

So I said, "No, no, I've already swished and sweated and looked like a complete idiot getting to this point. I doubt it can get worse. I mean, I'm sure you'll be fun to do it with. I'm just saying I don't think I can embarrass myself any more than I have already."

Benedict smiled this smile at me. It was so weird. I mean, I kind of liked it. It almost felt, I don't know, flirtatious. But it was so weird.

"Why are you looking at me like that?" I asked, finally, and not flirtatious back. But defensive. I'm such a bitch.

"I think that sentence before, about swishing and so forth, was the longest, most revealing sentence you've ever shared with me."

"Oh." Really? Yeah. I think about it. Thinking about it makes me feel like that sentence doesn't even sound like me. I mean, it sounds like the me in my head but not the me everyone else knows. The quiet girl who speaks only in single-word sentences.

"I enjoyed you speaking like that very much." He is *totally* flirting with me. In his Tin Man robot way, but for sure.

I think about saying something flirty back. Like "I like that you like it." Except that makes me want to throw up. So I just say, "Cool," and god, I suck, but whatever.

And then he tells me to follow him, that he did some research on how to ski properly, and he starts moving and I move with him. I know I'm going to fall and look like such a loser, but I don't care enough to stop. I want to follow him. And as we ski into the woods—woods I've avoided my entire life because I'm sure there are monsters inside them—I start thinking how I had said what I said to him. How I just admitted to being embarrassed, just said was on my mind, exactly like it was *in my mind*.

And I didn't do that with Paul, or my mom, or my dad, or Iris, or anyone ever. I did it with Benedict.

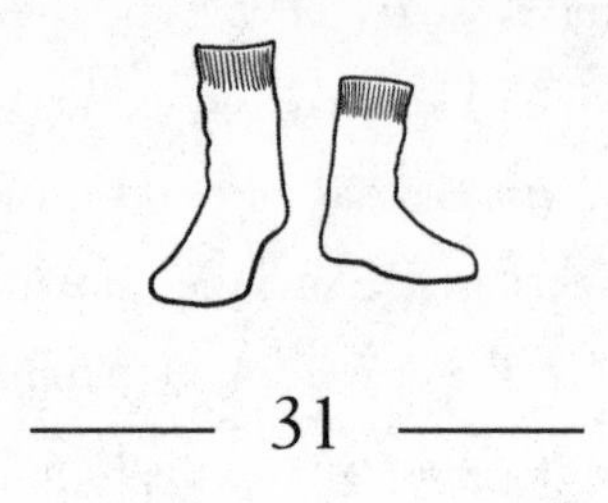

31

BENEDICT

PENELOPE FALLS THREE TIMES WITHIN THE first fifty meters and each time she says, "I'm so terrible at this! I look so dumb!" And I tell her she is doing an excellent job and that she doesn't look dumb at all.

This is, of course, a lie. She is terrible at skiing and she looks a bit like a giant white turtle on its back when she falls. But I don't tell her this. The old me would have. The new me concentrates on what she is probably feeling instead of what I am thinking. It's very difficult.

Yet, also, each time she falls, I must help her up and when she stands we are always right next to each other, our skis between each other's legs. Her scent of flowers, fresh laundry, and mystery floats between us. And there is not much space between us at all. If we were boyfriend and girlfriend, I would kiss her each time I helped her up. Yes, I think that's what I would do. It would be a nice thing to do, to help console her after a fall, but also it would be nice for me. To kiss a girl. I've imagined it many times. I think I'd be very good at it.

Evil Benny says I'd be terrible at it. Even worse than Penelope is at skiing. He says that a boy who has never even kissed a girl by the time he is seventeen (which I turn tomorrow) will probably be a terrible kisser forever. In fact, he says I probably should never kiss anyone ever because they would laugh at how terrible I am at it. . . .

"Penelope . . . sorry, Pen . . . can I ask you a question?" I start, though I really don't have a question in mind. I just wanted to stop Evil Benny from talking so much.

"Yeah," she says, out of breath. I look back to make sure she is capable of skiing and talking at the same time. Possibly not. I decide I must ask a question anyway.

"Do you like having a boyfriend?" This question was a logical progression from my thinking about kissing a girl, and so forth, but now it feels nerdy. Like a child asking a teenager if they liked being able to drive.

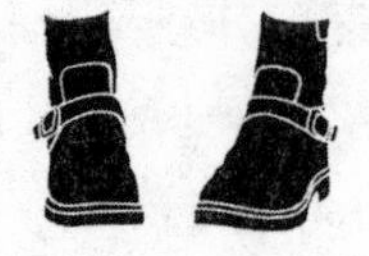

32

Pen

He asks if I like having a boyfriend. Does he know Paul and I broke up? How could he know? Maybe Paul's telling people and it's out there and he read it on Facebook or something. I'm half sweaty, half freezing, I keep falling on my butt, and Benedict's toying with me, isn't he? He knows I've been dumped. He knows I'm this desperate mess. He knows what I'm thinking every time he helps me up.

I fall again. I don't even know if I did it on purpose. I think I did. I totally did. So I don't have to answer the question? Maybe. But really so Benedict would lean over, so he'd grab hold of both my arms, lift me up, and my skis would then slide toward him, almost into him. Even though I'm the least attractive I've probably ever been in my life, I decide this time I'll give him my "fuck me" eyes. I'm good at this. Great at it. It shuts Paul up when I want and has made college boys cross rooms toward me. These eyes are like a gift of mine. Maybe my only one.

I imagine that after giving Benedict these eyes, he'll grab me. Grab me like Paul has never grabbed me. Grab me like a guy that can only tell the truth would grab me. Grab me, kiss me, throw me down into the snow, fall on top of me, and I don't know what else. I can't really imagine beyond that because just before I can give Benedict my "fuck me" eyes, he says:

"That was a totally dorky thing to say, wasn't it? Asking about having a boyfriend? I'm sorry. It must be hard to have conversations with me sometimes."

What? Huh? Oh-my-god. He has no clue. No clue about Paul. No clue we broke up. Benedict . . . he's just . . . He wasn't playing a game. Wasn't trying to get in my head. He was just asking a real question. Like always.

"No, it's not," I said, even though it *was* a dorky question now that I think about it, but what does that even mean? "It's cool to ask. Having a boyfriend is cool. . . ." Stop using the word "cool" so much, Pen, you sound so uncool saying "cool" so much. . . . "It's nice to have someone to be with. To talk to." Even though Paul and I have not had one conversation I can remember right now. But whatever.

"Okay. Thank you, Penelope. Sorry, I mean, Pen."

"You can call me Penelope. I don't care." I don't?

"That's nice of you, but I'll work harder on saying Pen. I'm not sure why I keep saying Penelope. I think it was the name of a Greek goddess. No, perhaps, from one of Homer's books?"

I shook my head even though I knew.

"I'm not sure either. But I think you have always been very mythical to me. How you transformed yourself in junior high from one of us to one of them. So maybe that is why I say Penelope. Because you are more mythology than reality." He stopped and looked at me. We were still only a foot away, our skis entwined. What Benedict had just said made me like my name for the first time in forever. But I couldn't tell him that. I couldn't say anything. I could, I suppose. But I wouldn't. I'd just stand there, looking at him like what he said hadn't just rewritten a part of my self-identity. He went on, while I was being a mute fool. "Am I talking too much? Elizabeth says I talk too much. Is everything I'm saying something no one should ever say? You could help me too, if you don't mind. My sister, she's socially smart, but she's only in eighth grade. You're my age and you're very popular. You could tell me what I should say. What's dorky, what's not. You could be my second teacher. Help me change . . ."

"Don't," I said. I couldn't take any more. Not of Benedict. Of my own invisibility. Of being not real when I want to be the opposite of not real.

"Don't what? Don't . . ."

"Don't change, Benedict."

"But . . ."

"You're awesome, Benedict. You're one of a kind. You say what's on your mind. You don't try to tell people only what they want to hear. You tell people what you want them to hear. You ask questions you want to know the answers to because you want to know things, not just to hear yourself ask things. Yeah, not everyone's going to love it, you'll get beaten up by idiots like Paul sometimes, but, man, you're what we all want to be."

As soon as I finished talking, I tried to go back in time and not say it. I don't talk like this! It was like I just made my soul naked and now it was about to freeze from the exposure. What the hell, Pen! Oh-my-god, I've got to get away from him. So I pushed back and skied past him. I skied like I knew how to ski. And I didn't fall. I went fast even. Maybe because the universe knew I needed to get away from Benedict, it granted me sixty seconds of athletic ability. It knew I couldn't look at him one more moment. I couldn't be so close to him for one more breath. Not just because I wanted him to kiss me more than I have ever wanted to be kissed in my life, but because I had just said all this stuff. All these words. It's like my mouth threw up sentences I didn't even know were inside me. It felt *so, so, so* uncomfortable to have my thoughts out of me, out in the world, for other people to judge.

So I push faster on the skis, faster, and faster. And there's a hill. And I think Benedict's yelling at me. But I can't stop. I don't want to stop. I want to go so fast that everything I'm feeling, everything I said, falls behind me and can never catch up. So I just go over the hill and it's bigger than I thought, like the size of a school bus on its end, and straight down. Or close. And I'm going so fast now. So, so, so fast. And now the speed is not me, it's nature, it's hurling me downward and there's a curve and I can't turn. I have no idea what I'm doing. I'm going to crash into a tree. I'm going to crash into a tree and I'm going to die . . . and as much as I hate that I said all that, I'm glad I said it before I die. I'm glad I was real at least once.

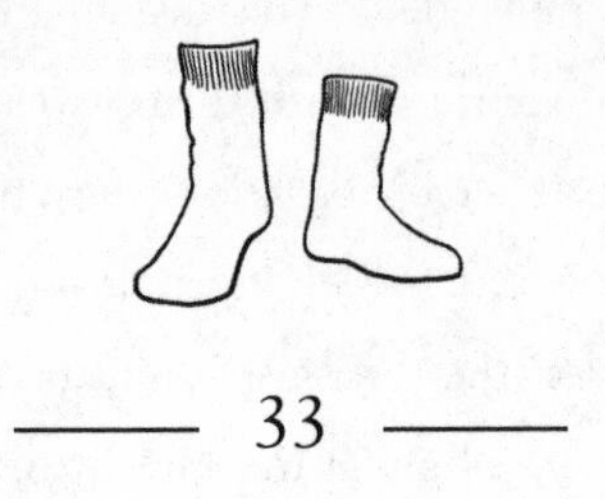

33

BENEDICT

AFTER PENELOPE SAID THE NICEST THING anyone has ever said to me, I entertained the possibility that she was lying or, worse, trying to fool me. (Evil Benny certainly voted for this possibility.) But no, I don't think so. I really don't think so.

I think . . . yes, perhaps . . .

I'm not sure. I'm very confused. A week ago, I was very confident that I was the smartest person in the world, with the possible exception of my father. Yes, Evil Benny tried to undermine this. But I always put Evil Benny in his proper place. Then Robert dumped me as his friend, and I got beaten up by Paul and his friends, and my father wanted to fire me as his son. And then I believed I was the opposite of smart. I was the weakest, dumbest person in all of school.

Then, last night, I was on the brink of losing my mind, so I admitted what I had long denied: that I had social problems. Except now one of the most popular girls in the junior class was telling me I shouldn't change. That I should be exactly the way I had always been.

But before I could ask her to explain further what she meant, or say thank you, or say anything because it's nice to acknowledge someone who has spoken so eloquently and kindly, Penelope pushed past me and skied ahead. Skied very well, I must say. I determined she wasn't going to fall again. She suddenly looked like an Olympic skier! Not precisely, but it was faster than I could ski. Was she trying to get away from me? Because I hadn't said anything?

"Pen!" I yelled after her. Again and again. But she kept skiing and we moved deeper into the woods. I was getting better, faster. I must really want to catch up to her to be learning so quickly.

That's a hill ahead, I believe. I really don't want Penelope going over that hill. "PEN!" But she didn't stop and so I didn't stop. I was descending, plunging, down the hill. Were my skis even on the ground? They must be. But it felt as if I might be flying. My stomach rushed upward into my lungs and exploded. Not literally.

Pen was going to crash and I didn't want her to crash alone, so I followed her right into the tree.

34

Penelope

The pine tree that I was sure was going to kill me had a large hole around it. Not a hole, more like a deep bowl of snow. Anyway, the bowl's edges collapsed and sucked me downward, flung my skis up and my back down into the snow. That sounds bad, but it was a lot better than smashing into the tree.

Which, two seconds later, Benedict did. Oh-my-god. The whole pine shook and every branch dumped on us. I wiped the snow from my face because it was freezing but also because I had to find him.

"Benedict!" I screamed, and I never scream at anyone except my mom but he had just bounced off the trunk and spun face-first down into the snow. Only the back of his hat and the back half of his skis weren't buried.

He's dead.

He's totally dead.

If he's not dead, I'm going to kiss him.

What a stupid thing to think when someone's probably dead. I couldn't really move because the skis had me lodged in place, but I twisted, then crawled enough that I could reach him . . . but all I could do was take off his hat, which wasn't very helpful. But then he turned his head toward me. Which was nice. It meant he wasn't dead.

"I think I broke my face," he said.

"Are you okay?"

"Yes, though I may be paralyzed."

"Benedict . . ." My brain went numb. I, uh—

"I was making a joke, Pen."

"Oh." I was mad at him, sort of, but also, I don't know, charmed. I wasn't going to let him know that.

"You didn't think I knew how to make a joke, did you?"

No, I didn't. Stop being charming; it's distracting me. "Benedict, seriously, you're not moving. Are you okay or not?"

He wiggled a bit. "I think my skis are stuck, so I am stuck facing downward."

"Give me a second. I think I can get out of my skis." I had to crunch forward, like the hardest sit-up ever, but I did it and unlatched my shoes. Scooting over to him, I undid his skis, which allowed him to turn over onto his back.

So with the branches over us, and him lying on his back in this small snow bowl, and me sitting there, I don't know, it's almost like a canopy at a beach. Except for it being cold and in the woods, but you get it. Like, if we were together, I could lean over and kiss him right now. I know I said I would if he wasn't dead. But that was me being an idiot.

He sat up before I could do it. I mean, I suppose I could have done it still, but I was never going to do it, so I don't know why I kept thinking these thoughts. Get me out of my head! Please!

So I said, "Are you sure you're okay?" Just because.

"Yes, are you okay?" he asked.

"Yeah."

"Suddenly you became a very good skier."

"Yeah, I don't know."

Then we both sat there, under this snowy tree canopy, saying nothing. Not really looking away, but not able to look at each other either. Wait, he's totally looking at me. Of course he is. Because he doesn't understand how weird it is to stare at a girl in a moment like this! Then he said, "Thank you for helping me out of my skis."

This felt like a delay by him. Wasn't it? Like something a boy would say before they worked up the guts to kiss you? So I said, "Thank you for crashing into the tree with me." This was the cheesiest crap I've ever said in my life. But whatever. I was doing my part. Giving him the time to find the nerve. Then I looked at him. Not with my "fuck me" eyes. That would be so wrong right now. But with eyes that said "KISS ME, BENEDICT!" I think they did anyway, in a desperate, pathetic way but whatever.

"Pen," he said, the way a boy does right before he kisses you.

"Yeah?" I said, the way a girl does to let the boy know it's okay for him to kiss her.

And then, and then . . . he talked again. Fucking Benedict. My whole body is beating with my heart and my heart is going to blow up and *he's* talking again! "I know you have a boyfriend who is very popular. And Robert is in love with you. Robert's my best friend. I shouldn't have said he was in love with you, but I cannot not say it right this second. I've always told Robert you were unattractive because I knew you would never like a dork like him. Or a dork like me. And before five days ago, I think I would insult people in my mind because I thought they'd insult me to my face. But before you skied like an Olympic skier and crashed into this tree, you said the best thing anyone has ever said to me. And every time I am near you, my brain stops functioning properly because of your smell. And you look at me the way girls look at boys in movies, but I think I just don't understand how girls look at boys because I am socially awkward."

And . . .

And . . .

AND

I should kiss him. If I was bold, if I was even half as cool as Benedict thinks I am, I would kiss him. It would answer everything he just said. It would be magical, wouldn't it? But, like, oh-my-god, my eyes are tearing up, what the . . . what's wrong with me . . .

"Why are you crying? I'm sorry, did I say something?" he said.

I don't say anything. No way. No more saying what's really going on inside me ever again. But if I was the type of person who I thought I wanted to be, the type who said what they really thought—And I'm not! And I never want to be this person again!—but if I was, I'd say shit like this:

So why am I crying, Benedict? Why? Do you want to know why I'm crying for the first time since I was probably nine years old? Because I feel alive when I'm near you, the real me feels alive, and that's terrifying but in a great, beautiful way. And feeling alive makes me like myself and liking myself is something I never do with anyone else and so liking myself liking you makes me love you even though we're both clearly insane.

But, like I said, I'm not saying that. No way. In fact, I'm never even thinking it again. I like being silent. I'm never going to complain about being silent again. "Pen, are you hurt? Is something hurt? Why are you crying?" he asked again.

"I need to go back to my cabin. Okay?"

"Yes, okay, of course."

And because he's socially awkward, or a gentleman, or both, he stood up, didn't say a word, didn't complain or pry, and helped us out of our little snow home and back into our skis.

As we pushed ahead, me in the lead this time because I didn't want him looking back at me, neither of us said anything. It wasn't awkward. I mean, it was unbearably awkward but less awkward than it would have been if either of us opened our mouths.

Then there was this sign that said WARMING HUT. I looked over and it was this tiny dark one-room wood cabin. It looked like the type of place you stepped inside and when you came back out . . . you came back out into a better world.

I stopped and looked at it. At this mystical warming hut. My imagination imagined all the things that can happen in a tiny hut in the middle of the woods. Then I turned back toward Benedict. He was so handsome, and such a dork, he was so interesting, and so impossible.

You know what I'm terrible at? Talking, telling the truth, being the real me. From now on, I'm only doing what I'm great at.

So, with my best, purest "fuck me" eyes ever, I said to Benedict, "Paul and I broke up."

And then I faced forward, skied ahead, not stopping, not looking back, not thinking about love or feelings or being alive. You know, all the things I can't control.

I could feel him chasing me, not knowing what to say to make me slow. The only noise was the glide of our skis and the swish of my pants. Everything—from the cold air, to my sweat, to our silence—felt erotic. Sensual. Foreplay. This on top of the insanity I was escaping. I couldn't take it anymore. My body was flooding. So I squeezed as I skied and without making a sound, I came.

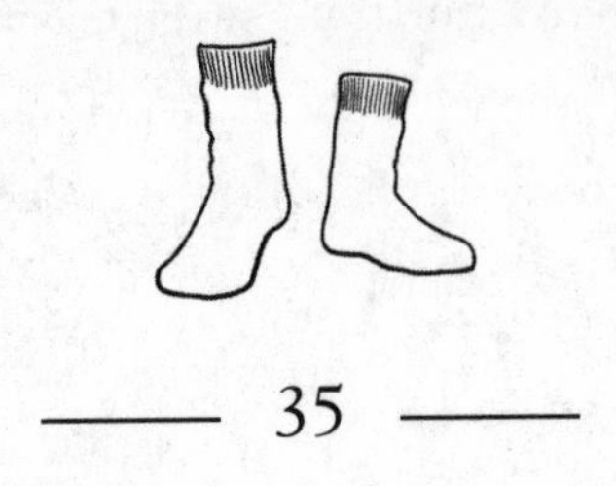

35

BENEDICT

I'M A VIRGIN. I'VE NEVER KISSED A GIRL. I KNOW I don't really understand how normal people communicate with each other.

But I'm very smart. I know I've admitted I'm not smart in *all* ways, but I'm still smart in a lot of ways. I know how to research topics and study very hard. I could tell you more about ancient Rome or the American Revolution than any other teenage boy. And I, obviously, wasn't alive back then.

Thus, even though I've never had sex with a girl, I know a lot about it. I've read a lot. I've watched a lot of videos. When I say videos, there are some educational shows, but mostly I mean pornography. I've studied them. Yes, obviously, I then masturbated. I'm not a robot. I'm very human. I don't talk about masturbating because, even though I'm socially awkward, I'm not *that* socially awkward.

So I've had, obviously, erections. In my penis. (Are there any other kinds?) This is very uncomfortable to talk about even inside my own mind.

("You're going nuts again!" Evil Benny said. No, I'm not, I'm just embarrassed to consciously think about these things. Very, very embarrassed.)

But even though I've had many erections at home, in my bedroom while I masturbated, and some uncontrolled ones when I woke in the morning or even at random times during school mostly due to how my penis had positioned itself in my pants, I don't believe I've ever had an erection like the one I had right now.

The one caused by Penelope looking at me with that madness in her eyes. That madness I had seen in school before many times. But now this madness was focused directly on me. It wasn't madness, was it? No, it was . . . primal, and by "primal" I mean biological, not diluted by intellect or even emotions. Just . . . lust? I'm not sure. I've never felt lust before. I don't think I have. I've liked girls before, but I've only liked them with my mind before. Not with my penis. This sounds ridiculous. But right at this moment, my penis was so hard—that's the slang term for erection—that I thought it would drain the blood from the rest of my body and I would pass out.

In addition, as Penelope gave me this gaze of biological lust, she said, "Paul and I broke up." My brain, even though it almost always translates things literally, instead translated her words from "I broke up with my boyfriend" to "I want to have sex with you in that warming hut." And because I have seen lots of videos of people having sex, I then pictured Penelope and me having sex in that warming hut.

This is strange to say, but I've never pictured having sex with a girl my own age before. Only the porn actresses in the videos. It was easier because I had seen those girls naked. It's much harder to imagine girls my age naked. I've thought about impressing high school girls with how smart I am, pictured them telling me how I am the best person they have ever met, but I've never had sexual thoughts about them.

Normal teenagers must think about sex with their classmates all the time. I've read they do. But I never had, so I didn't know how true that could be. It just seemed like a big waste of my time to imagine something that wasn't logically going to happen. But Penelope, with her eyes and her words, had made my brain allow for the logical conclusion that I could, possibly, have sex with her in that warming hut.

But then she skied away. I think Evil Benny had some negative things to say, but do you know who's even louder than Evil Benny? My erect penis. It said, "CHASE HER DOWN, BENEDICT! CHASE HER DOWN AND MAKE HER LOOK AT YOU WITH THOSE EYES AGAIN!"

So I skied after her, but she was, somehow, the best skier ever now. My brain hurt because it couldn't think of something to say. My chest hurt because it wanted her to talk to me. And, above all, my penis hurt because it had so much blood inside it. That's what happens to make it erect. The blood. Sounds very illogical when you think about it that way. Why did nature design us to need a rush of blood to our genitals in order to create babies? It seems very random to me. But it's true. And my ski pants were tight and that made it hurt even more every time I moved my legs to chase her. Not that I would ever stop chasing her, no matter how much it hurt, because . . . I'm not sure. Maybe it's lust that would make me never stop. Yes, I think so. I've never experienced it before, but I think that's what it must be. Lust. I've never kissed a girl, or had sex, or anything, obviously, but I wanted to do all those things with Pen no matter how much pain or torture I had to endure to make it happen.

When we got back to the cabins, she stopped at hers, unsnapped her shoes from her skis, and yelled, "I'll turn my stuff in later. I'll see you at dinner, Benedict!" without turning to me. She ran inside cabin 13 and closed the door behind her.

So, as I said, I've studied sex in books. Watched a great deal of sex online. I've masturbated a very healthy amount, even for a teenage boy, I believe. But . . . ummm . . . I'm not sure. I'm not sure how to process what I'm feeling. I'm standing outside her cabin; I can't even see her anymore, but my penis refuses to calm even the slightest bit. I can't move, neither toward my cabin nor toward hers. I can only stand here thinking about Penelope in that warming hut. Thinking about kissing her. Thinking about taking off her clothes. Thinking about her taking off my clothes. Thinking about her touching my penis. Thinking about touching her boobs. Her vagina . . .

. . . I'll be honest. The vagina scares me. No matter how many pictures or videos or diagrams I have looked at, it never stops being mysterious and intimidating . . .

. . . but being afraid of her vagina doesn't make me stop thinking about having sex. No, in fact, I think about it more and more.

I've had a lot of thoughts in my life, some thoughts I believed to be quite brilliant even, but I've never liked any thought nearly as much as I liked the thought of having sex with Penelope.

36

Penelope

Benedict just stood there outside my cabin for, I don't know, for a long time. My mom, who had been asleep on the couch, woke with her usual freak-out when I ran inside. ("Where were you!" That sort of crap.) But then she noticed Benedict, so she stared out the window at him even though I told her to stop. I mean, I was staring too, but I was staring from behind a corner so he couldn't see me.

"What's he doing?" she screeched. "He looks possessed!"

"I don't know," I said.

"Is he mad at you?"

"I don't know."

"What did you say, Penelope!"

"Nothing."

"What did you do to him, then?!"

"Nothing, Mom, nothing!" Which was a lie. I know, okay. I couldn't take my mom anymore, so I went into my room and locked the door. I still pulled back the curtains so I could keep watching him watch the cabin. He looked like an animal again, like he did at dinner last night, except this time I could almost read the thoughts going through his head. I knew he was thinking about having sex with me. I felt like a goddess. Like the goddess of sex. I had wielded my power, and this mortal man had chased me through snow and trees and now was left transfixed outside my door, waiting for me to reappear. This is so stupid to think, but I'm thinking it and I'm loving how powerful I feel and I'm turned on again except I don't want to masturbate. I mean, I do, but I'm not going to. I'm going to keep wielding my power.

Even after Benedict finally shuffled away back to his cabin, I knew I'd hold out because the more my want for him builds, the harder I'll work to make him want me.

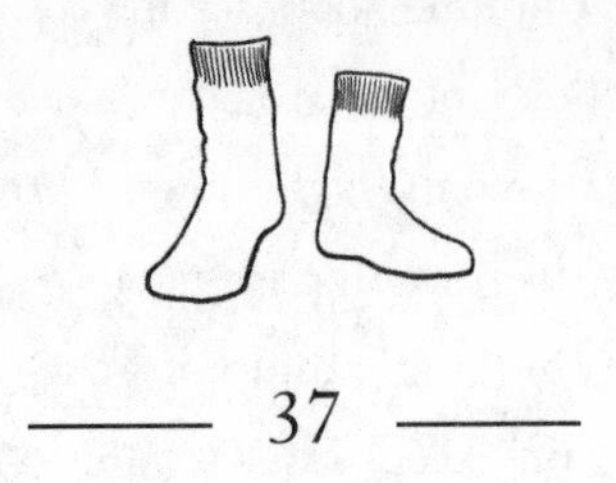

— 37 —

Benedict

THERE WAS NO INTERNET AT OUR CABIN. I HAVE never masturbated without pornography, but my penis told me if I didn't masturbate I probably would die. This is not true. I'm trying to say things that make me laugh at myself, but really I just am trying to not think about Penelope, which only makes me think about her more.

"I'm going to take a shower," I said the moment I walked inside. My mom and sister were sitting feet to feet on the couch, reading books in front of the fire.

"Aren't you going to tell us how your date went?" my mom asked.

"IT WASN'T A DATE, MOM!" I don't know why I yelled. My penis is making me very illogical. I turned back at the bathroom door, calmed myself as best I could, and said, "I'm sorry for yelling. I just am . . . very sweaty and . . . need to shower."

Once inside the bathroom, I stripped my clothes and grabbed Elizabeth's face lotion from the sink counter. It's not particularly ideal that

I had to use my younger sister's lotion, but mine was at home in my lower desk drawer and this was an emergency and emergencies require compromises.

Obviously people have masturbated for thousands of years without pornography, but now that it was so available on the internet, I just assumed no one ever masturbated without it anymore and never would again. But, as stated, this was an emergency.

Since I had been imagining having sex with Penelope in the warming hut, I started concentrating on that scenario as I, ummm . . . I'm not sure how much detail is appropriate here.

I suppose there's no point in pretending I'm not doing what I'm doing, so I'll just be frank. I was using my right hand to stroke my penis while my left hand pressed against the wall of the very small shower to steady myself because my legs didn't feel very sturdy and I had never masturbated standing up before. Much easier to be sitting at my desk. Maybe because of this, it was taking longer than I thought it would. (I was going to use all my sister's lotion.) Considering the long buildup and the sensation that my entire body was primed to combust, I just assumed this would be a rather quick operation.

Or, perhaps, I was enjoying it *too* much. That's possible. I really liked thinking about Penelope *and* touching my penis at the same time. My growing awareness of what normal people say makes me feel ridiculous for stating such a thing, but I can't help but acknowledge facts sometimes and this was very much a fact.

At first, I enjoyed trying to picture what Penelope's body might look like naked, trying to match her body size and type with girls I've seen in pornos. But then those girls' faces would enter my brain and this wasn't pleasurable at all. Not compared to envisioning Penelope's face. So that's what I did instead. I stopped trying to imagine her naked and just saw her face up close, like we were under the tree we crashed into.

Her dark brown eyes, with their lust, with their madness. Her skin, which was pale and tan at the same time. This might be a metaphor. There's, obviously, a maturity to Penelope, a sexual maturity. (Yes, I know she's had sex with Paul, but I don't want to think about that right now!) But there's an innocence too, isn't there? Those tears? They felt very innocent. I liked that Penelope had both innocence and experience. I think I have both too.

In my mind, my eyes kept looking at her scar. A week ago, I had never seen it up close. But this afternoon, I had seen it very close for a very long time and . . . I'm not sure. It didn't seem ugly at all anymore. In fact, it felt like the opposite of ugly. It felt exotic, like the defining brushstroke in a beautiful painting.

Obviously my thoughts make no sense. Obviously having this degree of erection for this length of time has made me the opposite of logical. But I couldn't stop. Couldn't stop thinking all these things about Penelope, imagining her eyes, and her skin, and her scar.

Until I orgasmed. In keeping with being honest, I orgasmed a lot. Despite all the disadvantages of doing it in the shower, cleanup was very easy.

By the time I finished the shower, the water was cold. My family would complain, they would ask why I took such a long time . . .

I moved quickly between the bathroom and my room, got dressed, and decided to avoid my parents and sister until dinner by rereading Forest Jackson's *If Only Girls Weren't Everything I Wanted I'd Have Nothing to Do with Them*, which was now my favorite novel ever. Theodore was so witty and eloquent around his love interest, Valerie! Me? I go mute around Penelope for long stretches and then jerk off for forty minutes in the shower. "Jerk off" is slang for masturbating.

Theodore would never use the term "jerk off"! He probably doesn't even masturbate!

You're losing your mind again, Evil Benny said. He didn't even laugh. In fact, Evil Benny seemed genuinely concerned.

My mom knocked on my door when it was time for dinner. When I walked into the living room of the cabin, my sister and mom were waiting by the door.

"Where's Dad?" I asked.

"Getting dressed," my mom said.

"He's mad about the hot water," my sister said. The way she said it, with that raised-eyebrow look of hers, I had this feeling she knew what I had been doing. If there is a worse feeling than knowing your younger sister knew you were masturbating in the shower, I'd prefer death over experiencing it.

My dad walked in a few seconds later. He didn't look at me, just marched toward the door. He said, "Benedict, please don't masturbate in the shower again at the resort. You can do that at home, if you must, but not here."

My sister and mother, usually my defenders, couldn't even look at me. My face was numb from the avalanche of shame. I used the term "avalanche" because I hoped a real one would fall on me that very second.

38

Penelope

When my mother saw what I was wearing to dinner, she wailed, "Penelope! Oh my, why are you wearing that! It's twenty degrees outside!"

I didn't say anything. Just stood there. I couldn't really argue with her. Yeah, it would be nice if she didn't act like I just chopped off a kitten's head, but I get it. What I was wearing wasn't appropriate at all: knee-high black leather boots with high heels, a black leather miniskirt that stopped uncomfortably close to my panty line, and a deep-necked white cashmere sweater. My boobs are kinda small, but I can make them look huge with the right bra and a tight-enough top. And tonight my bra was perfect and my sweater was as tight as tight gets.

"Really?" my mom said when she realized I wasn't going to say anything back. "Not my problem, then! Go ahead and freeze! Go ahead and have everyone in the dining room think you're a harlot! It's your life to ruin! Not mine! I'm too hungry to argue anymore!" (My mom had been using her "I'm too hungry" thing forever.)

Not to be weird, but sometimes when my mom looked at me and

screamed her crazy insults about how I dressed, I could see beyond it. Could see she might be jealous. When she was young, before marrying my dad, she was gorgeous. Just as thin as me, but taller, and far prettier. (She's northern Italian, so her skin is very fair. We don't even look related sometimes.) I don't know when but she started getting fat, then she stopped caring what she wore, and now she barely leaves the house. So it hurts to have her yelling those things at me, but it also makes me think a part of her likes that I dress the way I do. Like I said, I know it's weird. Never mind.

I had taken longer to get ready because, yes, I needed time to look good, but also because I wanted to make sure Benedict got to the lodge before us. Because I wanted him to see me enter.

So I let my mom walk ahead a bit as we entered the dining room, enough that when she turned toward our table, there was almost a straight, unobstructed line between me walking and Benedict sitting at his table.

And for that first reaction, it was worth it. I knew it the moment our eyes met. Those intense, deep eyes of his widened to twice their size, and I could see in them—even though we were thirty feet apart—his brain try to process what he was seeing and what I was doing. Saying his jaw dropped wasn't actually true; it's more like his whole body rose up. His shoulders, his jaw, his eyes, his forehead. In every sense he had risen and I knew, because I know these things, that things I couldn't see must have risen too.

His sister mouthed, *She's so sexy*, which made me feel almost as good as Benedict's response. His mother whispered, "I'm not sure that's appropriate," which made me feel more like a whore than my mother actually calling me one.

But then his dad, who I knew was sort of famous, said loud enough that I didn't even need to read his lips because I'm sure the whole dining room heard it: "Is that who you were thinking about in the shower, Benedict?"

Oh-my-god. This sort of made me proud (and yes! Turned on! Because I'm the freakiest freak to ever freaking live!) but—oh-my-god—who says that out loud about their kid? My mom says crazy stuff, but, I don't know, this felt worse for Benedict than any of her crap ever felt for me. Maybe, I don't know. Everything in Benedict drooped; he bowed his head in shame so far I thought it might hit his plate. His sister yelled at their dad. His mom gave that disapproving-wife look. But I had to turn away. I couldn't look at him anymore. I was mortified, like unable-to-walk-straight mortified, and I stumbled into another table before making my mom switch seats again so I didn't have to look toward any of them.

"What's wrong with you?" my mom asked after she sat back down.

"I don't know."

"So you *are* admitting there's something wrong with you?"

"Mom, please, stop." I said it quiet, but so pathetic that even my mom listened.

After we both ate pieces of bread in silence, her like a normal person and me like I should be in a straitjacket, my mom asked, "What about Paul?" She almost seemed concerned for me. Which my mother never seems.

"I don't know."

"I thought you said this boy was unpopular?"

"He is. . . . I don't like him. . . ."

"Penelope, I know you think I'm an idiot, but please. No girl dresses like *that* in *this* weather unless they really like a boy."

"Paul broke up with me, I'm, I don't know . . ."

"Exactly, Paul broke up with you . . ." she started. Please, no. I couldn't take any judgment of hers right now. My breath shortened, and I could feel another panic attack coming. Brace yourself, Pen, she's about to say something horrible: ". . . so you like whoever you like. You're a free agent. I'm sure this outfit will have this kid eating out of your hand for the rest of his natural life."

Wait.

Huh?

Did my mother just say something nice? Honestly, I needed to resay it in my head until I was sure. Yes, oh-my-god, she did. My body relaxed; my breath evened out. "Thanks, Mom."

My mother patted my hand, smiled, sort of, at me, but I could tell that was all the tenderness and understanding she had for right now. Which was enough. It was a lot for her.

So I said, picking up the menu, "What are you having?"

She got giddy because she loves talking about the food at Wild Wolf. "I'm getting the prime rib. And the mashed potatoes. And the strawberry shortcake. And maybe the soup . . ."

When Benedict didn't stop by our table on his way out of the dining room, like he had at breakfast and lunch, I assumed he was too embarrassed by what his dad said to hang out in the Bear Room tonight. Or worse, his mom wasn't going to allow him to hang out with the "slut in the short skirt" ever again. I don't know. It doesn't matter. My plan to drive Benedict so wild with desire had totally backfired. Which was fine. I don't even care. This whole thing was so stupid.

While my mom ate her dessert, I texted Paul:

ME

Miss you

Which wasn't even true. I didn't miss him at all anymore. But I felt like such a moron for dressing the way I did and then for Benedict to just leave . . . I, uh . . . I don't even know who I am anymore or what I want or anything about anything. . . .

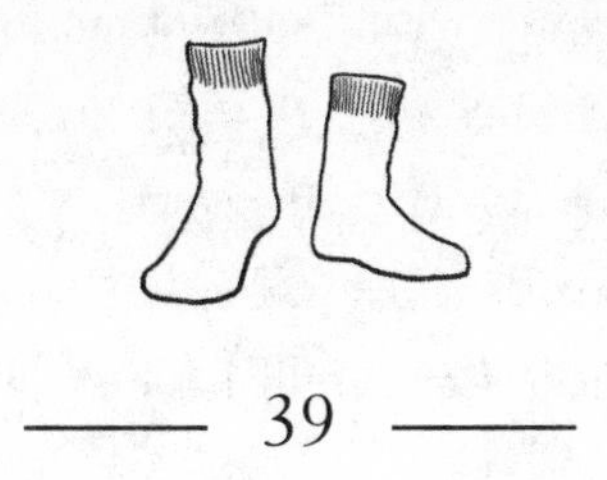

39

Benedict

FROM THE MOMENT WE SAT DOWN AT DINNER, I kept one eye on the dining-hall entrance waiting for Penelope to enter. I told myself not to look; I tried to listen to what my sister and parents were discussing. My father disciplining me over my time in the shower had left me feeling as if I had ruined my life. That every second that I spent thinking about Penelope was a second in which I was becoming a lesser person, a person my father would never respect. Thus I worked very hard to diminish our afternoon cross-country skiing. Yes, she said some kind things and she had looked at me with eyes that made my entire body excited. But nothing that happened would make me smarter, or a better student, or get me into a better college or get a better job, or I'm not sure what else.

So, yes, even while watching for her to enter, I believe I convinced myself that I shouldn't waste any more time with Penelope, either in reality or in my fantasies. And then she walked in.

I will try to replay the initial experience of seeing her. It's very difficult. My mind is at war with itself and not just in the usual Good Benedict versus Evil Benny way.

Because now there was Penis Benedict.

Calling him Penis Benedict makes him sound like he's dumb or ridiculous. Perhaps he is. I truthfully have no idea. That's why all this is so confusing!

Again, let me replay what I saw. From all three of me.

Penis Benedict reacted first. He saw her tan thighs. Seeing tan thighs in the middle of winter, he said, was like seeing a drinking fountain in the middle of the desert. (I'm not sure why he's speaking in metaphor since I frown upon it.) Then Penis Benedict noticed the swivel in her walk. It was very hypnotizing. In fact, if Penis Benedict was in charge, he said he would do everything Penelope asked him to do for the rest of his life. Last he noticed her eyes. They weren't the lustful eyes like from the woods, but rather they were eyes that told Penis Benedict, "I know you like what you see and now you know I know you like what you see."

Penis Benedict was the only one talking until my mom and dad said what they said.

After my mom said Penelope's outfit was "not appropriate," Good Benedict spoke up next. He said that looking at Penelope like that would only get me in more trouble. He said a girl who spent time making herself so attractive to boys probably did so because she didn't think she had anything else to offer them. Good Benedict suddenly felt very confident in my choice to not speak or think about Penelope anymore.

And then my dad, very loudly, asked if this was the girl I was thinking about in the shower.

That's when Evil Benny joined the battle. He said that Penelope was just bored and teasing me and had no real interest in me. But in the very next breath, he said if she *was* actually interested it was because she's desperate and an idiot and a slut. Then Evil Benny said my dad would never look at me like I was his son again if I dated a girl like Penelope.

My mom and sister tried to make my dad apologize for saying what he said, which I knew he never would. He never apologizes about anything. He shouldn't have to. He's always right.

As dinner went on, my sister and mother attempted to lift my spirits by asking me questions about school. (They knew better than to ask about my day with Penelope.) But the war waging in my head between the three mes left my vocal abilities paralyzed. I could only really nod and grunt.

"Benedict," my father said, halfway through the meal in which I had acted like a lobotomized monkey, "stop your pouting. I spoke frankly, which you should relish. Most parents lie to their children, telling them they are smart when they are not. Telling them they are talented when they are not. This makes it impossible for children to honestly self-assess. Would you prefer I lie to you so you can have a deluded sense of yourself?"

I found the words. "No, Father . . ."

"Of course you don't, because you're my son."

"Yes, Father."

"As for that girl, she is very obviously troubled . . ."

"Samuel, stop right now," my mom said.

". . . and I would be very disappointed in you if you wasted any more time in her company."

"Samuel, another word and I will leave." Mom used this threat very rarely but it often was the only way to derail my father once he had gained momentum in whatever point he was trying to make. He didn't say anything more about Penelope. It didn't matter. He had said enough to convince me: I could never talk to or spend time with Penelope again.

Once back at the cabin, my family wanted to play the card game Kings in the Corner, but I said I was tired and retreated to my room.

I was too defeated to even change from my clothes. I just lay on my bed and imagined what the night would have been like if my dad had never said any of the things he said.

Perhaps I would have asked Penelope to play Ping-Pong again in the Bear Room, as we did last night.

Though this time perhaps my sister would go back to the cabin before us and it would be just Penelope and me.

Perhaps then we would have gone up to the loft area to watch television.

Perhaps she would have sat close to me.

Perhaps she would have looked at me again in a way that allowed me to believe she liked me in the way that girls like boys.

And perhaps then I would have kissed her.

Even though I had spent a great deal of time fantasizing about having sex with Penelope this afternoon, I didn't think about sex at all. Only about kissing her. It would have been nice to get my first kiss before I turned seventeen tomorrow. Despite everything said by my dad, by my mom, by "Good" Benedict, and by Evil Benny, it would have been nice if my first kiss was with Penelope.

If I wasn't Benedict Pendleton, son of genius Samuel Pendleton, I think I would sneak out my window and go find Penelope. If I were the type of boy who disobeyed his parents' wishes, I would go find the girl they had forbidden me from seeing and I would kiss her.

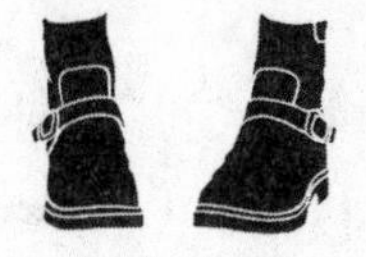

— 40 —

Penelope

My mother wanted to play double solitaire at the cabin after dinner, but I just wanted to change out of my stupid slutty clothes and go to bed and wish I was a different person.

"You better not be this moody for the rest of vacation or it's going to ruin my vacation too!" she said as I disappeared into my room. I guess sympathetic, supportive mom was gone. It was nice while it lasted.

I put on sweatpants and a sweatshirt, got under the covers, prayed unsuccessfully to the internet gods that I could get service, and then read Millie Dragon on my phone. You know, Millie and her creator, Zelda Zowie, are my heroes, but I hated both of them tonight. Yeah, great, Millie is brave enough to tell everyone that there are demons hunting them that no one but her can see. But you know what we never wonder? If Millie is doing the right thing. We *know* she is. Yes, a lot of bad things happen to her in both dimensions for doing the right thing. But

I guess it would be nice to know that Millie could screw up. That even heroes can make really shitty choices.

Anyway, I had to stop reading. I wasn't tired. Like, I was the least tired I've ever been in my life. Usually when I'm awake like this in bed, I feel like masturbating. In the past I've done it for hours. But it was the last thing I felt like doing. I felt so unsexual I might not masturbate ever again.

So my life is basically pointless. I have nothing I want to do, no one to talk to or do anything with. I don't even want to do anything with myself.

It's Benedict's fault, right? I mean, if he wasn't so weird and . . . oh, I can't even lie to myself right now. God, I fucking like him. I fucking hate him for making me like him. I like everything about him. Is that even true? There are so many things about him that should make me *not* like him but right now all those things—like him being the biggest social outcast at school—only make me like him more.

But I treated him like any other guy. Gave him my "fuck me" eyes, dressed in my "fuck me" skirt, and, yeah, it worked because it would work on all men but I don't want Benedict to like me for that! Okay, maybe a little for that because I'm a freak, but not *just* for that. I want him to like me for the same reason I like him. For all the crazy shit in my head. No, I want for him to tell me it's not crazy. If I had one more chance, that's what I would do. Just tell him everything.

But that's never going to happen. Because I screwed it up.

Oh-my-god, this sucks, this sucks that I'm stuck up at this lake with him, but now his family thinks I'm a whore and he probably will ignore me the rest of the week. I'll just hide out in this room. I'll tell my mom I'm sick. She'll get me food. She'll bitch about it, but she'll do it. Or she'll just say we could go home. God, that would be great. So much better than being stuck in this room, wishing I could be with the guy I'm also hiding from. . . .

There was a noise outside my window.

Raccoon? Bird? Probably. Who knows. Don't worry about it, Pen.

But then there was more noise. Like someone climbing through the snow. Breathing heavily. Oh-my-god, it's a murderer. There are all those stories I'd hear as a kid. Stories about Dwayne the Wild Wolf Killer. He'd snatch fishermen off their boats, he'd capture hikers in the woods, he'd take children from their cabins. As a kid, I always slept with my mom because I was so terrified of Dwayne the Killer. And now he was coming for me.

"Pen," he whispered. Pen? Oh-my-god. I leaped up, went to the window, pulled open the curtains in a quick flash, and . . .

There he was.

Benedict.

Standing up to his waist in snow, his hand held up in a wave, the dorkiest smile in the history of dorky smiles. But man . . . man, oh man . . . this was the most romantic thing anyone has ever done ever. I hate romantic stuff, and if I thought Benedict thought he was doing something romantic I'd probably hate it, but he had no clue; he just climbed through waist-high snow because for some reason he thought it was worth it. Worth it to see me.

What are you doing here? I mouthed super quietly because I didn't want my mom hearing us. I knew why he was here, at least the big reason, but I couldn't tell him I knew. I had to pretend I didn't. I had to make him say it.

"My father has banned me from seeing you . . ." he started. "I always do everything my father says because millions of people do what he says and I'm his son, so if millions of strangers listen to him, then I should. So my being here might be proof that I'm no longer making intelligent decisions—"

He'd go on and on if I let him, so I said, "Benedict . . . meet me in the lodge in five minutes, okay?"

"But . . . yes, okay . . . Yes." But he didn't move. So I closed the curtains on him. I had this fear he might change his mind and go back to his cabin. No, he won't. No more stressing about stupid fears, Pen. Just go.

I changed. I wore jeans this time instead of the skirt, but I put the tight white sweater back on. Meeting Benedict at the lodge wasn't about seducing him, wasn't about driving him wild with lust. It was about talking to him. Being real. Being my true self. But all that didn't mean my boobs couldn't look good.

Mom screeched as I rushed through the living room, "Where are youuuuuuu going?!" but I just ignored her, left the cabin, and ran to the lodge. Yes, ran. I never run *anywhere for any reason*. I even get out of gym with a semi-legit asthma excuse. But I was so nervous, and so excited, which made me more nervous which made me more excited. Wow, I was losing it. Didn't care.

Benedict was sitting on the same couch I was sitting on yesterday. He stood as I entered.

"Pen, I'm . . ." he started as I moved toward him. I didn't see socially awkward Benedict. I didn't see handsome stranger Benedict either. But this third Benedict, this combination of both. Maybe I saw all of him for the first time.

"Benedict . . ." I had all these things I wanted to say, about him, about me, about our situation. I wanted to ask him about what his dad said, tell him about my crazy mom. Tell him I loved him just how he was and I wanted him to love me just how I really was. And more, so many things . . . I HAD BEEN KEEPING ALL THIS CRAP INSIDE ME FOR SO LONG AND NOW HERE WAS THE ONE PERSON I FELT I COULD TELL IT TO, NOT JUST COULD *BUT HAD TO* and so—

I just fucking kissed him. Ignored my whole plan. Put my right hand around his neck, and because he's six inches taller than me, I had to pull him down, and I just kissed him. And his lips were dry and rigid and I'm like, crap, I screwed up, I should have talked, he didn't want me to kiss him. . . .

But then he opened his mouth a little, which made his lips wet, and I wet them more with mine, and then his right hand scooped across my lower back and lifted me up—like in the air!—and my legs looped around him. And we just kissed, no tongue at first, just rapid mini-kisses, lips against lips, and, yeah, I could tell Benedict had maybe never kissed anyone in his life, but the passion in him was just erupting from inside and the combination of his passion and inexperience made each kiss feel special. Made it feel like each time our lips touched something unique was being said between us. I know that sounds like cheesy romantic bullshit! But it is what it was and it was so stupidly perfect that I cried. Again. Twice in one day! Who the hell am I?

I guess the real me, the one I've been hiding all these years from everyone, is an emotional wreck. A romantic emotional wreck.

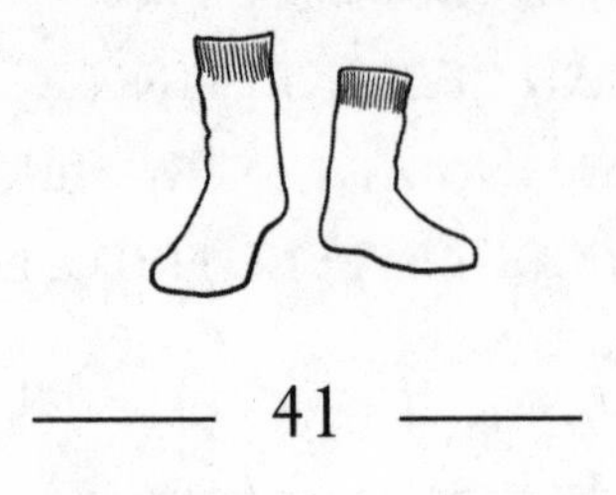

— 41 —

Benedict

SHE KISSED ME.

She kissed me.

A girl kissed me.

I always assumed my first time would be when I'd kiss the girl and then she would kiss me back. That I'd be the heroic gentleman who took a girl who admired me greatly and, with a strong sweep of my hands, pull her into my arms and kiss her. Like it happens in superhero movies.

But she kissed me first.

Penelope kissed me first and I kissed her back.

And, frankly, this is far better than any of my superhero scenarios. There's something about how Penelope kissed me, not just her confidence in making the move before me, not just her sensuality, but that she *chose* me. Chose me despite all my problems. Or maybe because of them. Or it doesn't matter why, what matters is that her kissing me first made me feel like I'm worth kissing first.

And, obviously, kissing Penelope is more than emotionally uplifting. It is also extraordinarily physically pleasurable. And not just because my penis is erect. In fact, right now, that's more distracting than pleasurable.

Kissing is not biologically necessary for procreation, so I always wondered if I would enjoy it the way other people do. I like logic, I like efficiency, and kissing didn't seem very logical or efficient.

Then why am I enjoying it so? Beyond the expected physical enjoyment of her wet lips against mine, her smell not just in my nose but in my entire body, and her legs wrapped around my waist?

I don't know. I don't like not knowing. But I like kissing Penelope more than I dislike not knowing. In fact, I'd be fine not knowing anything ever again as long as I could keep kissing Penelope.

Except there are tears in her eyes. My kissing must be so terrible that it's making her cry.

"Are you crying because I'm doing it wrong?" I asked.

She laughed a tiny laugh. For a moment, I felt even worse than I felt when I thought she was crying at my terrible kissing. "No, Benedict . . ." She stopped. Which I expected. Penelope really hated talking. But then she talked more anyway. "I love how you kiss. I'm crying, I don't know, I think because I'm just feeling a lot. You make me feel a lot."

"Is that good?"

"It's great. It's great, great, great."

"Good. Because I like kissing you. And I thought you were crying because you didn't like kissing me. You're the first girl I've ever kissed."

"I figured," she said.

"You figured because of how awkward I am?"

"I figured because you kissed me like you meant it. Like I was special."

"Okay, good." My arms were getting tired from holding her. But I didn't want to say that. . . .

"Your arms must be getting tired," Penelope said. Maybe kissing someone lets them read your mind. This is ridiculous. Obviously. "You can put me down and then we can sit on the couch, okay?"

"I like you close," I said, and then, instead of letting her down, I took a step back and sat on the couch with her legs still straddling me. More tears formed in her eyes, but I was starting to understand this was a good thing. But I didn't know how to say "What did I do to make you cry happy tears?" so I just stared at her in silence, our faces very, very close.

"I don't talk much," she said.

"I know. It's okay."

For another second, she was silent, but then Penelope took in a big breath and said, "But I want to talk. I've always wanted to say what's on my mind, but I just never do because, I don't know, maybe because I was afraid people wouldn't like what's on my mind. And I wanted to be liked more than I wanted to be me."

"I want to hear everything you have to say about everything," I said. Was this true? I'm not sure. I couldn't guarantee this was true because I hadn't heard everything she had to say. So I said, "Let me amend that. There may be some things I don't want to hear you say, but I am willing to risk hearing you say something I don't want to hear because I like hearing things I want you to say so much."

I'm not sure if what I said made any sense but Penelope kissed me again, so I didn't care if it didn't make sense. This kiss was a single long kiss. I didn't move because I didn't want it to end. When she pulled back, she said, "Do you realize how what you just said no other person could say?"

"No . . ."

"I love your brain, Benedict. I love how it works."

Strange. What's happening. My eyes. Ummm. This makes no sense. "Are you the one now crying?" Penelope asked.

"I don't see how that's possible, but yes, I think so. I'm not sad. . . ."

"I like that you're crying," she said, with this smile that made me like her even more.

"You do?"

"I do."

"It's just I want to understand why I'm crying. I'm usually very good at explaining myself. . . ."

"Take your time," she said, and kissed one of my tears away. Even though I started to have an idea of what I would say, I waited until she kissed away my other tears to speak.

I said, "I've always wanted girls to say nice things to me, but I always imagined them saying it in the way I would say it. Or the way I had seen it said in books or in movies. But you said, 'I love your brain.' I've never heard that before. So I think I'm crying because you said something I wanted to hear even though I never even knew I wanted to hear it."

Now Penelope's eyes were tearing up again.

"You're crying again . . ." I said.

"I am."

"I just explained why I was and now I would enjoy hearing why you are this time."

She said, "You . . . just said I had said something unique."

"Yes," I said. "One-of-a-kind unique."

"And, and . . ." Penelope was almost sobbing now. Smiling and sobbing at the same time. It was very strange. But also beautiful. She continued, "That's what *I've* always wanted to hear, and I have imagined hearing it, a million times, but I never imagined you, Benedict, would be the one that said it."

42

Penelope

Benedict and I sat there on the couch in the Bear Room for at least another hour, telling each other things, then kissing, then just staring at each other, then kissing, then talking, then staring. I think I said more to Benedict in that hour than I had to Paul in three years. That can't be true, but it can't not be true either.

Since I spent most of the time straddled on his lap, I could feel his hard-on. I'm a sexual freak, so of course I was aware of it. But I didn't say anything. We talked about our families, about school, and about Paul, and religion a bit, and a bunch of other stuff I never talk to anyone about. But I didn't want to talk about sex. Benedict's dad had basically banned him from seeing me because I wore a short skirt to dinner. What if telling Benedict about my weird sex obsession made him rethink not listening to his dad? Benedict had never kissed a girl before me. He was so innocent. He wasn't ready to handle my crap. So that's the one thing I kept inside my head. The one real part of me Benedict didn't now know. And maybe it'd be better if he never knew.

At midnight, the office lady came in and said the lodge was closing. After we stood and started walking outside, we felt like strangers again. We didn't know how to talk unless our faces were inches apart.

And then Benedict said, "Thank you for giving me my first kiss, Pen. It was the best first kiss in history."

"You're welcome."

"I'm very inexperienced. I'm not sure what I should be doing now. Does a boy usually hold a girl's hand when they walk outside after kissing?"

"Sure," I said, which felt lame. I loved how he put it all out there. So I said, "I mean, yes, Benedict. A girl likes when you hold her hand after kissing. I would like that a lot actually."

He reached over and took my hand. Our fingers entwined. I slowed down our pace because my cabin was close and I didn't want to say good-bye yet. It was freezing but I didn't care.

He said, "I'm not sure how my father's going to react when I tell him I kissed you. He may decide I'm no longer worthy of being his son."

"He's not going to say that."

"My father is very logical and I'm—"

I interrupted him, "Then don't tell him, Benedict. I don't tell my parents anything because they flip out over the stupidest things."

"But I want to see you tomorrow," he said.

"Can you sneak out again after they go to bed tomorrow night?"

"I don't want to wait until tomorrow night. I want to see you the moment I wake up."

I couldn't not pull him down and kiss him after he said that. I just had to.

"Does that mean you want to see me too?"

"Yes," I said. "We'll figure something out. You have your phone?" He nodded, took it out of his coat pocket. I put my number into it. "Bring it to breakfast. Only the lodge has Wi-Fi, so we can text then and find a way to see each other."

"You're very smart, Penelope," he said, but not like he was trying to say something nice. More like he was discovering it for the first time.

"Thanks," I said.

"It's past midnight."

"Like twenty minutes past. We've walked a yard a minute since we left the lodge."

"That means I'm seventeen now."

"It's your birthday?! Why didn't you tell me?" I was acting all girly. I felt stupid. Whatever.

"It didn't seem relevant."

"Well, happy birthday," I said, and then, because I'm still a sex freak even if I'm not going to tell him that, I pulled him down toward my lips again. Except this time I opened my mouth, this time I used some tongue, this time I wanted to drive him just a bit mad with lust. When I stopped, Benedict looked at me with these eyes, these hungry eyes.

Oh, wow . . . trouble, trouble, trouble . . . I pulled him down one last time, kissed him quick but deep, and then ran inside the cabin.

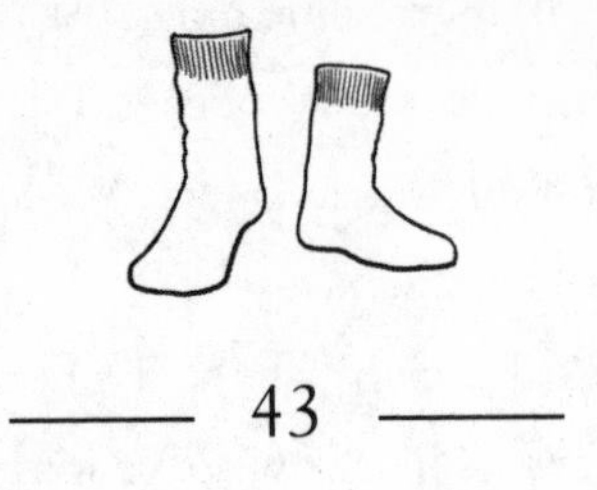

43

Benedict

I WOKE UP EARLY, LEFT A NOTE FOR MY parents that I needed to drive into town to buy deodorant. This was a lie. In fact, I took my old deodorant, which was barely used, and threw it out at the drugstore. The real reason I needed to go was to buy condoms. I had never bought condoms before. I tried to pretend I had done it many times, so I bought a newspaper along with the new deodorant and the condoms. I had not read a newspaper since I got my own iPhone at twelve years old, but I convinced myself a person who bought a newspaper and condoms together would look like a person who bought condoms all the time. This makes no sense. I'm clearly not being logical. But I have logically determined that doing illogical things in order to spend time with Penelope was worth it.

I didn't really expect to have sex with her. Of course, I lay in bed last night thinking about it. For hours. But I'll never ask Penelope to have sex. I'll only do it if she asks. It seems like the boy should take the lead, but I liked how Penelope took the lead with our first kiss. I'm not sure what this means. But I am sure that I would feel like a pervert if

I asked to have sex with her and she said she didn't want to. But if she asked first, I wouldn't feel like a pervert at all. Again, I know none of this makes sense. And again, I don't think I can care.

At breakfast, after they brought out pancakes with candles in them and sang me "Happy Birthday" (my sister and mother sang; my dad watched them sing), I took out my phone as Penelope had instructed. My dad always read a book at breakfast, so I knew he wouldn't pay too much attention to my texting. Penelope hadn't arrived at the lodge yet, but there were several texts from Robert. He wished me a happy birthday in the first. It was nice to get a birthday wish from the person you want to be your best friend again. But seeing his name also made me feel as if everything I was enjoying with Penelope was a betrayal of him. His next text said *Did Allison text you? She asked for your number.* She hadn't, which was good. Allison was no longer my dream girl. Maybe she was but I'm not sure I know what that means anymore.

Penelope was my real girl and when I saw her enter the dining room, my heart raced as if it wanted to race out of my chest and cross the room and leap into her hands. This is ridiculous. So I texted:

ME

Penelope, this is Benedict

She didn't look toward me. I worried she had changed her mind about me. What if she remembered that I was socially awkward? What if, while I stayed up thinking about having sex with her, she stayed up thinking she made the biggest mistake of her life kissing me?

But then I got this:

PENELOPE

Benedict, this is Penelope . . .

happy birthday ;)

She had sat in the chair facing away from me and my family. This made it look like she didn't want anything to do with me, but really it was just her being very good at keeping our secret romance secret.

I tried to do the same. Turned to face the cereal bar, which was the opposite direction of Penelope. Maybe Penelope and I would grow up and be professional spies. Who are married. And have lots of sex. This is ridiculous. I texted:

ME

What do boys text girls that they like?

PENELOPE

They text them they like them.

ME

I like you.

PENELOPE

They also text them they thought about them all night.

Penelope was being very forward. I liked it. My penis liked it too.

ME

I thought about you all night.

PENELOPE

I thought about you too.

Even though I had thought about her a lot, I had not come up with any viable plan to see her without my parents finding out. Luckily, Penelope is much better at espionage than me:

PENELOPE

So here's my plan: remember the warming hut we saw yesterday?

This was the easiest question I have ever answered and I'm smart so I find a lot of questions easy to answer:

ME

YES

PENELOPE

I'll go skiing first at 10 so it doesn't look like we are going together. But then you leave fifteen minutes later and meet me there. Okay?

This plan was genius. I'm not exaggerating. I don't know how the greatest strategists in history could think of a better plan. Maybe Penelope isn't just not dumb; maybe she's so smart that she gets bad grades because school isn't smart enough to measure her intelligence. This is ridiculous. This is probably Penis Benedict thinking. This was definitely Penis Benedict texting:

OKAY

My mom asked if she could take me shopping to buy a birthday present for me, but I said no, that I wanted to be by myself. She thought I was still upset about everything that happened last night, which I suppose I was in a small way but mostly I didn't want to do anything but spend time with Penelope. But I couldn't tell her that since she was married to the man who would rather see me dead than with Penelope. This isn't true. I'm being dramatic. I'm never dramatic. Well, I'm never aware I'm being dramatic. I'm not sure what's happening to me.

At 10:10, I told my mom I was going for a walk. She asked if she could go with me. I told her no.

Elizabeth said, "Stop being mean to Mom. She didn't do anything." My sister then pointed at Dad sitting at the table by the cabin window. But he was typing at his computer and when he's writing he might as well be in China.

"I didn't say she did," I said. Then I left.

I got my skis from the boathouse, ran up the stairs to the trail, and then skied. Honestly, I probably skied faster than anyone has ever skied before. This is not true, obviously, but my penis has been hard since breakfast and I'm unable to think anything but crazy things.

It would probably be best if I stopped obsessing about my penis. It can't be healthy. I doubt other normal teenage boys think this much about their penises. But how can I not think about it when it hurts AND feels good at the same time? I really, really hope my sexual thoughts stop by the time I get to the warming hut. As experienced as Penelope is, she's not some sexual freak who thinks about it as much as I'm thinking about it. If I only talk about my penis, she'll think I'm very dumb and boring.

Evil Benny said, "You are dumb and boring!"

And then he said a bunch of other stuff, but he was distracting me from Penis Benedict, so I sort of listened to Evil Benny in the hopes that when I arrived at the warming hut and saw Penelope, I didn't just grab her and kiss her. I would try to act like a gentleman. Ask her about how she's feeling, and other things like this that normal people ask about.

By the time I was taking off my skis outside the hut, I was sure my plan had worked. I could almost feel my penis retreating. It would be easy to be calm and collected now.

But when I opened the door to the warming hut, Penelope stood up from the bench. She had already taken off her coat and snow pants. It's not as if she was naked. She still had jeans and a long-sleeve T-shirt on. But she *felt* naked. And then she looked at me with those eyes again. Those biologically primal eyes.

I had absolutely no control over my body. That's not true. But I wanted it to be true. So I took two giant steps across the length of the hut, picked her up, and kissed her and used my tongue and squeezed her into me and I was so dizzy—because all my blood was in my penis, obviously—that I fell back to the floor of the hut, and Penelope fell back on top of me.

44

Penelope

When I was texting Benedict my plan to meet him at the warming hut, other texts showed up on my phone. Texts from Paul. He was responding to my *I miss you* text from last night, which I forgot I sent and never meant.

PAUL

Babe! I miss you! God I miss you!

I'm so stupid! I didn't do anything!

I shouldn't have broken up with you!

But I didn't do anything!

Stacy's a fucking liar, so don't believe a word she says.

Babe! Call me!

I love you!

God I love you!

And . . . nothing. His words made me feel nothing. I was done with him. Done. Over him and that life. Over that me. I deleted his texts. I'd never text him again. Never. Never. Never. Never. I could not think of one reason I'd ever need to say a word to him ever again. I wanted this to be true. I just don't know if Paul would let it be true.

Benedict.

I want to think about Benedict, not Paul.

I get to go meet Benedict.

Which in theory is awesome.

But then I realized I had volunteered to go into the woods *alone* on *skis*. I mean, who the hell am I? What exactly was I willing to do to spend time with him?

Anything.

Fucking anything.

I'm insane.

I don't care.

And you know, after I got over the terror that the Abominable Snowman was going to rise up at any moment, the skiing wasn't bad. I've always enjoyed looking at nature, but now I was *in* it. Gliding through endless trees, the snow, the silence, the cold. Instead of having a panic attack about being out here by myself, everything inside me began to calm, to get as quiet as the forest.

And then I saw the warming hut and, well, I'm still me and I, well, I got turned on just at the sight. Took off my skis, knocked on the door just because, I don't know, and then pushed it open.

There was a bench to the left and a window to the right. The entire hut was the size of my bathroom at home. Big enough for . . .

For what? What did I think was going to happen here? You can't have sex with him! I mean, you can't. I'm not going to. He would think I'm such a slut if I even talked about it. So no way.

I did take off my jacket and those stupid puffy snow pants. It was warm enough in here. Not really but it's okay to be a little cold for the sake of not looking horrible.

What if he didn't show up? What if his parents found out? What . . . Crap, I'm going nuts and I've been here two minutes. Calm, Pen. Calm. I'm sure he'll show up. We'll kiss, we'll talk for a bit. Definitely no sex. We'll both get bored I'm sure and then we'll go and you'll see him again after dinner.

So . . .

Yeah . . .

I waited . . .

And . . .

I heard him. Heard him approaching. Should I open the door? Wave? No. No. Just sit here. Act relaxed. Pretend you're not thinking about what his penis looks like. Pretend you're not some sex-starved chick waiting in a tiny hut in the middle of the woods hoping he steps in here and rips off your clothes. Oh-my-god, you have to ask him some dumb question about nature or something as soon as he walks in here or your mind will . . .

He walks in. Oh. Wow. Those eyes . . . into me, he, my, how do I say this . . . his eyes, Benedict the dork's eyes . . . they are . . . he has . . . they're "fuck me" eyes. Like mine. For me.

He steps in, picks me up, and kisses me.

Tongue, hands, my legs around him again, my mouth, my lips, they want to be inside his lips and mouth, and his eyes are open and mine are and we fall, stumble, and we're on the ground. . . .

I'm on top of him, kissing him; he's leaning up, into me. Everything tingles. Inside, yes, of course, but outside too, my skin, my head, my eyes . . . but I can barely feel *him* because of those ski pants of his, which I would take off, but I can't, he would know I'm a crazy sex freak— but maybe he is too! That stare, this kissing, maybe he is . . . but I can't risk putting myself out there . . . I want him too much, not just his body, I want *every* molecule of his soul. . . .

"Benedict . . ." I say in a breath when our mouths are free. No idea what else I'm going to say, but we can't just kiss forever. We could. Maybe we should. Just kiss forever. But he doesn't kiss me again, maybe I ruined it, but someone should talk . . . or not . . . Yes! But not me . . .

"I'm sorry I wasn't a gentleman. I wanted to be a gentleman. . . ."

"What do you mean?" I ask, even though I know, sort of . . .

". . . I just saw you and I had to kiss you. Obviously, I didn't have to. But yes, ummm . . . I want to be eloquent and witty right now like characters in books but I'm just very, very, very . . ."

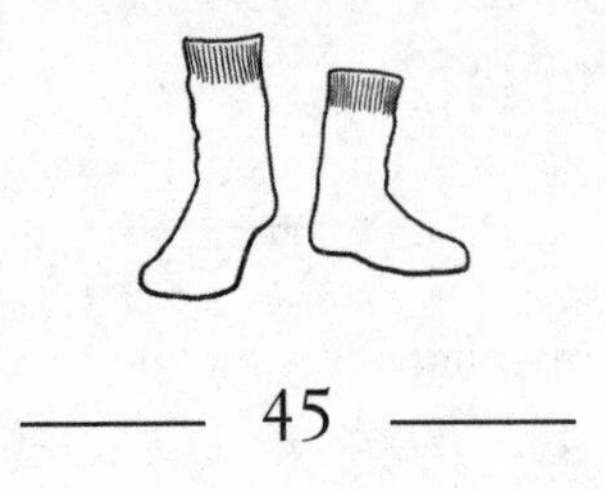

45

Benedict

"...VERY..." I'M NOT SURE WHICH WORD I should use. I don't want to be false. But I don't want to be crude either. So I said, ". . . very . . . excited by you."

But Penelope said, "What do you mean?"

This was very frustrating! I'm the one that has no idea what I'm doing! But, no, Benedict, you can't blame her. She told you to be you; she told you she loved your brain. But I cannot just tell her my penis is excited by her. "You make my thoughts excited . . . and my life. I'm very, very excited by my life right now because of you. I thought I was always excited about my life but now I see my old life as very safe and predictable. You are the opposite of safe and predictable. Which is very, very exciting. I wish I could think of another word for 'exciting.'"

"What do you mean?"

"Uh . . ."

She laughed. Then said, "I was just going to keep saying 'What do you mean?' so I could listen to you talk. I love watching your lips as they form words, your eyes as your brain thinks of those words. That must sound so weird. I'm sorry. . . ."

"Pen, you always apologize. You told me yesterday that I shouldn't change. Which was the most important thing I think anyone has ever said to me. I like to say grand things, but I think that's really true. And I want you to know I feel the same about you. The exact same. I love how you express yourself. Telling another boy that you like watching his brain think of words might be weird, but to socially awkward Benedict Pendleton, it is the best compliment ever."

She loved what I said. I could tell because her eyes were glistening. I kissed her tears because I really liked when she did that to me yesterday. Then she said, "What do you mean?" Which was very funny. I laughed. I never laugh at other people's jokes. I never get the jokes or I never feel comfortable. But I got Penelope's. I feel so comfortable with her. What does this mean? Oh, ummm, this . . . I feel . . . ummm . . . something is happening to me . . . my body, it is opening up and closing down at the same time . . . this . . . is . . .

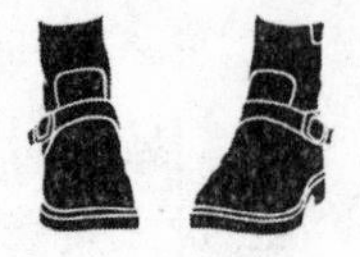

46

Penelope

After he laughed at my joke, Benedict got this look, and then he started stumbling through words under his breath, and I just knew. Just knew what he was feeling. I shouldn't know, but I do and it sounds stupid or like I'm full of myself, but I know. I know, I know, I know. . . .

I knew he, at that second, had fallen . . . I just have to say it. He fell in love with me. I knew it. Just *knew* it. Even though people say it and think they feel it and who the hell knows what love really is, but WHATEVER it is, Benedict was feeling it and I had been feeling it ever since yesterday. He's like this genius, this one-of-a-kind warrior of truth, but he's also just this kid, this kid who right now is so terrified he can't talk . . . and I'm barely talking and . . .

"Benedict . . ."

"Yes?" he said with these eyes as big as the earth.

"I love you too."

And for a moment, he stayed silent. He nodded, just kept nodding, like some voice in his head was talking.

"Pen . . ."

"Call me Penelope."

"But . . ."

"Only you get to call me it. Only you make me like it."

He smiled. "Penelope . . ."

"Benedict . . ."

"Love . . ."

"Love."

"It feels differently than I thought it would," he said.

"What did you think it would feel like?"

"I thought it would be very logical. That two people decided it would be mutually beneficial to have mutual feelings." I laughed, he laughed, and went on. "But instead it feels like I could stay in this warming hut with you for ten thousand years and never want to leave. Which is not very logical."

"I love that you're not logical with me," I said. Which was cheesy, but also kinda original so that made it less cheesy. He kissed me again, a little kiss, but it restarted that hunger of his, almost at once, and his hunger restarted mine, and his kissing is so good, it's so good it should be enough, but it being so good almost makes it impossible for me not to want more . . . but he's still innocent, this boy, this amazing boy, but this boy who I just witnessed the *very* second he fell in love with me . . . so we should just kiss, just kiss, just kiss and kiss and kiss and . . .

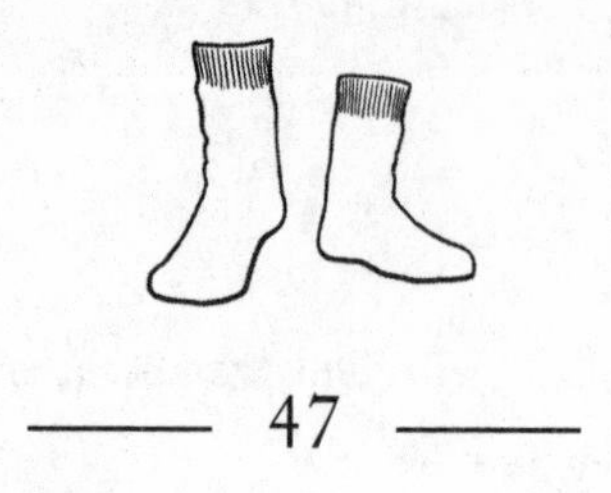

— 47 —

Benedict

...KISS, WE KISSED. WE WERE VERY GOOD kissers together. I know this is the first girl I've ever kissed, but I don't see how if I kissed every girl on planet earth that I would ever find someone who kissed me like Penelope kissed me. I should tell her that. That sounds romantic.

Do you want to know what's not romantic? Penis Benedict said: I AM IN EXCRUCIATING PAIN TRAPPED IN THESE TIGHT SKI PANTS. I KNOW YOU WANT TO BE A GENTLEMAN BUT THIS IS TORTURE. INHUMANE TORTURE!

Ignore him. Yes. I should. Obviously. Penis Benedict would ruin everything. But maybe I just tell her. . . .

48

Penelope

He said, "You make me so excited," in between our kissing. That's the second time he's said that. If it wasn't Benedict, I'd assume he was giving me the universal guy code of "Please touch my penis," but Benedict couldn't know that. He couldn't. Yes, I could feel him. I knew how hard he was. But he's so innocent, right. . . . Yes . . . If I did something, suggested something, it would freak him out. My freakiness would freak him out. I like him too much to scare him off. So I can't. I just can't.

But . . .

Don't, Pen.

But . . . how could he really love me if he doesn't know that part of me?

He couldn't.

He could!

No, he couldn't.

So I have to. Just have to say something. I love how his brain works. I have to see if he loves how my brain works.

"Benedict . . ." I pulled away from his lips, still caressing his face with my hands.

"Yes . . ."

"I'm not normal."

"I'm not normal either!"

"But you're not normal because you're brilliant and you say what's on your mind and . . . other great stuff . . . I'm, I think . . . I have . . . thoughts . . . I . . ."

"Penelope," he said, and, wow, I really did like him saying my full name. "I know love may not be logical, but I still am. And I could not love it that you do not judge my thoughts but then judge your thoughts. . . ."

"People do, everyone does . . ."

"Yes, ummm, okay, let me say it a different way. I've thought about this a lot recently. I've thought about all the times I've judged people and I realized I only did that because deep down I didn't feel confident about myself. So we judge to inflate our self-worth. Thus, if I ever judge you, you can say, 'Benedict, why is your self-worth low today?' " He smiled, and, damn, what the hell, this kid, this man, wow, what the . . .

"Benedict, that was genius, do you realize what you just said? Do you?"

"Yes, I think, ummm, now I'm not sure. . . ."

"You know. You KNOW stuff. I think it, and then you say it, and I feel like this world isn't totally screwed. If two kids like us, if we could just put stuff out there . . ."

He kissed me. He loved hearing me talk, didn't he? Yeah, he did, and so it's time, Pen, it's time. . . .

"So," I said, "what you just said, and how you looked at me when you walked into the warming hut, all of it. Do you know what it does to me? It makes me feel everywhere. My whole body just tingles everywhere. And I'm just gonna say it, it makes me throb, down here. . . ."

I drifted my hand down to my groin, just grazed it, his eyes followed down, held there, then came back to me. I had said so much, if he was going to run off it was too late so, what the hell, I might as well say more. "And yeah, I've read about girls like me. Women. But they're all older, grown-up, and it's not the same. None of my friends talk about it. No teenage girls online talk about it the way I think about it. So I feel like a freak. Like I'm screwed up. So screwed up. So I've never talked about it. Not with Paul. Never. But I'm telling it to you and I'm so scared what you're going to think of me . . . but I had to tell you. I had to."

"So . . ." he started, and all my abilities to read his mind were gone. God, I hope he doesn't hate me. ". . . I was very scared to talk about my penis because I thought you would think I was a dork or a jerk for talking about my penis. But you talking about your vagina makes me feel like I could talk about my penis. Which I don't think is normal . . . but I like being not normal with you."

"I like being not normal with you too," I said. So lame, maybe not, I don't know, screw it, I love it. And now: "So, Benedict, I can't believe I'm going to say this, I'm not sure if it's hot or dorky or whatever, but I want to tell you all my thoughts, all the dirty thoughts."

"Yes. This is the best idea ever." He laughed and I laughed.

I went on, "I want to undo your pants. I want to see it. We don't have to if you don't want to. . . ."

"I want that. Penis Benedict wants that very much."

"Penis Benedict?"

"I didn't mean to tell you about Penis Benedict."

"Do you have a voice in your head that you've named Penis Benedict?"

"Yes. You think I'm crazy. I am crazy. I'm sorry."

"Yes, you're fucking crazy and I love it. We're crazy and we're alive and we have penises and vaginas and I'm going to undo your pants now and I'm just talking, talking, talking, talking like I think in my head except I'm saying it out loud and a boy is hearing me say it as I unbutton his pants and unzip his pants . . . and . . ."

"I can help pull them down," he said.

"Yes, help me pull them down, and I'm just going to touch your underwear because I know that feels good for you, doesn't it?"

His face went to this blank, serene place. "It feels so good."

"God, I love you, Benedict, I love talking like this, I love being here like this, I love touching you. Is it okay if I pull down your underwear?" He nodded. "And there's your penis . . . it's . . ." And I almost couldn't say it because it's the freakiest thing I've ever thought in my history of freaky things, but I was beyond the walls I had been trapped behind my whole life, I was free, and once you're free, you can't stop being free, so I said, "It's beautiful, Benedict. You have a beautiful, beautiful, beautiful penis . . ." and . . .

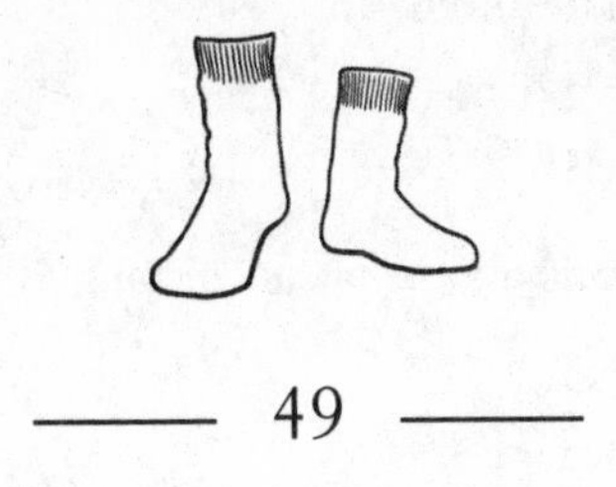

— 49 —

BENEDICT

I CAME. FOUR SECONDS! HOW EMBARRASSING! It took forty minutes in the bathroom yesterday! Took all the hot water! Took all the lotion! But today, when even four minutes would have been acceptable, it took *four seconds*. But the touch of her hand against my bare penis was too magnificent. And not just her hand, her telling me how beautiful my penis was. It overwhelmed any chance I had to not become overwhelmed.

"I'm sorry."

"Don't be sorry," she said.

"I went so fast. I've read about men with this problem. . . ."

"First off," she began, "I'm sure you don't have that problem. This is the first time a girl has ever touched you. We've had, like, twenty-four straight hours of foreplay. It would be weird if you didn't go fast. Second, it turns me on that you're turned on by me. That my touch . . ."

"And your voice."

"And my voice . . . that I could do that to you. That I made you come so fast makes me feel like I have this power. That sounds weird. . . ."

"You do have a power," I said. "Umm, so even though I orgasmed so quickly, you are still turned on?"

"Yes, like the most turned on I've ever been. You do it for me. I'm going to say something strange, but screw it, we've already said so much, but I've been fantasizing about you since you said that thing to Stacy in the hall on Tuesday."

"Fantasizing about me?"

"Masturbating."

"You masturbate?" I asked.

50

Penelope

Crap. Benedict is weirded out by me fantasizing about him. Maybe. Please don't let him hate me, please, please . . . "Yeah," I said, "I'm sorry. . . ."

"Sorry? You should not be sorry! It makes me feel much better about masturbating in the shower yesterday for forty minutes thinking about you."

"But you're a boy; boys are supposed to masturbate."

"So should girls! I know I am very inexperienced. But I have read a great deal about this and studies show that it is very healthy for girls to masturbate. But most teenage girls feel ashamed about it, so they don't do it. Penelope, you are very evolved. I'm the luckiest boy ever to have an evolved girl like you to be the first one to touch my penis. A girl that wasn't as evolved would have made me feel bad about coming so fast, but you made me feel good about it. . . ."

I kissed him. Had to. I leaned into him again. I knew he was done. If this was Paul, the TV would be on already. But I was still so horny, maybe if I rubbed against him . . .

He said, "I don't want to make you messy, so I am going to pull my underwear back up so that it can clean my . . . semen up."

I laughed. "I can't believe you just said the word 'semen.' "

"That's very dorky probably."

"Yeah, maybe, Benedict, like if this were a movie people would probably think you're a dork for saying that word. But fuck them. I think saying things just like they are is the opposite of dorky. It's cool. No, 'cool' is not a good enough word. It's evolved."

"So we are both evolved," he said.

"Yes, your brain, Benedict . . . I don't just love it . . . I want . . ."

"It turns you on?"

"Yes . . ."

"Can I touch you like you touched me?"

Yes. Yes. Yes. Yes. Yes. But all I could do was nod. He laid our coats and pants on the ground, making a sort of bed. Then he lifted me up and laid me on it before moving on top, his arms on each side of my shoulders. Then he leaned down and kissed me before maneuvering back between my legs and reaching for the button on my jeans. It took him a while.

"I'm very nervous," he said.

"It's okay. You being nervous turns me on."

"Why does me being nervous turn you on?" he asked as he inched down my jeans. (They were my tight pair.)

"Because," I started, "this means something to you. We get nervous when we care . . . if you weren't nervous, it would mean you didn't care. It turns me on that you care." My jeans were off. Underwear still on. Both our shirts were still on. He gazed down at my bare legs.

"Can I study you for a little bit?" he asked. I nodded. He ran his fingers up and down my thighs, my calves, up to my hips. Slowly. Carefully. As if I was precious art. I shivered. "Are you cold?"

"No, it just feels good."

"I am surprised by how much I enjoy touching you. It's not very logical. It should only be enjoyable for you to touch me."

"You're very good at it. . . ."

"I am?"

"You are."

"You make me feel very good about myself, Penelope." Then as he said this, he pulled down my underwear, exposing me to him. It felt vulnerable, him sitting up, between my legs, staring at my nakedness.

"Kiss me," I said, pulling him back on top. But he soon moved to his side and reached his hand toward me.

"Is it still okay that I touch you?"

I nodded again. He reached his hand there, but then hesitated. "Penelope, I don't want to do it wrong. I would hate if I did it wrong."

"You can't . . . I mean, yes, it can be done wrong . . . but just go slow. Do everything slow. Like you were touching my legs. Just go slow and you will be perfect."

He did. Go slow. Using two of his fingers, he brushed against my pubic hair. It felt nice. I wanted more.

I said, "You can touch me more."

"How?" he asked.

"More inside."

"But I thought the clitoris was outside."

I laughed. Fucking Benedict.

"Why are you laughing?"

"Because I love that you not only have read enough to know the clitoris is on the outside, but that you actually said the word 'clitoris.' "

"I'm glad you love this. But can you show me where it is?"

"No!" I said before I really thought about it.

"Why not? You know where it is. I do not. It feels much more logical for you to show me where it is instead of me guessing."

He was right. "You're right . . . you're right . . ."

"I'm socially awkward, but I'm still very smart." He laughed at his own joke as I took his fingers in mine and guided them past my hair, past my . . .

"There," I said as my body tensed and released from the sensation. "Can you feel it?"

"Oh, yes, it's not that small. Comedians make jokes about how hard it is to find, so I was very nervous I wouldn't have been able to find it on my own."

"Most guys don't even try, so they pretend it's hard to find."

"Did Paul try to find it?" he asked.

Paul. Paul. Paul . . . He felt like another life suddenly. Like a life I would never go back to. It would just be me and Benedict in this warming hut forever.

"Should I not bring up Paul?" he asked. "It's okay if you don't want to talk about him."

"I just don't want you to compare yourself to him," I said.

"Is he much better at this than me? I can learn, I can study . . ."

"Benedict! Oh, my gosh, no . . ." I laughed. "No, Paul never tried to find my clitoris. He never asked. I never asked him to find it either. I wasn't real with him like I am with you, so I don't want to blame him, but no, he never tried to touch me the way you are touching me."

"So I'm doing a good job?"

"Yes."

"So will this make you have an orgasm?"

"Benedict, no . . ."

"Then you should tell me how to do it so that I can make you have an orgasm like you made me have an orgasm."

"I've never orgasmed with a boy before, so I don't know if I can."

"But it feels good?" He was so concerned about me. So concerned. The boy I'd thought of as a robot had the biggest heart I've ever seen.

I said, "It feels so good, and I love how you talk to me, and how you ask me questions. I love how much you want to make me feel good. How much you care. See how I keep shivering? That's because of how good everything is. I don't need to have an orgasm to enjoy this very, very much."

Then he just went and said, "Can I try giving you cunnilingus?"

"Oh-my-god . . ."

"What?"

"You're . . ."

"Am I being awkward?"

Yes, he was, but was he? I don't even know. He *was* awkward but only if awkward meant being different from anything I'd ever seen or even imagined. He was just so matter-of-fact about it. So I said, "No . . . no . . . you're not. I mean, oh-my-god, it just won't taste good. Paul refused to ever try because he said he hated the smell so much."

Then, OH-MY-GOD, he put his fingers, the fingers that had been rubbing me, *into his mouth*.

"Benedict!"

"What? I'm tasting it."

"I can't *believe* you just did that."

"Penelope. You told me I wouldn't like the taste. But how could I know unless I tried? And so I tried without having to make you uncomfortable."

"You're a bigger freak than me." I shouldn't have said that. All I ever wanted was someone to tell me I wasn't a freak and now I'm calling a boy who may be my sexual equal one. "I shouldn't have said that. Or I should have said, I love that you are. I love that just put your fingers in your mouth. I really do. I'll probably masturbate thinking about you doing it tonight. You're just *so* comfortable, Benedict, so confident. . . ."

"You have made me feel confident about myself."

"You have made me like myself," I said. Saying that made me feel even more vulnerable than having him kneeling between my legs. Maybe he could sense it because he leaned back into me, kissing me. Calming me.

Then he said, "So you have never had a boy lick your vagina before?"

"No." I tried not to laugh, still did a little, but I tried.

"I know you are very experienced sexually. You know I am very inexperienced. It would mean a lot to me if this could be the thing we experience for the first time together."

That was beautiful, but . . . "I'm scared. . . ."

"Scared of what?"

"I don't know. . . ." Just tell him. "That you'll think I'm gross. Or that I smell. Or that it's not as good as the ones you've seen. . . ."

"Your vagina is the first one I've seen."

"Then the ones you've seen online. All those actresses are perfect, with perfect vaginas. . . ."

"You're perfect," he said.

"I'm so *not* perfect."

"You're perfect to me and your vagina will be perfect to me."

"You're saying that . . . Don't just say things, Benedict. Don't be a guy that just says things."

"I'm not. . . ."

"I know I'm not perfect. I know you don't think I'm perfect. I get crappy grades, I smoke, I drink, I have this scar. . . ."

Without asking, he reached and touched my scar. He ran his finger along the length of it. Paul had never touched it. Three years together, never mentioned it. Never touched it. Never saw it. Never saw the real me.

"It's so ugly," I said, and tried really, really, really hard not to cry.

"Yesterday, when I masturbated in the shower, I started out imagining having sex with you. But it was hard to imagine your body because I'm a very literal thinker. . . ." He laughed, then stopped, and leaned toward my face. Studying my scar. I hated him looking at it. But I needed him to look at it just as much. He continued, "So I just imagined your face. Up close like I am right now. I especially imagined your scar, which, from afar, I would rationalize made you unattractive, but once I saw it up close yesterday . . ." He stopped, I tensed, he kissed my scar, I calmed, he went on, ". . . it became the thing I found most attractive. This confused me in the moment. I do not like metaphors because they are not very logical, but I was very horny and perhaps being horny makes me think in metaphors, but when I was in the shower, I was thinking, 'Her scar is like the best brushstroke on a beautiful painting.' And right after I thought of this, I had an orgasm."

I shook my head because . . . he was too good, *he was perfect*, and it was too much, I loved him too much right now, and I felt so afraid but also so ready to face my fears. . . .

"Okay," I said, and nodded.

"What do you mean 'okay'?"

"You can do it. You can go down on me."

"I was not telling you that . . ."

"I know. I want you to."

"If you ever want me to stop, you tell me and I will stop."

"Okay," I said. Benedict then positioned himself again between my legs and began inching backward. He pushed up my shirt on his way downward, kissing my belly button.

Then he kissed my pubic hair.

Then he kissed the inside of my right thigh.

Then the inside of my left thigh.

Then he looked at me, his head framed by my legs. "Hello," he said.

"I love that you just said hello." And I giggled.

"Are you still scared?" he asked.

"Yes, but also very, very, very turned on."

"So I've studied this, obviously. . . ."

"Obviously."

"And in all the porn videos male actors go very fast with their tongue, but the online articles said I should go slow. And you said I should go slow with my hand. . . ."

"Go slow." I braced myself as he leaned his head in. And . . . it tickled. At first. Then. Oh. Yes. Okay. He wasn't really going near my clit, but his tongue was so light and delicate compared to a boy's fingers . . . made me feel light and delicate and, oh—

"I found it," he said, his mouth still on me.

"You did. . . ." Which was great, then too much, then—

"Go around it too, Benedict . . . everything around there . . ."

He nodded and then my body just melted downward, like butter on a pan . . . not everything, though, no, his tongue was sending gentle waves from its tip to my tip, and my pelvis raised ever so, and . . .

I didn't think about anyone else. Didn't imagine another person or situation. No, but I didn't just enjoy what he was doing either. It was incredible, yes, but still, not as good as I could do it myself. But that's not the point. And that's not what was making this so good. . . . It was that Benedict wanted to be down there, for the excitement of doing something new, and to please me and only me . . . that he didn't just see my scar, but that my scar turned him on . . .

I spent three years with a boy who I loved being with because he allowed me to be invisible without being alone . . . and Benedict, in one day, and with this one act, made me so comfortable in my own skin, so alive in my own life . . . and that's what did it, that's what allowed me to do what I never had done with Paul.

I rose, and I shook, and I moaned, and I came. . . .

Still twitching as the orgasm subsided, I finally opened my eyes and looked down at him smiling up at me. Like a boy. Like a boy who knew he got an A-plus on the semester final.

And there, still between my legs, with my wetness on his mouth, with that grin of his, he didn't look cool, or sexy . . . he looked fucking adorable. He looked like the boy I was meant to love.

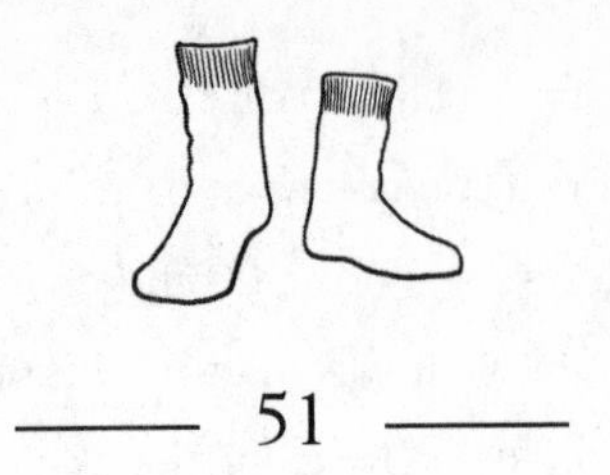

51

BENEDICT

SHE ORGASMED. ON MY MOUTH.

As I lay there, on my stomach, with her vagina six inches below my face and her bare legs on each side of my head, I tried to remember my old life. You remember, the one from yesterday. The life where I had never kissed a girl. Where I had barely spoken to a girl. Or two days ago, when I almost had a mental breakdown because I couldn't say a single word to a girl. And now I was here. With Penelope. The girl I'd insisted was not attractive but who was now the most attractive I could ever imagine a girl being.

Moving up beside her, I kissed her. Because that's what you can do when you have a girlfriend. Was she my girlfriend now? I shouldn't presume. Don't ask, Benedict. Yes, that was not important right now.

"So you didn't hate it?" she asked.

"I enjoyed it very much."

"But how could you?"

"Because it made you happy like you made me happy."

"But you didn't actually like doing it, you just liked the end result?"

"Penelope, look at Penis Benedict." I pointed down to my groin. "He is erect again. Just like you get turned on giving me pleasure, it is apparent I get turned on giving you pleasure."

Her eyes did their now-very-common water producing. I kissed the tears away. "Benedict, I . . . oh-my-god . . . I . . ."

I could tell what she was thinking. Just as she could tell what I was thinking earlier. "I love you too."

"I believe you. I don't think I ever believed Paul. I don't believe my mom when she says it. But I believe you."

"At Riverbend High School, we do not have much in common. No common classes or friends. But here, in this warming hut, our ability to freely communicate and our very strong sexual chemistry . . ."

"And our kindness . . . We are so kind to each other, Benedict . . ." she said, then kissed my cheek.

"Yes, this is true. I also think we are both very smart."

"I'm not as smart as you."

"Oh, Penelope, I think you have a genius I didn't know existed. My intelligence is very common. But yours is rare. It is special."

"Yours is rare, Benedict. . . ."

"YOURS is rare, Penelope," I said.

"I love YOU, Benedict." She emphasized a word just like me. This felt like flirting, and even though I didn't know how to flirt, I decided I should yell:

"I LOVE YOU, PENELOPE!" Maybe that was me being awkward, not flirtatious. But then she yelled back:

"I LOVE THAT YOU YELLED THAT!"

"IT IS VERY ENJOYABLE TO YELL THAT I LOVE YOU!"

And then, Penelope yelled, "I WANT TO HAVE SEX WITH YOU!"

I couldn't yell that back. I couldn't say anything.

"I'm sorry," she said. "I just don't, I don't know . . . I shouldn't . . ."

"I want to have sex very much too. I didn't want to say it first because I was afraid you wouldn't want to. . . ."

She sat up. Made me sit up beside her. "Oh, I want to, and I'm so happy you want to . . . but maybe this is too fast. Maybe we should wait."

"Yes, you are being very smart."

"Yes . . ."

"But I don't want to be smart, Penelope."

"Me neither," she said. She lunged into me, kissed me, then pulled my shirt over my head. I pulled her shirt off, then she undid her bra and—

"There are your boobs," I said.

She laughed. "Usually that's the first thing boys see, not the last."

"Can I touch them?"

"Oh-my-god, Benedict, you've already licked my vagina! Of course you can touch my boobs!"

"I wanted to make sure it was okay with you."

"Yes, yes, you can . . . and I like how you ask."

I reached out and touched them. Fascinating. "They *are* fun to touch. It's biological. Breasts give us nourishment as babies, so we subconsciously place high value on them even though they serve no sexual purpose. . . ."

"Benedict . . ."

"I shouldn't talk about boobs like that, should I?"

"No, I love that . . . it's . . . We don't have condoms. . . ."

"Oh, I have some." I reached inside my coat to the zipped pocket and pulled out two condoms.

"I can't believe . . ."

"I am very excited to do something very dumb with you, but I was very smart before."

She kissed me. "Do you really think this is dumb? Everything has been great. More than great. The greatest day of my life . . . I don't want to ruin it."

"You are right. . . ."

"I am . . . ?"

"No," I said, "you are right that I called this dumb. I apologize. I don't think this is dumb. Not precisely. I'm nervous. Very nervous. But I don't think this is dumb, I just think it is something I can't predict with my thoughts and so I call it dumb. But I think, when I die one hundred years from now . . ."

"You're going to live to one hundred and seventeen?"

"Obviously." I smiled.

"Obviously." Penelope smiled back.

". . . I will think back on this day and think it was the smartest thing I ever did, having sex with you." I then took her hand and put it on my penis. "Penis Benedict doesn't need one hundred years. He already thinks this is the smartest thing I will ever do."

Penelope took my hand and put it between her legs. "Vagina Penelope agrees."

She put on the condom because she knew how to do it right. I liked watching her do it. Then she lay back on our bed of coats and I got on top of her, my body pressing into her.

"Am I squishing you?"

"No. I like you against me like this."

"I'm not sure how to start."

"Scoot up a little and I'll help," she said. As I did, she reached around, grabbed my penis, and guided it inside her.

I'm not sure I had ever thought about how it would feel. I guess I thought it would be like masturbating but masturbating inside a girl's vagina. But it didn't feel anything like that. I didn't really concentrate on what my penis was feeling at all.

So I asked, "How does it feel for you?"

"Very good. How does it feel for you?"

"It feels . . . very good . . . obviously . . . but I'm mostly feeling . . ." My eyes started watering. I was crying. What kind of boy cries when he has sex the first time? "I'm being socially awkward. . . ."

"You're being beautiful, Benedict." She kissed my tears.

"I know you told me not to change, Penelope. But you changed me. I can never go back to what I was before."

"You changed me too."

"Maybe that's what love is," I said, and I didn't even know what I was saying but I said it anyway, "that someone loves you just the way you are, but love changes you for the better anyway."

"Oh, Benedict . . . that's going to make *me* cry. . . ." And she did. I kissed her tears because that was our special thing. Then she said, "Are you close to coming?"

"I think so," I said, even though I hadn't really been thinking about it.

"Can you wait just a little bit longer?"

"I think so."

"I want to come at the same time. . . ."

"That would be the best thing in the history of planet earth."

"I've never done that. I want to do that with you. I want you to be my first. . . ."

"That would make it the best thing in the history of the universe." I was being dorky. I know this. That's okay, I think.

"But, Benedict . . ."

"Yes?"

"I'll need to use my fingers to help. . . . Is that okay?"

"Of course! Why wouldn't that be okay?"

"Other boys might think . . ."

"I'm not other boys, Penelope."

She reached between our bodies, and I could see her body respond to her touch and I just had to say, "That is very, very, sexy . . . very sexy . . ."

"I love that you think it's sexy. . . ."

"It might be *too* sexy because it's going to make me . . ."

"I know . . . two more seconds . . . I'm close . . ."

"I can't . . ."

"One more second . . ." she said, and grabbed the back of my head and we locked our eyes together and . . .

52

Penelope

We came. Together. Our eyes open.

Then, after a bit, I pulled him down and held him against me. On top of me. And then, sometime later, after he put the condom into a plastic bag he had somehow thought to bring, he rolled over and we lay next to each other. We didn't say much. Just stared and enjoyed staring.

While keeping our coats beneath us, Benedict slid us both into my mom's snow pants to keep us warm. Like a cocoon. A cocoon for our love, for our magical day. I know I hate the cheesy, fake crap. But when it's real it's not fake and when it's real . . . it's everything.

So . . . in our safe, wonderful cocoon, we fell asleep. And slept for a long, long time.

If only we hadn't, if only we could have stayed awake in that warming hut forever.

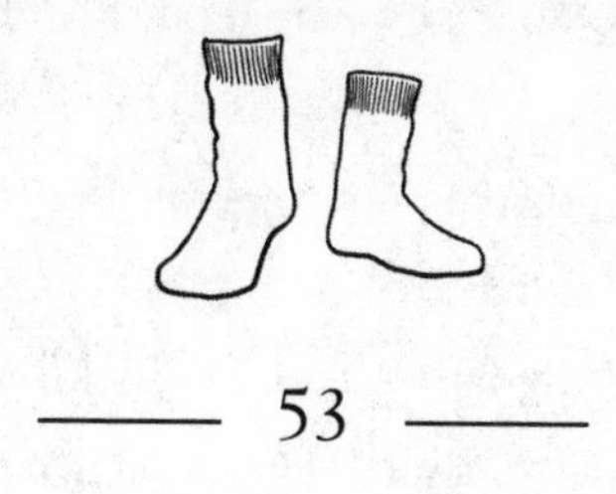

53

BENEDICT

I AM A VERY SOUND SLEEPER. THIS IS WHY I set up two alarms at home, one on my phone and one on my clock.

I didn't wake until Penelope woke me. Only after I sat up, and saw the terror on her face, did I hear what she heard. Voices. Footsteps. Idling snowmobiles.

The door to the warming hut swinging open. My father. My hero. Seeing me with the girl he banned me from seeing. Judging me with his eyes and with the force of a jumbo jet falling on my head.

Behind him was her mother and mine, the bearded boathouse man behind them both.

I heard Penelope's mother scream first, "OH MY GOD! OH MY GOD! THEY'RE NAKED! OH MY GOD! THEY'RE NAKED! OH MY GOD!"

My father didn't say anything to me. He didn't need to. Whatever kind of disappointment I had been to him so far, this was a hundred times that. This was more than a fireable offense. This was, his look told me, a crime that should be punishable by death. I know I exaggerate. I know. But you don't know my father. How my father's brain works. And he does not exaggerate. And he wished, at that moment, that I were dead.

Penelope's mom pushed past my dad into the doorway. "You whore! You whore! YOU WHORE!"

"She is a whore," my father said, but looking at me, "and that is what my disappointment of a son deserves." Then he turned away from me. I assumed he would never look at me again.

Penelope's mom now screamed at my dad. "She may be a whore, but your son is retarded! RETARDED! HE KIDNAPPED HER! I'M GOING TO SUE YOU! YEAH! MY DAUGHTER WILL PAY FOR BEING A WHORE! BUT YOU'LL PAY FOR YOUR SON BEING RETARDED!"

Penelope slammed the door closed. Her mother screamed for it to be opened, but my mother, who never yells, told them to give us time to get dressed.

Penelope was shaking and she tried to look at me, she tried, but her body was shrinking before my eyes. I couldn't move. I couldn't move or speak. I couldn't . . .

"You have to get dressed, Benedict, you have to . . ." she said, handing me clothes. "I'm so sorry, so sorry. . . ."

I wanted to say it wasn't her fault. Because it wasn't. We did nothing wrong. We were two teenagers who fell in love. How could that be wrong?

Evil Benny, who had been so quiet for so long, said: If your father thinks what you did was wrong, then it's wrong. Because you are nothing compared to him. You literally wouldn't exist without him. He deserved a smart, good son. But he got you.

Penelope, somehow dressed, tried to put my underwear on. My paralysis eased, but instead of telling Penelope it was going to be okay, or holding her, or doing anything I wanted to do, I ripped my clothes from her hand.

I'm sorry, I should say.

I love you, Penelope. . . .

But I only watched as she scooped up her coat and snow pants and walked out into the snow in bare feet. Her mom screamed more. Screams that cracked my skin with their force. I was still in the hut. But Penelope was feeling those screams up close. I should protect Penelope from her.

Move, Benedict, move. I did. I tried. But by the time I got outside, the boathouse man was driving his snowmobile away, Penelope and her mom with him. Within seconds, she was gone. As if she had never been here.

My dad said to my mom, "I'm not waiting for him. I'm not wasting another second on him. If he's old enough to ruin his life, he is old enough to find his way back."

She ignored him. He got on the second snowmobile, never once looking toward me, and drove off. After he was gone, my mother picked up Penelope's skis and poles. "I'll walk these back. You can ski if you wish."

I shook my head and picked up my skis as well. She waited until I stepped beside her then started walking in the direction of the lodge.

"Do you want to talk about it?"

I shook my head.

"Then we won't."

My mother didn't say another word on the way back. It was a long way back too, to walk through the snow trail as we did. I didn't think much. Not in the usual way my brain likes to think about things.

We left the skis at the top of the stairs to the boathouse. My mom then steered us toward the road where her SUV was waiting. We were going home. My actions had not only destroyed my dad's respect for me; they'd also destroyed his vacation.

But inside, behind the wheel, wasn't my father. It was Elizabeth. Who is thirteen. She climbed over the console to the passenger seat as my mom got into the driver's seat.

Elizabeth asked the question I wanted to ask: "So we're really leaving Dad here?"

"He needs some time by himself," my mom said.

Wait, I wanted to say as my eyes turned toward Penelope's cabin. Their car was already gone.

"I saw them drive off, Benedict," my sister said. "Her mom never stopped yelling the whole time."

As soon as my phone got service, I texted Penelope. I called her. I texted her. I called her. I texted her. But the calls went straight to her voice mail. My texts were never answered.

When we stopped for gas, my mother went inside to use the restroom. Elizabeth turned back to me and said, "You're my hero, brother."

I didn't say anything back.

Halfway home, I finally responded to Robert's birthday text:

ME

Thanks, Robert.

He soon texted back:

ROBERT

Did you get a text from Allison Wray?

ME

No.

ROBERT

Check Facebook. She might have written you there. I think she really likes you!

ME

Okay.

But I had no intention of checking Facebook for Allison's message.

ROBERT

Did you ever have a chance to talk to Penelope?

Honesty.

ME

Yes.

I also kissed her. I also fell in love with her. I also had sex with her. I also failed her.

ROBERT

I heard she broke up with Paul. Maybe we can go on a double date!

I didn't respond.

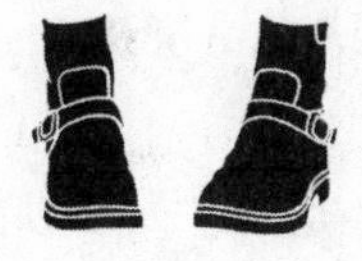

54

penelope

I never yelled back at my mom. She yelled for hours. Hours. I never yelled back. I never said anything at all.

She had thrown my phone out the window back when we first started driving home. It probably didn't matter. The look on Benedict's face when he snapped his clothes from my hands in the hut . . . I knew. Knew he was done with me. No matter how much you say you love someone, no matter what you share, you can't just forget about your father calling the girl a whore. You can't forget the girl's mother calling you retarded.

You just can't.

I could forget all that stuff because I have to forget horrible stuff to survive. But a person like Benedict, even though we were so similar in a lot of ways, he wasn't damaged like me. He didn't need to forget. If you don't need to forget, then it's impossible not to remember. I don't even . . . I don't . . .

I felt like I should open the door of the car and just fall out. Fall away. We were going almost seventy miles per hour. The pavement would just suck me into nothingness. Into the darkness. I could feel myself falling anyway. Could feel myself being swallowed by it. At least if I jumped from the car, the pain of the darkness would go away.

I could take the pain.

I could take the darkness.

I just couldn't take both at the same time.

— 55 —

BENEDICT

BY THE TIME WE GOT BACK HOME TO RIVERBEND, I still had not heard from Penelope.

She was just lonely up there at the lake, Evil Benny said, she was lonely and you were the only one around. Do you think you're worth seeing again when she'll have to listen to her mother call you a retard? Do you think she ever wants to see a boy again whose father called her a whore? Use your brains, retard. She was using you and now she's done with you.

I could feel my brain crumbling. My body felt cold outside and my insides were burning up. I must distract myself.

So I texted Penelope again.

And again she didn't respond.

So I signed on to Facebook. I'd write her there. But before I could,

I saw the message from Allison Wray. Before I could tell myself to delete it, I read it:

> **Hi, Benedict! Robert said it would be okay to write you. Hope you are having a good vacation with your family! If you have some free time when you get back, it would be really special if a cute boy showed me around Riverbend. Talk to you later! Allison**

See, retard? Evil Benny said. Your father was right. Allison Wray was the right girl for you. She even sounds like you! You two would have been a couple people would admire! You and Penelope would have been a freak show! The stoner and the Tin Man! You're so stupid. You went and made your father hate you for no reason.

I didn't write Allison back. I didn't delete her message either.

56

penelope

I never opened the car door on the highway. I'm too pathetic to even kill myself.

My mother drove straight to the church recovery center in Gladys Park.

When she got out, still screaming as she walked around toward my door, I noticed the keys still in the ignition. I couldn't just abandon my mom here. She's a horrible mother, but I couldn't. Then, as she swung open the door to grab me, she seethed, "You can stay here the rest of your life as far as I'm concerned!"

And suddenly I could. Suddenly I had to. I jumped into the driver's seat, put it in drive, and despite her still holding the passenger door open and her red-faced raging, I drove. She let go and the door slammed shut when it bounced off another car's bumper.

I went to the pizzeria. I needed my dad. Needed him to tell me my mother was nuts, that he was divorcing her, that he would protect me from her. But when I walked inside the restaurant, despite there being two tables of customers, he yelled at me the way he usually yells at her.

"WHAT THE FUCK IS YOUR PROBLEM? LEAVING YOUR MOTHER LIKE THAT! DRIVING LIKE A CRAZY DRIVER! I THOUGHT YOU WERE A GOOD PERSON BUT NOW I'M NOT SO SURE!"

He took two steps toward me and he could tell I wasn't going to stay. He could tell I was in a place I had never been. He tried to calm himself, to calm me, but it was too late. And he was too slow, too old, and I was back to the car and driving away from my dad just as fast as I drove away from my mom.

Where could I go . . .

nowhere . . .

nowhere to go . . .

not home . . .

nowhere . . .

nowhere but back . . .

back in time . . .

back to who I was . . .

back to being invisible . . .

back to Paul . . .

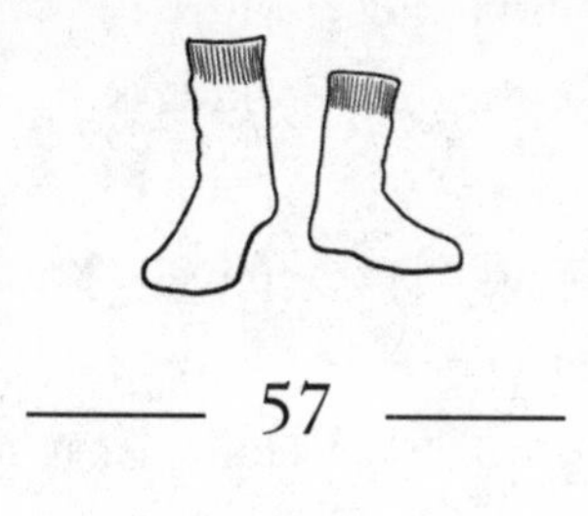

57

BEN . . .

IT WAS 8:03 P.M. WHEN WE PARKED IN THE garage at home. I said the first words to my mother since breakfast: "Am I grounded?"

"No," she said. And for a moment, I felt I should say something to her. Something kind. But I couldn't make myself do it. So I said:

"Then I'm leaving."

I found Penelope's address on my phone and drove there. No intelligent things formed in my head to say to her mother or to Penelope, but I had to drive there anyway. But when I got to the house, it was dark. Not a single light was on.

Next, because I would not cease my search for her until it was successful, I drove to her family's pizzeria. I went to the register at the front and asked, "Do you know where Penelope is?"

At the sound of my voice, a man, a round man with a round face and a round waist and round hands, lumbered out from the kitchen.

He carried a dough roller and anger. I knew it was her father because I just knew. "Who wants to know where Penelope is? Who are you? Are you that boy she was with up at the lake?"

"Yes."

He yelled, "Get out of here. You made her crazy. You made my good girl crazy. Get out of here!"

I became a robot. I would not let him get to me. I would not leave until I found out what I came to find out. I said, in my monotone robot voice, "I want to know that she's safe."

"She is crazy! She steals her mother's car. She leaves her. She comes here. She drives off again instead of talking to me. I should call the cops on you! I'll call the cops and they'll arrest you!" He points the roller at me. Waves it around. He could swing it at my head. I still wouldn't move. "Why do you just stand there?!"

"Where did she go, Mr. Lupo?" Flat voice. No emotion. No fear.

"Why are you talking like that? What's wrong with you? Why you talk like that? Are you retarded like my wife says? Are you?"

"Where did she go, Mr. Lupo?"

"Not to you! Not to you! You make her crazy! She go home. Or she go to Paul. He's a good boy! He's a good man. You're in trouble with Paul when he finds out about you making Penelope crazy! YOU ARE IN TROUBLE!" he screamed as I left.

As I got in my car, a tiny, frightened voice said, She wouldn't have gone to Paul's.

But then Evil Benny, in a strong, confident voice—in the voice of a general, of a grown man, in a voice like my father's—said, That's exactly where she fucking went, you fucking retard.

So I found the address online and drove to Paul's. I knew, as I drove, if I found Penelope there that Evil Benny would win. I had always been able to outthink him. I could always find a reason why he was wrong. But if he was right this time, if she was at the house of her ex-boyfriend, the house of the boy who'd beaten me up, on the night of my birthday, on the night of the day she had sex with me, on the day I fell in love . . . then Evil Benny would win.

Her mother's car was parked on the street in front of Paul's house.

Evil Benny told me not to even slow down.

So I didn't.

58

penelope

As I parked in front of Paul's, I felt like throwing up. I hadn't eaten anything since breakfast, almost twelve hours, but my stomach felt poisoned. It needed to purge itself. But I couldn't throw up my life. So I got out of the car and walked to his front door. I hadn't knocked in years but, I don't know, I couldn't just walk in. We had broken up. I had fallen in love with a beautiful boy from another dimension, and now I was back on this broken plane because I had failed to be who I wanted to be. So I knocked and waited.

His mother answered. His pretty, always perky mother. With her black hair and her nice sweaters. "Pen! Oh, I'm so glad you're here." She pulled me into their house, my second home, and hugged me. "Paul has been driving us all mad talking about you. Thank you, thank you, thank you for forgiving him. He's just a boy. You know boys are boys. You can't blame them for being what they are." I wanted to tell her *she* was an idiot, but I was doing exactly what she was telling me to do so really I guess that made *me* the fucking idiot. She hugged me again. I needed to be hugged. She never called me a whore. Paul's dad never called me a whore. This was my real family. Maybe they'll let me live here. I'll marry him. I'll marry Paul and I'll live here and I'll never see my parents again and I'll never think about Benedict ever, ever again.

Footsteps raced up from the basement. Paul burst out through the door, galloped over to me, and lifted me in the air before I could even let out a breath. "Babe, babe, babe, babe, babe, my babe, my baby . . ."

He was squeezing me so hard I couldn't breathe. Which is how it should be, I suppose.

He dragged me down into the basement a few minutes later. This was where we usually hung out. This was where we usually had sex. I'll marry Paul, fine, I'll do it to survive, but, man, I don't know if I could have sex with him. . . . I'm sure I could eventually. I'm sure I'll forget about my three days at Wild Wolf Resort with Benedict Pendleton. I'm sure I'll eventually convince myself our hours in the warming hut were just a dream.

"Babe, babe," he said, sitting me down on the black basement couch. "What did you hear? What did Stacy tell you?"

I just shook my head. He thinks I'm going to care if he screwed another girl. I don't care at all. I don't care at all, Paul, just let me live here and don't try to kiss me. You can have sex with whoever you want, just let me stay here with you and your family.

"Stacy told me to come over and her parents weren't home and we got drunk, so I'm not sure any of what she said even happened but you believe me, right?"

"Yes," I said, even though I didn't believe a word he said. But I don't care, Paul! Stop thinking I care! I think you're a moron! But I don't care!

"She's a fat pig anyway. She's a fucking whore. . . ."

Whore. *Whore.* I don't know. That word. I hate him saying that word.

"So I don't want you talking to that whore ever again. You hear me? Never again."

"Don't use that word." I couldn't not say that. I'll live here, I'll pretend I still love you, but please don't use that word.

"What? What's your problem?"

"Just don't use that word."

"Why the fuck are you telling me what to say? What's wrong with you?"

I should apologize. I just need to hide. Hide here.

"What happened? Your mom called earlier in one of her rampages. Said something about how I better keep you away from the retard. What the fuck did she mean? I thought she was in one of her moods, but now, you talking back to me, I don't know. . . ."

"Don't use that word either."

"WHAT THE HELL IS YOUR PROBLEM?"

Become invisible. Become invisible. Become invisible.

"Have you been talking to that Benedict kid? Is that the retard? Have you been talking to him? If I hear you've been talking to him, I'm going to be pretty pissed, Pen. Pretty *fucking* pissed."

Stay invisible? Stay invisible? Stay invisible?

He stood up, loomed over me. "Where's your phone? If I find his name on your phone, I'll murder him. Fucking murder that retard!"

Oh . . . Benedict . . .

Oh, Benedict.

It was never going to work. I know. It was only a matter of time before you saw my mom go nuts. When you saw that, you would know I was doomed. You would know I wasn't worth it. I wish it wasn't today. I wish that wasn't the way it happened. But it was always going to happen.

I'm glad we happened anyway.

I'm glad our mystical trip inside the warming hut happened.

Because I can't go back.

I can't be invisible.

I have to be me.

The me you loved.

The me I like.

"Paul, I'm sorry I came here. I don't care that you slept with Stacy. Over the past three days, I fell in love with Benedict. . . ."

His open palm was descending so fast I didn't even realize it was coming at my head until impact. My body went limp, bounced off the couch, and onto the ground. Paul was yelling. He was half apologizing and half blaming.

Yelling and screaming and hitting . . .

I get it, Mom and Dad. I get it. My whole body is flowing with adrenaline. I feel alive. Not alive like I felt in the warming hut with Benedict. Not alive like I'm excited to be alive. More like alive in that I need to fight to *stay* alive. So I get it. If you had to choose between death and this, I guess I'd choose this. But all this, all this yelling and screaming and fighting . . . was my parents' way of feeling alive. They can fucking have it. I want my own.

I stood up, taking in as brave a breath as I could even though I was sure he was going to hit me again. He was pacing, circling, like a dog. Maybe I could escape.

"Paul. I'm leaving."

"No you're not, Pen! No you're not!"

"I'm leaving. If you hit me again, or ever, ever even talk to Benedict, I'll tell everyone about—" He didn't let me finish. He hit me again. I was ready this time, but he still caught me across my mouth. I managed to stay on my feet, but my face burned. Fire. Flames. I said no more yelling, but I have to yell so that I can save myself. It's okay to yell to save yourself. You can't be silent if silence is death.

"AAAAAAAAAAAAAAAAAAAAAAAAAAAAAA AAAAAAAAAAAAAAAAAAAAAAAAAAAAAH!"

He tried to tackle me, to quiet me, but I screamed until his mother came downstairs.

"What's wrong? What happened?" his mother said, then saw my face. Her reaction made me taste the blood in my mouth. "Oh, no, no, Paul . . . no, no . . . Why'd you do this? Why? Come on, honey, I'll get you some ice." But I could see her darkness building. I'd never seen it in her. It looked just like my mom's. She twisted back at her son and yelled, "Paul! Why'd you do that!"

And she slapped him.

I had never seen her do that before. But it all made sense now. Why he was drawn to me and I was drawn to him. Why this felt like a second home. Because it's just like my first home. They just did a better job of faking it.

Maybe if I were writing the fictional version of my life, I would have said something super wise and witty like "He learned it from you." Or maybe "That's why." But I'm not fictional. I'm just me. So I just left.

Once back in the car, I thought about not telling anyone. Just being happy I got away.

Screw that.

I went to the cops.

I could never report my parents' craziness toward each other when I was a kid. But I could report it being done to me.

My mom's cop friend, Officer Roberts, was there, but I avoided him. I'm sure he'd call her. Who cares now?

I got lucky. I got a girl cop. Officer Sansone. She was sweet but serious, told me we didn't need to call my parents if I didn't want to. She drove me to the hospital. Talked to me while her partner wrote down the report. They took pictures.

When we got back to the police station, they said they were going to arrest Paul. It felt real. Good. They asked if they could call anyone for me, but I said no.

I had absolutely no idea what I was going to do. I had absolutely no one I could go to.

Oh. Yeah. Wait. Maybe there was one person. The person that had seen and heard so much of my life and yet had said so little.

The priest.

Father Jeremy.

I could go to him. Not to him. But maybe he'd meet me somewhere to talk. I went back into the station and used their phone. He answered. His voice had always annoyed me, but tonight it felt gentle. I needed gentle.

"Can you meet me at Roth's Diner?" I asked.

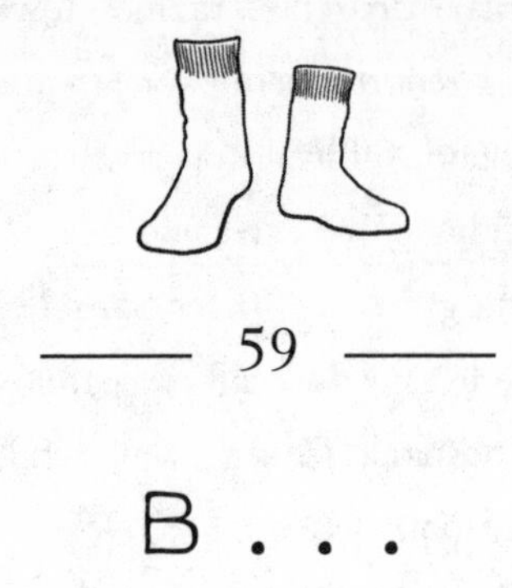

— 59 —

B . . .

I DIDN'T KNOW WHEN MY DAD WAS GOING TO come home. Perhaps tonight, perhaps tomorrow. I didn't know. Not knowing made me not want to go home even though I had nowhere else I could go. Eventually I would have to, but I would avoid it as long as possible.

Because you're pathetic, Evil Benny said.

Yes.

I pulled over on the side of the road and took out my phone. I signed on to Facebook because I knew why, but I didn't want to admit I knew why. I wrote her back. I said, *That would be nice. Are you free tonight, Allison?—Benedict.*

Evil Benny said, You sound so desperate asking her out at 9:22 p.m. on a Monday.

"I am desperate," I said out loud to the voice in my head. This was not a good sign for my mental health.

Even if Allison did write me back, I didn't think she would respond right away. So I went to my Facebook wall to look at my birthday messages. I have four hundred friends because everyone agrees to be your friend on Facebook even though no one really wanted to be my friend. (Except Robert, but Robert wouldn't want to be my friend when he found out I had sex with the one girl he ever told me he liked.) Of my four hundred Facebook "friends," only eight had wished me a happy birthday. I think if you were to do a survey of all the people on Facebook who got the smallest percentage of birthday messages on their wall, I would be the smallest by a lot.

One of the eight messages was Robert. One was my mother. Three were my cousins who live in Cleveland and Atlanta. One was Allison Wray. (*Happy birthday, Benedict!*) One was Gator Green. (The only unexpected one. It said, *happy birthday to my fellow library ghost*.)

The last was from Penelope. I got excited, as if my heart had launched into my head, until I realized she had written it this morning while we were still at breakfast at the resort. That was after our first kiss, but before the warming hut. So it was like a message frozen in time. Not literally. I'm not sure how anything could be literally frozen in time. Not important, Benedict. Penelope's frozen Facebook message said, *hb b*.

It was very simple. Three letters. But I could hear Penelope's voice saying them, and once I could hear Penelope's voice saying them, I could see her mouth saying them, and once I could see her mouth, I could see the rest of her and then I cried. I cried like a little boy would cry; my shoulders shook and snot came out of my nose, which I wiped on my car seat because car seats are a stupid thing to care about being clean when you have a broken heart.

My phone beeped. It was a message from Allison. *Okay! That would be fun! Where do you want to meet?*

I responded with the only place I knew stayed open after ten in Riverbend:

Roth's Diner.

60

Penelope

I felt naked without my phone. But, I don't know, I also felt free. I'm sure if I had it, I'd be checking it every second to see if Benedict would have called or texted and he wouldn't because I'm sure he was banned from ever even thinking about me again and even if he wasn't I'm sure he banned himself from ever thinking about the "whore" . . . yeah . . . yeah, anyway, better without my phone tonight. Better.

When I walked into Roth's Diner, Father Jeremy wasn't there yet, so I asked the host if I could sit in the closed section. I'd need to say some crap about my parents that I didn't want anyone else hearing but I knew the only way they'd sit me there was if I told them who I was meeting, so I said, "I'm meeting Father Jeremy." Everyone knew him at Roth's, mainly because my mom and him came here for breakfast whenever she decided not to be a hermit, which was like every third day. And he's a priest. Everyone respects priests, which is stupid but, hell, I was the one needing him now and I'm the last person who ever thought I'd need one. Not that I need a priest; I just need someone and he's the only person I have left that could meet me.

The host said of course and let me past the rope and to a booth around the corner. Without my phone, I had to just sit there and wait without doing anything, which I can't remember ever doing.

He arrived pretty quickly for an old guy and he scurried to the booth once the host pointed him my way. If he was an actor, he could play one of those hobbits in those movies.

"Good evening, Penelope, thanks for meeting me," he said as he took off his jacket and laid it on the booth behind him. He wasn't wearing his priest uniform, the collar thing, just a sports jacket and corduroys.

"You came to meet me, Father Jeremy. I owe you a thank-you."

"Oh, yes, I guess so. . . ." He looked at me like I just spoke Latin. But all I did was speak in a complete sentence to him, which I hadn't done since maybe ever. "Well, then, thank you for giving me a good reason to get out of my apartment."

A waitress with burnt-orange hair came over and slid two waters onto the table. "Hiya, Father."

"Hello, Dolores. This is my friend Penelope."

"Hiya, Penelope."

"Hi," I said. I felt like I was in some alternate reality where we were possessed by spirits who like to spend a lot of time saying hello.

"Would you like something to eat, Penelope?" Jeremy asked.

"No," I said, even though I was starving.

"Maybe order something just in case? You don't have to eat it if you don't want to."

"Okay," I said, and ordered eggs because I like ordering breakfast at night sometimes. Jeremy the Priest ordered some pancakes and coffee. I guess he liked ordering breakfast at night sometimes too.

After the waitress left, Father Jeremy leaned forward onto the table as if he needed to confess something. "Before we begin, and I am open to whatever you wish to discuss including the quality of the pancakes, I would like you to know your mother called me." I braced myself. He continued, "I didn't tell her you called me nor that we were going to meet. But I thought you should know that I am aware of some of what happened today."

Well, I . . . I don't know . . . She had already won, right? My mom gave her side before I could give mine. Father Jeremy was always going to be on her side anyway, but now it all seemed pointless.

"I am also going to tell you that my relationship with your mother is more complex than you are entirely aware. . . ."

Oh-my-god, they *are* lovers or something, oh, no . . . wait, just too impossible . . .

"I do not believe in advising parents in front of their children nor children in front of their parents. It makes the person defensive to receive advice in front of others and therefore it's not very helpful. That is why I have never said anything about your mother's behavior in front of you."

Which was true. I always assumed it was because she had him brainwashed with free pizza. But I guess he had never said anything critical to me either. In fact, he might be the only person who never has.

"But, when it's just me and your mother, I try to advise her toward a more patient and understanding approach when it comes to communicating with you. I am only telling you this now because I feel we have reached a critical point and I don't want you to think that I have, or will ever, defend some of your parents' behavior."

"Okay," I said. All he said actually made me feel better, but I couldn't tell him that.

"Fantastic. Then, if you wish, we can discuss what happened today.

Or I can tell you about my very exciting day doing inventory in the church kitchen."

Yeah . . . "Okay, but I guess you should know . . ." I can't believe I was about to tell a priest this but I guess this me, this post-Benedict me, just couldn't waste my time not being real. ". . . that I don't believe in God. Or at least a God like the one the church or my mom talks about. I sure as hell don't believe in religion or Jesus the way she does. So it's not really going to help me if you start talking about it like it's going to mean anything to me."

"I appreciate you saying that, Penelope. I appreciate someone who understands themselves the way you do." This conversation was already weirder than I thought it could be. But then Father Jeremy made it even weirder and said, "I don't really believe in God the way the church does either. I suppose I did when I started out, but we all change in our hearts even if the circumstances around us can't change."

I'm pretty sure Jeremy the Catholic Priest just told me he wasn't a Catholic. Not sure how to process this right now.

"Though I do ask you keep that in confidence between us. I am very grateful that my life in the church has provided me with the opportunities it has. Such as the chance to have breakfast at ten o'clock at night with someone like you."

"I would never."

"I appreciate that. It makes me feel safe to know that I can tell you something and it will remain between us. I hope you know I would do you the same honor."

And . . . yeah . . . and so I did. Told him everything. *Everything.* Okay, let me clarify everything. I told him I had sex with Benedict, fell in love, all the yelling, screaming, name calling, getting hit by Paul, the police, all that. I left out details like Benedict making me orgasm. I don't care how wise and understanding Father Jeremy is, he's still seventy years old and a priest and there are just some things that don't need to be said and not saying them doesn't make you any less honest, it just makes you respectful of who's listening.

Anyway, after I was all done, I felt better. The eggs and a few bites of Jeremy's pancakes helped too. You know, even if he didn't say another word, it would have been worth meeting him.

Then he said, "Today sounds like it was one of the most difficult, and special, and important, days of your life."

"Yeah."

"And I am very honored you shared it with me."

Yeah . . . okay. I thought that was it. I "confessed." He thanked me for confessing. I feel better. He feels like he did his job.

But then he looked off, and I could see him thinking, and then he turned back toward me and he said, "There comes a time when we must all accept that people are not going to change no matter how much we wish they would change."

Yeah . . .

"Penelope, I don't think your parents are ever going to change."

Yeah . . .

"But I think you have the power to change. I know you do. So I am going to break the very confidence I've just spoken about . . . and tell you about something that happened to your mom. And to you. And to your dad."

My head started doing a tiny shake back and forth. I had no idea what he was going to tell me but I could tell, just by his tone, by the pace of his words, that what he was going to say would change *me*. . . .

"When you were young, very young, I think just over a year old, your parents had moved to Brooklyn for the summer. Your dad, as you may know, had always wanted to move back there and your mom had agreed to spend the summer there to see if she liked it. I believe he was the chef at an Italian restaurant near the courthouse and your parents had rented a little apartment close by. In the evening, your mom would have an early dinner with you at the restaurant and then walk you home to put you to bed. . . ."

My heart started beating faster. Like every second it was doubling in speed. I didn't know why . . . what could have happened?

"Your father worked late and then he would go out drinking with the waitstaff."

"My dad almost never drinks."

"Not since then, no. On this night, your mom was carrying you in through the apartment door and a man came up behind her. He had a knife. He reached around with it, and pressed it . . ." Father Jeremy reached his hand out, just far enough so that I knew where he was pointing.

To my face.

To my scar.

He went on, "The man told your mom that if she screamed, he would kill you both. You were already bleeding. This man then pushed you both into your apartment, allowing your mother to put you in your crib before he forced her to the floor and raped her."

My eyes bloomed fast with tears, and my heart stopped racing and maybe stopped altogether, and I thought I was going to have a panic attack, but, no, I couldn't. I wouldn't. I was okay. I broke, but I put myself together before I became permanently broken.

"Your father didn't come home until morning, when he found your mother still in shock on the floor and you in a blood-soaked crib. If he had come earlier, they might have gotten you stitches sooner. . . ."

"And it wouldn't be such a big scar." I touched it. It's okay. All I have is this scar on my face. Not like the scar my mom has. . . .

"I told you this because I thought you should know. I came to the conclusion that your mother would never tell you. She hasn't brought it up to me in almost a decade. It's buried very deep now, all that pain. I didn't tell you it to excuse your parents' actions . . ."

The yelling. The blaming. The hatred of Brooklyn. The hatred of sex. The paranoia. The fighting.

". . . but I do think it might help you understand them."

Yeah.

"Their shame about what happened is so profound that they don't know how to express it except with blame. Sometimes violent blame. Mostly toward each other but also, most tragically, toward you."

Yeah. And. So. What do I do now?

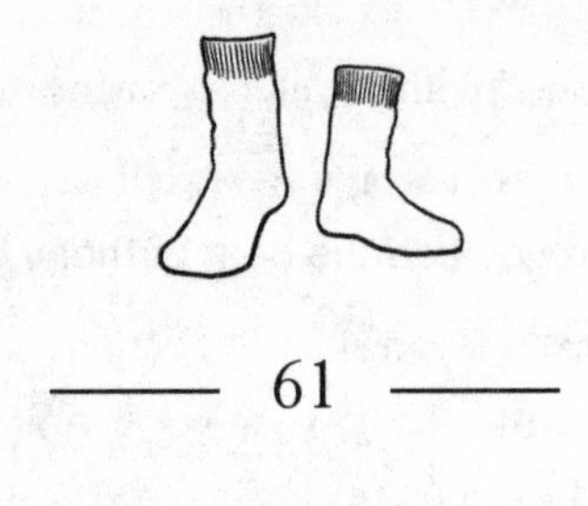

— 61 —

BENED . . .

I DROVE TO ROTH'S DINER, ASKED THE HOST for a table for two, and then sat in a booth facing the entrance. I took out my phone, opened Facebook, and messaged . . . Gator Green:

Thanks for saying happy birthday.

After I sent it, I realized this was a not very effective way to make a new friend. So I decided to send a second message:

I celebrated by spending the day in the library bathroom.
I hope you don't mind.

This was, obviously, a lie. But I think it might be funny. It would be even funnier if Gator knew I spent the day having sex for the first time in a warming hut with Penelope Lupo and then being caught naked by our parents and called a retard by her parents and then discovering Penelope had gotten back together with her ex-boyfriend who beat me up last week. Perhaps it wouldn't be funnier. In fact, it sounded very depressing.

Gator did respond a moment later by saying:

So you're saying you had the best birthday ever then ;)

That was a nice thing to say. So I wrote: *You have no idea.* Of course, this was true. He literally had no idea that it was the best birthday ever. Well, and the worst birthday ever. But I was just exchanging light banter in hopes of solidifying a platonic bond with a male classmate. When I state it like that, it makes me feel like I still have social problems.

If only Penelope were here at the diner, she would tell me she loves how I state things. I was about to get depressed again when Gator wrote:

Want to see a movie over break? Or just get together and talk about how awesome the library bathroom is?

It appears I was being successful at making a new friend. I told Gator yes. Then I heard someone say, "Hi, Benedict!"

Allison Wray had entered the diner and walked to my table while I was staring at my phone. I got to my feet and reached out my hand to greet Allison, but she said, "Can I just give you a hug? That's what we do in South Carolina." And then she opened her arms, so I did too and we hugged. She smelled like I always expected a girl to smell. Which was fine. It wasn't the smell of fresh laundry, flowers, and mystery. But it was a scent that was very commonly admired.

After our hug, we both sat down and faced each other. I had not prepared any topics of conversation and was now sure I would be very socially awkward with Allison Wray without being able to state that I knew I was being socially awkward like I could with Penelope. But then the words just formed in my head: "How was your day?" This was an incredibly boring question to ask. Though I now knew it was better to do that than to just sit in silence trying to find the perfect question to ask.

Allison then told me about her day, which I didn't find particularly interesting. But she was very pleasant to look at. Her overtly friendly tone was also very inviting. If she were my girlfriend, I'm sure many of my classmates would be envious. They would think as we walked through the halls together, "There goes Benedict, who is not only one of the best students in school but also has a very pretty and nice girlfriend." Perhaps I would be popular soon after. Perhaps after I became popular, my father would again love me.

Yes, I would have a girlfriend, the envy of my peers, and the respect of my father. Inside my own mind I would know that I was merely a puppet listening to Evil Benny's every thought. But on the outside, my life would seem very successful.

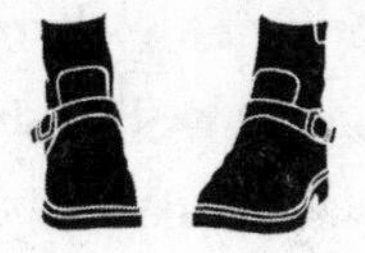

62

Penelope

Father Jeremy paid for our breakfast-dinner and then we walked to his car. I hugged him good-bye. Told him thank you a hundred times.

You know, I still think religion is kinda stupid and not really for me. I sure as hell don't think religion makes people good people. But, you know, I do think good people can make religion not all bad.

Then I got in my car, which was facing the restaurant. Like straight on. Like directly into the windows of the late-night section, where everybody (except me and Father Jeremy) sat.

Like . . . it faced, *lined up perfectly with*, one booth in particular. And in that booth was a very pretty blond girl. If I was a boy, she'd be the exact type I'd like. And this very pretty blond girl was with a boy.

My boy.

Well, he was mine for a day. Maybe just a few hours.

And now, I guess, he was somebody else's.

I almost cried. Really almost cried a lot. But no, no, no, no . . . I'm going to just drive away. I love him. I love Benedict Pendleton. I love him *so much* . . . that I'm going to let him go.

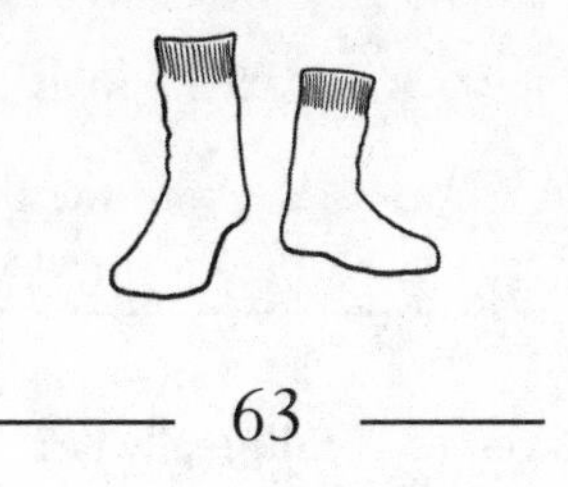

63

BENEDIC . . .

WHEN ALLISON WRAY WAS DONE TELLING ME about her day, she asked about my day. This is what normal people do. Ask generic questions so that each person can exchange generic information that allows each person to think they aren't different or weird or a freak or a dork.

I, obviously, would not be able to tell Allison how eight hours ago I got to lick my first vagina or that I fell in love or that I have a voice in my head I've named Penis Benedict. This would be *unique* information that would make her feel that I was not normal and the only way she could feel normal is if she bonded with another normal person.

Stop overthinking this, moron, Evil Benny said.

I suppose you are right.

Allison Wray is your dream girl!

I suppose you are right.

Just lie to her. Tell her you had a great day with your family celebrating your birthday and the day was ending even better now that you two were here together. Trust me, she'll love it.

I suppose you are right.

So I said, "Allison, my day . . ." Talk really fast! "Actually, I've been curious about something first. If you don't mind . . ." (Evil Benny tried to object, but I really was talking faster than he could think.) "Why would you be interested in me? You're a very attractive girl with a very nice personality, but I'm not sure how I would be appealing to you."

Her face turned a bit red, which was cute, I guess. Then she stumbled through her words as she said, "Well, I thought you were very handsome when I first saw you . . ."

I like being thought of as handsome.

". . . then you said that odd thing after I sat down and I thought, okay, maybe he's not a good match for me . . ."

Ah, yes, my social awkwardness.

". . . but then I talked to your friend Robert, who told me how smart you are. Which is very important to me."

I like my intelligence being appreciated.

". . . and then I found out your dad wrote *Being a Perfect Person*, which is my mom's favorite book and she told me, 'Allison, I bet Benedict will be just as brilliant and successful as his father.' And so I thought I'd write you to see if we were a match after all. And I'm so glad I did because I think it's going very well so far, don't you?"

Yes, I do, Evil Benny said.

Huh?

This is where you say, "Yes, I do," Evil Benny said.

I believe she just informed me her interest in me is largely based on my father's book being one of her mother's favorites.

So?

I, just . . .

Evil Benny didn't like me hesitating. So he yelled, YOU WON'T EVER GET A NORMAL, RESPECTABLE GIRL TO LIKE YOU UNLESS SHE LIKES YOU BECAUSE OF YOUR DAD! SO JUST TELL HER YOU THINK IT'S GOING WELL AND THEN LIE ABOUT YOUR DAY AND STOP BEING A RETARD!

"Benedict," Allison Wray said, "I didn't mean to say I was only interested in you because of your dad. I just think the apple doesn't fall far from the tree. So your father is like a glimpse of you in the future."

"Yes, I get it. . . . You're very right. . . ."

I'll go to Northwestern like him. Then I will become a very successful psychiatrist like him. Then I will have two children like him. Then I will become a bestselling author. Then I will tell my son he can't date girls who have nose rings and wear short skirts. If he does, I will tell him his girlfriend is a whore and then I will fire him as my son.

Evil Benny added, SOUNDS LIKE A PERFECT LIFE TO ME!

"Yes," I said. "Yes . . . Allison?"

"Are you okay?"

"Yes, no, I'm fine. Do you want to be normal?"

"I don't know what you mean."

"You're right. I wasn't clear. I'll rephrase. Do you want other people to think you're normal?"

She wasn't that excited about answering, but she tried: "I guess I don't want people to think I'm *not* normal. Like a freak or a dork or anything."

"Being considered a freak or dork would be the worst." I was attempting sarcasm for one of the first times. Allison didn't notice.

"But I don't want to be boring either. I want people to look up to me. So I guess, yes, I want them to think I'm normal but the best version of normal."

"The best version of normal. I've never heard that before. That's a good description. That's exactly what I wished for too."

"Thank you," Allison said, and smiled. But then her smile died because she registered exactly what I said.

"But as much as I wished for this, it was impossible. I'm chemically unable to feign normalcy. I have a voice in my head that I call Evil Benny that has been yelling at me for the past few hours and by telling you about this voice I'm giving you evidence that I can't be normal. But if I didn't tell someone about this voice, I would become exactly like my father. Which would be outstanding in every respect except that I would hate myself."

It took Allison thirty seconds to register everything I said and then come to the conclusion that I was, in fact, insane. She then, with a great deal of normalcy, said, "I'm just so tired suddenly. Thank you so much for meeting me, Benedict! I'll see you in school in a few weeks!" Then she stood and left.

Evil Benny said, You fucking blew that, reta—

Shut up, Benny, you're boring me.

He waited a beat, but then said:

Yes, okay.

64

Penelope

I let him go. I let him go. I let Benedict go.

I really did.

I swear.

I just didn't *actually* go.

See, I kept telling myself I just wanted to watch.

Watch Benedict being happy, being normal.

But man, even through the car's window and the restaurant's window, I could see his brain work. Spin . . . "spin" is not the right word. His brain was a fucking tornado.

Yeah, so I just watched his tornado brain—AND YES, I WAS GETTING TURNED ON BUT THAT'S NOT THE POINT—and then he unleashed it. Not all of it. Not like in the warming hut. That probably would have torn the whole diner down. But he unleashed a few gusts of that brain and this pretty blond girl went from thinking

Oh, this is nice, having a coffee with a cute boy to *I must run for my life!* And puff, puff, puff, those gusts blew that girl right out of the diner.

And then Benedict was alone.

And I was happy he was alone.

Until I was sad he was.

If only I wasn't sure he was done with me. If only I wasn't sure that we had no hope of repairing the damage done today. If only the universe could offer me a sign, any sign, no matter how small, that Benedict the dork and Penelope the freak still had a chance. . . .

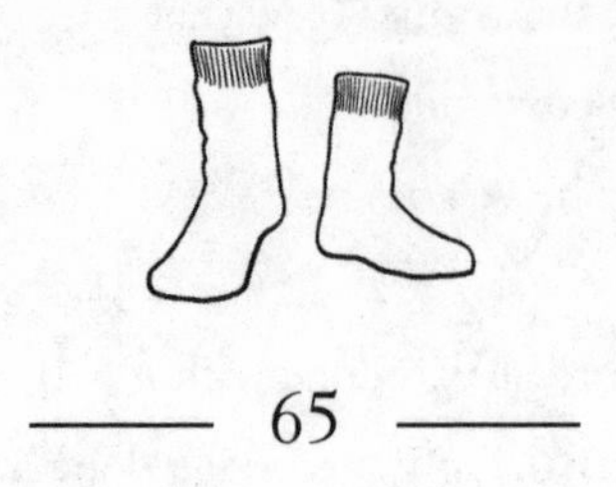

65

BENEDICT

I'M NOT SURE WHAT HAPPENS NEXT. I BELIEVE I achieved two moments of clarity at almost the exact same time. One, I no longer wished to be like my father. Two, I had slain Evil Benny. Not literally. He's just a voice in my head. If I had slain him literally, I probably would be dead. But I am the opposite of dead. I feel as alive as I have ever felt. It would be nice not to be alone. It would be nice to feel so alive *with* someone. But I think it's better to be alive alone than dead together. Never mind. I'm talking nonsense. I guess what I'm really saying is I wish Penelope hadn't gone back to her ex-boyfriend. I wish I were waiting in this diner for her. I wish she were in the parking lot right now—

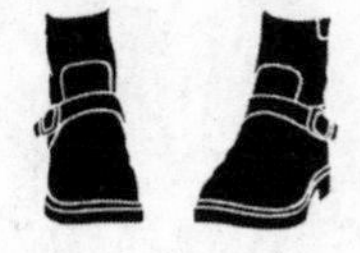

66

Penelope

He turned toward me. Oh-my-god. I know this sounds crazy, but it's like he was turning to look *for* me.

It was too dark, I was sure he wouldn't be able to see me. But maybe this was the small sign I was looking for. Maybe—

He saw me.

And he jumped up onto the booth seat. Nope, not gonna stop there. Onto the table. Benedict was now on the table. Benedict was not only on the table; he was pounding on the window. Benedict did not believe in sending small signs.

"PENELOPE! PENELOPE!" he was yelling. "PENELOPE! IT'S ME—BENEDICT! I'M INSIDE! DON'T LEAVE! I'M INSIDE! CAN YOU SEE ME?"

I nodded. Oh, oh, oh, oh . . .

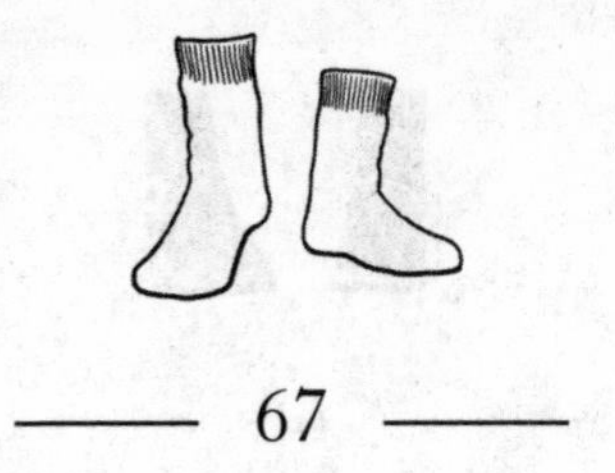

67

BENEDICT

SHE SAW ME. PEOPLE WERE LAUGHING. THE host was yelling at me. They concerned me not at all. I screamed one more thing: "I'M COMING FOR YOU!"

I leaped down from the table and sprinted toward the front door just as—

68

PENELOPE

I said <u>I'm coming for you</u> in my mind, and I threw open the car door and ran toward the diner entrance. The moment I stepped inside, he stepped into me. He lifted me up in the air, our lips found each other in a breath, and if we weren't us . . . if we were normal, let's say . . . we probably would have twirled once in a circle, then he would have put me down and, blah, blah, blah . . .

Well, we twirled, except we twirled right into the host stand and that made us lose our balance so we fell onto the floor but we kept kissing and kept holding each other. Someone was yelling, "You two can't do that!" and someone else was yelling for us to get up except Benedict wasn't letting go, so I sure as hell wasn't going to let go either.

A VERY LONG

EP*il*OG*ue*

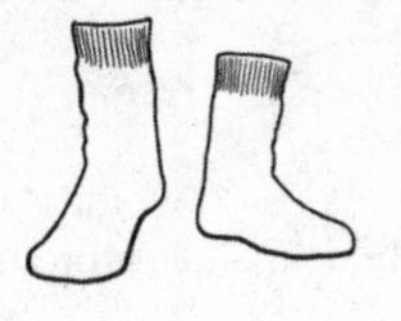

Benedict

AFTER PENELOPE AND I PERFORMED OUR dramatic public display of affection on the floor of Roth's Diner, I explained the Allison Wray situation. Penelope then explained the Paul situation, which was, obviously, a lot more serious than the Allison Wray situation. I got angry at Paul, but Penelope said I was getting mad at Paul because I felt responsible but I wasn't responsible and she had taken care of it and the best way I could support her now was to be proud of her, not angry at Paul. She's basically the smartest person alive. Perhaps tied with me. Well, since I've been valuing other types of intelligences besides those I understand, perhaps we are all tied. Though that's less interesting to say.

Then we told each other about our parents. I didn't have much to tell besides how my mother took my sister and me home and that I did not know what was going to happen with my father. I did tell her about

Evil Benny and, for one second, I worried she would think I was insane like Allison thought I was insane, but then she said, "You tell me if Evil Benny ever starts talking a lot again and I'll tell him to go fuck himself."

Which I believe can be translated into: I love you, Benedict.

Penelope

And then I told Benedict about my parents. I couldn't not tell him everything. I knew I had to, but as I was telling him everything—all the stuff Father Jeremy told me, but also every fight and crazy thing that's happened since—I kept thinking at some point he was going to stop me and say, "Penelope, I'm sorry, but you are way too psychologically damaged for me to consider romantically any longer."

But, fuck, he never said that. Not even close. Instead, after I had poured it all out, Benedict told me, "Now I better understand your profound source of wisdom. You have been, in many ways, your own parent since infancy."

Yeah.

It was almost midnight by then and we needed to go somewhere, so he called his mom and asked if his dad was there. He wasn't. He asked if I could spend the night. She said yes.

So we went to Benedict's house, which was this huge, sprawling mansion on a lot that used be a farm or something. I mean, I don't even know what to think about this right now.

Elizabeth and his mom met us at the door and they both gave me a hug, which I don't know how I could explain how good it felt but it did. Benedict at some point asked if it was okay if I slept in his room with him.

His mom said, "You're seventeen. You're old enough now."

But, to be honest, if this whole crazy day had happened a week ago, I bet Mrs. Pendleton—who's a fucking saint—would have probably said the same thing except she wouldn't have mentioned being seventeen.

His sister lent me some old clothes of hers for pajamas, which was a bit embarrassing since she's younger than me but so much taller. But seriously, it was awesome and I'm going to stop stressing about crap I can't control, like my height . . . and my parents.

Except I should tell them I'm not dead.

Which I told Benedict, who said, "I could tell them."

"What do you mean you could tell them?"

"I could call and tell them. If they yell at me, I will not get hurt because they are not my parents."

"Okay."

So I gave him my mom's number and he called her with his phone. He put it on speaker so I could listen. After she answered, Benedict said, "Mrs. Lupo, this is Benedict—"

"OH MY GOD—DO YOU KNOW WHERE PENELOPE IS? WE ARE SO WORRIED! IS SHE ALL RIGHT? YOU TELL HER WE ARE GOING TO SUE PAUL AND HIS FAMILY! NO ONE HURTS OUR DAUGHTER!" My dad was in the background, seconding everything she said. I love how my mom was going to sue Benedict and his family ten hours ago and now she was going to sue Paul. For the record, my parents have never sued anyone. It's just what they say. Anyway, she went on like this for a while and I kept wanting to say something, but Benedict squeezed my hand gently before I ever could. After my mom's rant slowed,

Benedict said, "Penelope will be staying at my house tonight. She is safe."

She yelled, "BUT YOUR FATHER CALLED—"

"Yes, he did. He is not here nor will I allow him to be here if Penelope is here."

"Okay. Tell her we love her. I STILL DON'T THINK WHAT YOU DID UP AT WILD WOLF WAS OKAY! But tell her I'll pray for her."

"I will," Benedict said, but then he mouthed to me, *No, I won't.* He's getting funnier by the hour.

I heard my father tell her he wanted to talk. They fought for a second over the phone, but my mom relented. My dad got on and said, "Hello, thank you for taking care of our baby girl. I'm sorry for saying what I said at the restaurant. I get crazy because I love her so much and I just want her to be safe." And then my dad started sobbing on the phone. "I just want her safe and you make her safe and I love you. I love you for making my daughter safe, so thank you, thank you, you come in anytime and I give you free pizza for you and your family anytime. Okay? I love you, I love you. Okay, I go." Even though he was telling Benedict he loved him, which was nuts, I mouthed, *I love you, Dad.*

Then my mom got back on and said, "Everyone thinks I'm the crazy one, but you see what I have to deal with? What are we supposed to do now? Just wait for her to call us? We are so worried. Tell her we can go shopping tomorrow. Tell her I'll buy her a new phone tomorrow." And since that was my mom's way of telling me she loved me, I said, in my heart to both the mother on the phone and the mother that did what she had to in order to protect me back in Brooklyn all those years ago, *I love you too, Mom*.

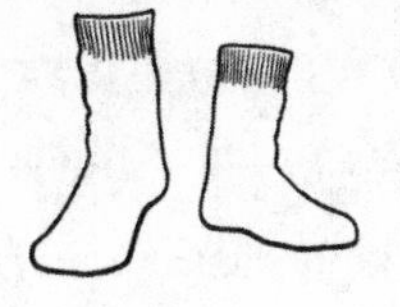

Benedict

THAT NIGHT, AFTER I GOT OFF THE PHONE WITH her parents, Penelope and I got into my bed. The last time I slept in this bed, I had never kissed a girl. Now, I was lying on my mattress with my girlfriend's head on my shoulder.

Penis Benedict wanted to have sex, but I didn't. Not exactly. So I told Penis Benedict to go to sleep.

Penelope thanked me again for talking to her parents. She then came up with a plan. Tomorrow, she said, she would text her mother from my phone. Her mother hated texting, but Penelope said, "If she wants to talk to me, she'll have to learn." She would tell both her parents that when they yelled she was going to walk away and only communicate by text until they calmed down.

"And you can spend the night here any time you need to," I said.

"That would be so nice."

"I think your plan is brilliant. *You're* brilliant, Penelope."

We lay there in silence for a little bit. Penelope rubbed my chest with her hand to which Penis Benedict said, REALLY? YOU EXPECT ME TO GO TO SLEEP WITH HER DOING THAT?

I think Penelope heard him because she reached her hand down there. "I love you," she said and then we had sex. Quietly but as if we had done it a thousand times even though it was only the second time.

"Benedict," she said afterward, when we were lying still again. Only this time I had my head on her shoulder. "What would you say to your dad if he came home right now?"

"I don't know. If he said anything bad to you, I think I would tackle him."

"I'd tell him the highest form of intelligence is kindness and his son, my Benedict, is the kindest person I know."

As she said this, these thoughts started forming in my head and I just said them even though I didn't know exactly what I was saying. "I bet my dad has an Evil Benny like me. His would be named Evil Sammy. Obviously. Except Evil Sammy is one hundred times more evil to my dad than Benny ever was to me. And the only way my dad can feel good about himself is to make other people feel bad about themselves. That's why he wrote a book about being a perfect person, which only ever made me think I would *never* be perfect. That's why he tells my mom she's dumb and calls his son's girlfriend names and fires me."

"So you're saying he's got social problems." Penelope smiled.

I smiled, but only a little, as I said, "Yes, obviously, but maybe it's worse that that. Much worse. I'm not sure. No matter what, I guess if I saw him, I'd say, 'Dad, stop listening to Evil Sammy tell you how horrible you are and start listening to the voice that likes you no matter how imperfect you are.'"

I never got a chance to say this to my dad. Maybe I will someday. He still hasn't come home. He didn't call on Christmas. My mother eventually tracked him using his credit cards, but she didn't tell us where he was or what he was doing and neither Elizabeth nor I asked more than once. My mom did get a court to freeze most of the bank accounts. I think she was prepared for something like this. She knew he had more than just social problems a long time ago. Honestly, my dad is smart, but he is only smart in one way. My mom's smart in so many ways I'm not sure I even know all of them yet.

Even though it's odd not having him in the basement, our house feels the same. In fact, we feel more like a family without my dad down there. I think when he was down there, all three of us were worried about him. But now we can just concentrate on worrying about people that worry about us back.

PENELOPE

Paul got released on bail. Dean Jacoby called me—so weird—and told me everyone at school was on my side. They expelled Paul and have asked the Riverbend police to keep an eye out.

I don't think Paul would ever try to hurt me again. I don't think he's some kind of homicidal maniac. I just think he's a scared, angry child that needs an adult to tell him it's not okay to take your fear and anger out on other people. I'm just not going to be that adult for him. I've got enough problems being an adult for my parents.

Stacy sent me some rambling text about how she always knew Paul was an asshole, blah, blah, blah. I didn't respond. No interest in talking to her ever again. Hopefully she gets the hint.

I did go shopping with Iris (with my mom's credit card) and it was nice. I told her some of what had gone on, but didn't really get too far into it. I told her I wasn't going to talk to Stacy anymore and she said she wasn't going to either. When I asked why, she said, "A lot of reasons."

Iris did agree to go on a double date with Benedict and his new friend, Gator Green. Both Iris and Gator have lost a parent, so I thought, I don't know.

Anyway, the four of us went to a dumb action movie that Gator picked and then had pizza at my dad's place afterward. I thought Gator looked pretty cute (even though he's probably more out there than Benedict and me put together), but Iris didn't seem to have any interest at all. I found out later that Iris likes girls, not boys, and her and Stacy weren't just friends, so the whole Paul/Stacy thing ended up breaking her heart a lot more than mine.

On that night, and any night he saw him, my dad would pick up Benedict in a big bear hug, kiss him on the cheeks, and repeat, "I love this boy!" Benedict was super understanding about it. In some ways, my dad was exactly the kind of dad Benedict needed now. Just someone who tells him how much he loves him and feeds him pizza.

I downloaded the new Millie Dragon book the second it was available Christmas morning. And . . . guess what? She got a boyfriend for the first time. He, of course, doesn't believe she can see demons at first. But then, blah, blah, blah, he finally believes her and they fall in love. Kinda stupid. Kinda perfect. I cried at the end.

Benedict asked me to read his new favorite book, *If Only Girls Weren't Everything I Wanted I'd Have Nothing to Do with Them*. When I told him I already had, he could tell I didn't like it. I explained, "It's just hard to care about a boy who cares about a girl that doesn't care about him."

He said, with a wounded puppy face, "But what if I was in love with you but you didn't love me back. You don't think people would care about me?"

"You would never love a girl that didn't love you back."

"How do you know?" Benedict asked.

"Because you will never love a girl besides me." I really liked when I said this. So did Benedict. If I do ever write a book about my life—which I'm not going to, probably not anyway—I probably would include this line even though it would sound like a line a writer would say instead of a real person.

Benedict and I have sex a lot—*a lot*—and I never thought about any other guys (or girls) while I had sex with him until suddenly I did a couple times, and I worried that meant I loved him less but it didn't *feel* like I loved him less so, what the hell, I told him and he said, "I've read a lot about this . . ." Of course he had. ". . . and it's very normal. Just tell me when you are doing it next time and perhaps it will make it exciting for me too."

And I still think about sex all the time but maybe just a little less than before. I don't judge myself as much, so maybe I think about it less because I'm not thinking about it just to make myself feel bad for thinking about it. I have no idea what I mean by that. I mean, I do, but I'm not explaining it any better than that.

Benedict and I talked about this because, well, we talk about everything, and we both decided sex—doing it, talking about doing it, thinking about doing it, thinking and talking about other people doing it—makes us feel alive. Not exactly in the same way for each of us, but close enough. Yeah, we get why it's not important to everyone like it's important to us but we promise not to judge you for what makes you alive if you promise not to judge us.

Benedict

THE DAY AFTER MY BIRTHDAY, ROBERT TEXTED me, asking me if I had talked to Allison Wray yet. I had been avoiding all thoughts of Robert for days because Robert is the best friend I have ever had but I fell in love with his dream girl and this was a difficult thing to explain to your best friend.

But Penelope told me that if Robert and I are really meant to remain best friends, then he would forgive me and respect me for telling the truth. This sounded impossible, but I asked Robert to go to Midnight Dogs for lunch the next day. We talked about video games and TV shows until after we started eating. Then, while staring at his hot dog, Robert asked, "Did you talk to Pen about me?"

"Robert," I said, and waited until he looked up from his hot dog, which took an awfully long time. "You were right about almost everything, from us being dorks to Penelope being beautiful. I didn't like that you were right, so I said mean things, for which I am now asking you to forgive me. While I was on vacation in Wisconsin, Penelope was on vacation at the same resort. We fell in love, which I did not expect at all, but maybe it makes sense if I think about how I love you, as a friend, and you loved Pen, from afar, and now I love her. It's like the associative property. Maybe this doesn't make sense. All I know is—you are my best friend and if I could go back in time and only say nice things to you, I would, but I wouldn't go back in time to change how I feel about Penelope."

Robert didn't say anything. But then he took a bite of his dog, and with his mouth full and his eyes again locked on his food, he said, "So Pen's your girlfriend?"

"Yes."

"And I'm your best friend."

"Yes."

"So, using the associative property, Pen's my best friend now too."

I laughed at his joke.

"That's the first time you've ever laughed at my jokes, Benedict."

Yes, it was.

PENELOPE

After Benedict picked me up for school on our first Monday back from break, but before we picked up Robert, I asked him, "Are you nervous?"

"Yes. Are you?"

"Yes."

"Why are you nervous?" Benedict asked.

"There are just so many unknowns. We've spent like every second together the past two weeks. But now we're going to school, *school*, where you're brilliant . . ."

"And you are popular."

". . . and we don't have any classes together. We don't have any mutual friends. . . ."

"Yes, we do," he said. "We have Robert, and Gator, and Iris."

"The five of us . . . wow, we would be a sight if we all sat together."

"The Freaky Five."

"You just came up with that now?"

"Yes, I'm very smart."

I said, "It would be a good title for a book."

"You should write it," Benedict said.

"I can't fucking write."

"I bet you would be a writing genius." Of course he would say that. The kid was whipped by Vagina Penelope bad.

"I don't know . . . okay . . . I have a question. A strange question. Ready?" I asked.

"Yes."

"Let's say there was a book about us."

"Called *The Retard and the Whore.*"

"That's a horrible title—"

"I'm making light of our most dramatic moment." He grinned.

"No one will know that."

"How about *The Dork and the Nympho*?"

"Forget the title, that's not even my question. My question is, how does the book end?"

Benedict thought for a second, then he said, "It would end with us holding hands as I died on my one hundred and seventeenth birthday."

"I knew you would say that."

"I like happy endings."

"But I don't believe in happy endings, Benedict, because they're kinda bullshit. See, even in your version, you die one hundred years from now and leave me *alone.* So our book can't end with us just skipping into the sunset holding hands and singing love songs, blah, blah, blah. It's got to end feeling real."

"Are you worried that our love story won't end happily? I'm not worried at all about that unless you are, in which case I am worried a lot."

"I'm not. . . ." I was. But I didn't say it like that, I said, "I just don't want people to think all our problems are solved because we love each other. It's lame. Life is so much more fucking complicated."

"Then end it now," he said.

"What do you mean?"

Benedict went on, "If you were to write a book about us, you should end it before we get to school this morning. A lot can go wrong once we go back to school." We parked outside Robert's house.

"Yes, you're right."

"You were supposed to disagree with me, Penelope!"

Robert got in the car. He said, "Good morning, Pen. Good morning, Benedict."

"Robert," Benedict said, "Penelope wants to write a book about us."

"I do not!"

"Yes, she does. It's going to be called *The Dork and the Nympho*."

"No, it's not," I said. "The word 'nympho' confuses people." Especially boys.

Robert thought for a moment then said, "I think *The Nerdy and the Dirty* would be a fantastic title. It's humorous and the rhyming y's are very appealing."

"He's right," Benedict said. "Robert's always right."

I liked it, not that I'm going to write a book, probably not anyway. So I said, "No one would ever publish a book about teenagers with the word 'dirty' in the title."

"Why not?" Robert asked.

"Because," I said, "the world's not ready for that."

We turned onto Kirby Street and Riverbend High School soon came into view. As he pulled in behind a line of cars waiting to turn into the parking lot, Benedict reached over, took my hand in his, and squeezed. He said, "I think the world's ready for us."

“Now I could *never* end the book here because you saying that makes it sound like a happy—” But he kissed me before I could finish.

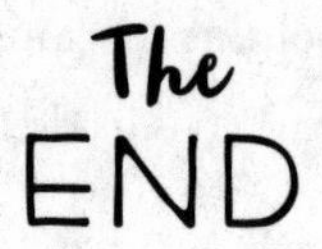

ACKNOWLEDGMENTS

For the acknowledgments in my first book, I asked my two main characters—Carolina and Trevor—to help me thank everyone. It felt right to ask Penelope and Benedict to do the same for *The Nerdy and the Dirty*.

But when the three of us finally found time to sit down and talk, and I explained that their story was being published, neither seemed particularly excited by it. In fact, Pen was almost hostile. I don't know why I say "almost." There was nothing almost about it.

"Are you allowed to do that?" Pen asked, her body shifting beneath her even as her eyes shot straight and still at mine.

"Do what?" I asked back.

"Just write about us without asking our permission?"

"I did ask," I said, even though I knew it would be hard to explain the author/character "permission" to them.

"That's not fair, Brad, and you know that." And she gave me this look. And, crap, you know what? Pen didn't like me. I really didn't like Pen not liking me. She's one of my favorite characters ever and she didn't like me! (I also wasn't a huge fan of her using my real first name but it felt inappropriate to ask them to call me b.t.)

Benedict, who had taken hold of Penelope's hand in order to help calm her, whispered something in her ear. She nodded. Then Benedict said, "We'd like to read the book and then decide if we will let you publish it. If we decide to let you, then, and only then, will we help you with the acknowledgments."

Because I really wanted Pen to stop hating me—and because I liked the odds of them liking the book—I agreed. Benedict said good-bye, Pen didn't say a thing, and I emailed them both a copy of *The Nerdy and the Dirty* that night when I got home.

Two days later, I got an email back. Attached was a marked-up manuscript with changes I was to make to the book in exchange for their approval. Before I read their demands, I worried they would want to make themselves look better during the more painful and awkward points of their story. But, honestly, they wanted the opposite. Penelope and Benedict, as they stated more eloquently than I could, ". . . want teenagers, and adults, to know every crazy, mean, self-destructive thought that went through our heads. We're sure everyone else has just as much self-doubt as we do and pretending we had even one percent less than we did is not real and one of the main reasons we're together is because we were real with each other."

Without fully admitting how much they improved my book, I agreed to their changes and they agreed to meet me again. But this time they insisted I meet them on their turf. At Penelope's Pizzeria in Riverbend. I tried to explain this was impossible, but Benedict and Penelope said I'd figure out a way.

How I did "figure" out a way to Riverbend was even more difficult than I imagined and probably a novel in itself. For brevity's sake, let's just say I did get there and found not only Penelope and Benedict waiting for me, but a large, hot Margherita pizza in the center of the table.

"This is my favorite type," I said as I grabbed a slice.

"Obviously, we knew this, Mr. Gottfred," Benedict said, smiling. I don't know what was worse: Pen calling me Brad or Benedict calling me Mr. Gottfred.

"How did you know that?" I asked. Pen was still giving me a strong "I loathe your existence" vibe, so Benedict said,

"Penelope said we will talk about how we know your pizza preference—and other information—at the end." He then laughed. He seemed so relaxed in his body from the last time I saw him. Very strange to find your characters have grown up without you.

Benedict and Penelope shared a look—a look that mostly made me think they shared part of the same brain now—and then she nodded, and he said, "So we've been emailing with Kate Farrell, your editor at Henry Holt, and thought you should know."

"How did you get her email?" I didn't believe them.

"He doesn't believe us," Penelope said.

"I believe you, I just want—"

"You don't," she cut me off. "It doesn't matter if you believe us or not. But you asked us to help you with the acknowledgments and, after talking with her, we think you should start with Kate."

I started, "How about I say—"

"We wrote something out," Benedict said before I could finish.

Then he retrieved a printed sheet from a folder in his backpack. He read from it, *"Kate, your loyalty to truth surpasses even my own."*

Pen added, "Surpasses yours, Brad. No one's surpasses ours." She smiled—well, almost—for the first time.

"Obviously," Benedict said as he kissed Penelope on the cheek.

Pen continued, "Kate told us all about the people at Henry Holt who took our story and helped transform it into an actual, readable book that people will spend actual time and money on."

Benedict spoke now. "I memorized all the names to show you how important we think they are: Kathryn Little in marketing, Allison Verost in publicity, Anna Booth the designer, Jackie Hornberger the copy editor, Starr Baer the production editor, Jennifer Healey the managing editor, and Tom Nau the production manager." As he finished accessing that Rolodex in his head, I realized how jealous I was of Benedict's brain sometimes.

Penelope kept her focus on me. "Next we want you to thank your always awesome agent, Jill Grinberg, and every awesome person in the office."

Benedict and his brain had those names ready too: "Those awesome people are Katelyn Detweiler, Cheryl Pientka, and Denise St. Pierre."

Penelope pulled the sheet from Benedict's hand and read, *"Jill, thank you for letting me be your wild card in your stack of aces."*

I said, "Maybe I can edit some of these? It might be confusing if you're saying it."

"No, people are really smart. They'll figure it out," Pen said, and handed the sheet back to Benedict.

"To the Wolfpack. The greatest writing group ever assembled. Jennifer Bosworth, Nadine Nettmann, James Raney, and Gretchen McNeil."

Penelope said to me, "You know there's like a zero percent chance you would have finished this novel of us without their help, right?"

"I know. They're great writers and better people."

"Don't do that, ugh," Penelope started.

Benedict explained, "Mr. Gottfred, I told Penelope she needed to try and stay positive no matter what, but it would help if you just let us do the thank-yous. We've written them in your voice. We would never talk like this normally." His confidence was so unshakeable now. A girlfriend who loves you for you will do that for any teenage boy, I suppose.

But that only made me realize I needed to ask Penelope a question. "Why are you so mad at me?" Just had to know. Couldn't take it anymore.

"She'll address that at the end as well, Mr. Gottfred."

"Please don't call me Mr. Gottfred, Benedict."

"But you're really old." He said this with a straight face. For about five seconds. Then he let out a big laugh. "I'm really funny now."

"I can see that," I said.

Penelope read from the sheet again: *"To Amy Makkabi, for liking my brain, and valuing uniqueness everywhere."*

"I insisted on that one," Benedict said.

Penelope went on, *"To Joanne Mosconi . . ."* She stopped as tears formed. Fighting through it, she finished. *". . . who inspired so much with her own journey to truth."* On that mention, Penelope and I shared a look of common and profound appreciation.

Benedict then kissed the corner of Pen's eyes before continuing. *"To my family. All of them. Not just my parents and sisters but my nieces and nephews and cousins and uncles and aunts and grandparents. Those here and those gone. They are all wonderfully loving and complex people who encourage growth in me, themselves, and each other."*

I started, "You forgot . . ." but couldn't finish because Penelope said,

"Your wife. Of course we didn't forget Danica. She deserves her own separate mention. She deserves her own special chapter. Do you know how lucky you are to have her as a wife, Brad?"

"Yes . . ."

"Do you really? I don't think—"

I cut her off for the first time. "I actually do. She is the partner to a better, more fulfilling life than I imagined. It's not a perfect life, but it's a—"

"Real one," Penelope completed my sentence for me as she looped her arm through Benedict's. For some reason, the way she said this, and the way she pulled Benedict close to her, made me want to ask,

"Are you two doing okay?"

After their seemingly shared brain waited a moment, Benedict answered, "I understand now why Penelope was hesitant to end our story on an overtly happy moment . . ."

"And I . . ." Pen paused, pulled him even closer, and continued, ". . . know and understand and love his brain and his heart more than ever." Now Benedict was the emotional one and she was kissing his tears away.

"You want to talk about it?" I asked, wanting back in their lives more than I was prepared for.

"No, that's between us," Pen said, then read the final thank-you. *"To my sons, Axel and Leif. It will be fifteen years before either of you can read* The Nerdy and the Dirty, *so if I die before you do, just know that I love you for being exactly who you are, no matter who you are, and love every dream you have, whatever those dreams may be."*

That's great, but wow, "I'm only forty!" I said.

"Which is really, really old." Benedict laughed again at his joke.

"Brad," Penelope said, "at some point, and maybe it's fifty years from now and not fifteen, your kids are going to read this and you're going to be dead and they'll want to know you love them for being their true selves no matter how old they are."

"And . . ." Benedict's laugh died. He tried to restart with a smile but couldn't. "Some kids might read this and not have a dad—"

"—or mom—"

"—that tells their kids what you just told your kids. And this note is for all of them too."

I nodded. They were right. Penelope and Benedict were two of the best people I knew. What else could I add? Maybe I should thank—

"We don't want you to thank us," Penelope said. "We know you thanked Carolina and Trevor and that's great for them, but we want something else from you."

This, strangely, scared me a little bit.

Benedict said, "This is the end I warned you about."

Penelope went on. "What we want—not just Benedict and me, but Trevor, Carolina, Zee, Art, and everyone else in Riverbend. Not just Riverbend. Everyone on this side of the page."

I got what they meant.

"Of course you do," Benedict said. "Because you're almost as smart as us." He really did think he was hilarious now.

But Penelope was on task. I could tell this was what it all was building toward. All her anger at me. Maybe it wasn't anger. It was her passion. It had become so amazingly purposeful. "Brad . . . *what we want* . . . is for you to admit that we may be real."

"Of course you're real!" I said. "That's what this whole book was about!"

"No," she said. "That we may be as real as you."

Oh. That was more complicated.

She continued, "I want you to admit, as you sit in a Riverbend pizzeria and talk to two characters you think you made up, that maybe, just maybe, Benedict and I are sitting here, alone, writing a story about a character named Brad. A character named Brad that is so hopeful of being understood and accepted for his true self that he writes a book about characters searching for the same thing."

Oh. Yeah. Man. There were tears in my eyes, weren't there? Yes. Yes. "Yes," I said.

"Yes, what?" Penelope wanted me to say it out loud.

"She's very good at making people be clear now," Benedict said, and kissed her yet again.

Okay. I'll say it. "I agree. There's just as good a chance that you're the writers and I'm the character as the other way around. That everyone reading could be more characters of yours, all with my same common goal. Hoping and searching to be understood and accepted for their real selves."

"Obviously," Benedict said. But Penelope wanted more. I knew she would.

I sat with my thoughts for a moment and then tried to say it in a way that would make them both proud: "Maybe what you really want me to say is if the writer of two characters can admit that those characters have just as much a right to be real as the writer himself does, then everyone has that right. That no one—no parent or teacher or group or society or even reality itself—can take the right to be real away."